I0630488

HIDDEN HEARTS

JADE RIVER SANCTUARY

SAVANNAH KADE

GRIFFYN INK

This book is a work of fiction. Names, characters, businesses, organizations, places, events and incidents are either a product of the author's imagination or are used fictitiously. Any resemblance to actual persons, living or dead, or locales is entirely coincidental.

Published by Griffyn Ink

www.griffynink.com

Copyright © 2023 Griffyn Ink

All rights reserved.

No part of this book may be reproduced, stored in a retrieval system, or transmitted by any means, electronic, mechanical, photocopying, recording, or otherwise, without written permission from the publisher.

For ordering information or special discounts for bulk purchases, please contact Griffyn Ink at Mail@GriffynInk.com.

CHAPTER ONE

The beer in her hand was as warm as the tears on her cheeks were cold.

Pounding at the door had her taking another sip of the beer, certain that the lock would hold and that—if it didn't—surely the fact that this was a *church* would keep them from breaking it in.

"Come out! *Please.*"

She didn't even answer. Just sipped the beer. The mounds of tulle around her made it look as if she were in an insanely frothy bubble bath. Oh, the irony.

Each time, it was longer and longer between visits. Longer and longer between when they tried to coax her out. Maybe they were learning that they couldn't.

The guests had to have all gone home now. Maybe they'd eaten the food and had a grand party, or a solemn one, while her heart broke. Damn, she'd missed the baked salmon and the chocolate cake.

That fucking chocolate cake was supposed to celebrate the happiest day of her life, not this shit.

She sipped at the beer again.

Kicking off the insane white pumps she'd bought just for this —of course it was just for this—brought a soft clank. Sucking in a sharp breath, she almost dropped the beer in a mad scramble through the tulle. She had to find that penny. She'd forgotten she'd tucked it into her shoe this morning when Gamma had given it to her.

Her heart pounded. She could not lose that penny!

Gamma would be so disappointed with all of them if she ever found out. But Brandy managed to snatch the penny just before all her shuffling around made it slide down the drain. So much for good luck. Hers had been the exact opposite.

Heart rate slowing, she leaned back again, sliding down until she lay in the tub the way it was intended. Though probably not in the dress.

One fist held the penny tightly now, the other still clutched the beer.

Her eyes fell closed—her puffy, red, irritated eyes. *How long could she stay here?* She didn't know . . . but she might try to find out.

She was almost asleep when the pounding came on the door again.

"Let us in!" the feminine voice pleaded.

Nooope. She never wanted to hear that voice again.

Then his voice. "Please, at least let us know you're still alive."

Barely, she thought. They'd ruined everything. Her mother had come by asking what had happened and in that moment, as Brandy had opened her mouth to spill everything, she'd snapped her jaw back shut.

They'd broken her heart. But if she told, she would *completely destroy her family.*

Had her heart stopped beating? She'd given her mother enough trouble for one day. So, she'd lied through her clenched teeth then and with a false calm said, "I'm okay, Mama. I just can't do this."

But these two would keep bothering her until she said something.

Still, they could wait while she took another sip of this nasty, warm beer. It tasted as bad as the day.

They pounded again and she sucked in a deep breath before calling out in her most irritated voice. "I'm alive!"

No thanks to either of you.

CHAPTER TWO

The drive had been beautiful—what he was staring at now was *not*.

Ash Cooper put his hands on his hips and turned around to face the other way just so he didn't have to see what he'd just seen.

Looking down the long gravel path, he saw across the mountains. Thick trunks grew upwards into the tops of the trees. In the distance, he could see the Jade River flowing through the valley below. His breathing calmed just a little with the sight.

With a slow, supposedly cleansing breath that did absolutely jack shit, his brain started churning through the implications.

The view here was spectacular, but he'd still seen what he saw.

He couldn't do this again.

Did he even have a choice though? Was there anywhere else for him to go?

The only thing to do was turn back around and face it. His car was the only one in the large gravel lot. Had he gotten the time wrong? Or, God forbid, the *day*? She was supposed to be here to greet him—and it wasn't supposed to look like this.

Ash thought about unclenching his jaw, but it wasn't even clenched. Had he already given up?

He couldn't tell.

The building in front of him—what had to be the main lodge —was filthy. "Dirty" would be a massive understatement. A large spider had spun an intricate web on one side of the porch from roof to railing. Black and yellow, it was beautiful, but it shouldn't be here.

From the looks of the place, the spider fit in a hell of a lot better than he did.

Broad, wooden double doors would have been welcoming if older, dustier webs hadn't hung from the knob. If leaves hadn't built up, blocking the threshold . . . and it wasn't even fall yet.

He would have rolled his eyes, but Ash wasn't one for wasting effort.

The window on the right was broken and the others were so grimy, that without the broken one he wouldn't have been able to see inside at all. The wide front porch had once been white. The roof now listed to the right.

Ash peeked in and slowly stopped breathing.

He'd signed a contract. Had he legally bound himself to this place for several years? Or was this enough to break the contract?

Climbing the front steps, he tested each one as he went. They looked sturdy enough but given the state of the windows and the grime on the place, he wouldn't have been surprised if he fell right through.

He thought about checking the doorknob but wasn't willing to brush away the old cobwebs draped over it.

Not my circus, not my monkeys.

But he was here to help build the circus. God help him.

He told himself he didn't have to know what was inside. He

5

was supposed to meet her here. But as he turned back around and surveyed the view off the front landing, he realized something was wrong.

Hopefully, it was him. Surely, he'd come at the wrong time.

The grounds were empty—at least of human sounds. When he stopped and listened, he heard the birds in the trees, the kind of twittering sounds that only came from mountain birds. He hadn't heard that in a long, long time. In fact, he almost hadn't taken the job just because of the location.

Rustling noises came from the underbrush in the trees just beyond the clearing. *Hopefully not from inside the building.* Although from the state of it, if they opened the door and found a family of raccoons, he wouldn't be that surprised.

Holy Hell. What had he done?

He listened again, wondering if that was the river he was hearing in the distance. Was it loud enough to reach up to the sanctuary?

Some sanctuary, he thought. Good for spiders who wanted to live undisturbed, not for people. Not for dogs. Not for anything civilized.

What he didn't hear was the sound of tires coming up the gravel drive. He made his way off the front porch, at least a little more trusting of the foundation this time and headed around the back.

Part of his contract was that he had a cabin on the premises. God help him if the cabins were in as bad of shape as this main building was. As he cleared the back of the building, he saw chain link fencing that might have been dog runs at one time, though now it was cut in places, rusted and rolling away. Absolutely not suitable for use and probably even a hazard.

He'd expected to help design some things. He hadn't been told he'd have to help repair and build the whole sanctuary.

He sighed heavily, wondering why he wasn't more upset than he was. Was he just so burnt out that he couldn't feel anything? Had he gotten used to losing, and this was just the next thing in line?

He'd burned so many bridges on the way here, could he burn one more?

And if he didn't stay here, what would even be left for him?

Ash didn't know. What he did know was how to keep moving.

The cabins weren't in sight yet. When he thought about it, that might be good design. It was going to be enough living where he worked—*if he stayed*. The nearest city was Charlottesville, over forty-five minutes away. The local town, Jade River Valley, was barely big enough to support a small chain grocery and basic supply store. There were two fast food restaurants that he had seen as he drove through. He was hoping there were a few more that maybe weren't on the main road.

So it might be good that the cabins weren't right next to the main building. They might afford a little bit of privacy, and he might very well want it in case he needed to scream into the void, or in case he found a spider at night.

Right now though, the privacy made him very, very nervous. Still not hearing tires behind him, he headed down one of the walkways. At least the paths remained relatively clear. Once upon a time someone had taken the care to put down paver stones. That kept the small plants and weeds from fully taking over. In a few places, tree branches had reached across and he had to hold them back as he passed.

Had Roz simply banked on the *potential* of this place? Because even now he could see that it had once been beautiful. At last, he stopped in front of the cabin.

Taking a good hard look, he felt his heart sink.

CHAPTER THREE

He'd heard the tires as he was heading back toward the main lodge, and as he came around the corner, he heard the door of the large SUV slam.

The woman had climbed down, and Ash instantly recognized her from the tiny headshot he'd once seen. This had to be Roz. But the headshot hadn't done her justice—her black hair was bobbed, ending just above her shoulders, marked with a few faint streaks of gray. Her wide hazel eyes were luminous and frantic. Worry showed on her brows and at the corners of her mouth.

"Did I give you the wrong time?" She leaned forward as she asked. "I got held up in traffic, but I thought I'd still be here before you."

"I may have read it wrong. You must be Roz." Ash held out a hand. Despite what he'd seen he was still going to be nice.

"And you must be Ash Cooper." Her grin didn't quite reach her eyes, he could hear the fear in her voice. "Did you get a chance to look around?"

Oh, dear God, if she was asking him that . . . He'd barely begun to nod before she said, "Is it all as bad as this?"

She waved her long, slim hand at the front of the lodge.

"Have *you* not been here before?" He had to ask. He could see something at the edge of her eyes that looked like a combination of regret and anger.

"No, but I was given detailed images."

"That didn't look like *this?*" he asked.

"Is it even safe?" She ignored his question, then immediately switched topics as she looked back at the building. "Are there snakes inside?"

He had to laugh. As much as this was a complete shit show, her anger and fear and irritation were comforting. "I was guessing raccoons."

"Are we placing bets on it?" She moved toward the porch, fishing in her pocket for a key.

"Twenty dollars?" He might get enough for dinner out of this. It wouldn't hold him until he got a new job. He'd been hoping for a paycheck starting in a few days, but clearly that wasn't going to happen here.

She pulled out the key ring, the plastic tag from the realtor still dangling from it and headed up the steps. She took the first one quickly, then—like he had—seemed to think better and slowed down.

"Can I ask what you paid for it?"

She began testing the wood in front of her, muttering something under her breath. She turned back at the last moment. "You can ask, but I'm not going to answer."

He saw her hesitate only for a moment before she reached out and wiped away the cobwebs with a bare hand. Somehow, they magically didn't stick to her, or else she knew a trick he didn't. But she was fitting the key into the lock and seemed pleased to find that it worked.

Interesting. It hadn't just been him thinking this place was not as expected. But she should have come out and seen it for herself before she bought it.

Still, she had some kind of resolve. Putting her hand on the knob, Roz turned back to him. "Raccoons or snakes, twenty bucks!"

She swung the door wide, letting a beam of sunlight sweep across the open floor. Sure enough, they watched as several small animals scurried away.

Disappointed, she looked back at him. "Possums."

He shrugged. *There were no winners in this game.* He was not looking forward to this. And honestly, this wasn't safe. Anywhere the animals were inside, they would leave droppings inside. It would all have to be cleaned. Before—

"This all has to be professionally cleaned," she announced, echoing his thoughts. Then she sighed. "Do you have anywhere that you can stay for the next couple of days? If not, I'll put you in a hotel nearby."

Ash wondered where *nearby* might be, because there certainly wasn't a hotel in Jade River Valley. In fact, he thought they'd be lucky if there was even a *mo*tel.

"The good news is," she announced with forced cheer, "I don't close escrow for three more days."

He watched as she reached back and flipped the light switch, showing that *luckily* the electricity seemed to work. No flickers. Ash thought that was a good sign. One good sign out of many red flags.

Then he put the pieces together. "They gave you the keys before you closed on the place?"

She nodded over her shoulder toward him but still didn't look at him. She was too busy taking it all in.

Tall and slim, she held court in the center of the room. He could tell she was cataloging everything. Absorbing the feelings and making new plans.

It seemed to him she'd been lied to about the place, or at least grossly under-informed.

"I'm going to make sure that they get this repaired. Or at least drop the price, so that I can get it fixed."

He didn't interrupt. She clearly couldn't afford to get taken on this place. And he couldn't afford for her not to be able to afford him.

Where else was he going to go?

He should have been more angry, frustrated, *anything*. Had he simply run out of the energy to care that he was getting screwed over? Maybe.

They spent a while checking through the main building, inspecting every room. Most of the inside doors had stayed closed and therefore the rooms behind them were in much better shape than the main area. That part had been accessed by the broken window, but it didn't seem the rest of it had.

Another piece of good news. But was it good enough?

Roz whipped out her phone and was taking copious notes.

"Before you go any further, you'll want to see the kennels and the cabins," he told her. He hated to be the bearer of bad news, but he'd been specifically trained in how to deliver it. Not about real-estate, but surely it was a relatively universal skill.

They headed around back, going the other direction around the lodge from how he'd first looked. It wasn't any better over here. Trash wood—old plywood, rotted two-by-fours, and plastic—was piled up against the side of the building. An old wheelbarrow still held water though the wheel itself had long since deflated.

He should stop looking.

Roz pulled up short as they cleared the back corner.

"These were supposed to be usable dog runs!" She was mad. Spitting nails now. If only those nails could repair things. "I'm so glad I didn't bring the dogs today!"

His eyebrows rose. She was going to bring the *dogs* today? He barely choked out, "How many?"

She must have seen that he was petrified at the idea of filling the broken spaces and dirty rooms with dogs. They wouldn't stay contained and everything out here was more harm than help. "Oh, just Shadow and Astra. My dogs. Not . . ." she waved a hand at the broken and empty spaces in front of her, "—these dogs."

He was mildly relieved. She seemed too competent to have bought a place site unseen and have gotten taken like this. But clearly, she'd done it.

"Cabins are over this way," he pointed. Though he thought they could get to them the other direction as well. He'd gotten the impression that the trail would loop back to the other side of the lodge, but he hadn't followed it all the way through, and he wasn't willing to try it.

As they walked along the path he'd found earlier, they passed six of the cabins along the way.

"Damn, each one is worse than the one before it." She sighed. "I was hoping to stay here tonight, since the power was on and all. What a mess."

Ash discovered that he liked Roz. He felt he should trust her, despite the shitshow that he'd blindly walked into. Then again, he'd trusted the wrong people before.

So he promised himself he wouldn't make any big decisions about this job until it had been at least a few more days. Until he got a better idea of whether she, too, had been had. Whether she was competent despite this first massive error. Whether she was going to be able to make a go of this or not.

As he opened the door to the last cabin, he watched her face fall and imagined it was a similar expression to the one that he had made when he first saw it.

She stepped inside, shaking her head.

And he wondered if he even had a job at all.

CHAPTER FOUR

B randy pulled up to the front of the lodge already feeling out of place. Her little car, perfect for city life and fitting into tight parking spaces, had seemed like it might not make it. The bumps and ruts in the gravel drive had been more than she'd expected.

But what had she expected? This was a much-needed escape, not the trip to the Bahamas she'd been promised.

The drive had been well paved all along the side of the river and the view was gorgeous. She'd almost driven off the side of the narrow road a few times, it was so captivating. Trees lined the edges, glimpses of moving water peeking through the thick trunks, begging her to dip a toe in. It was all so . . . *green*!

She'd rolled down the window, taking deep breaths of air clearer than maybe any she'd ever breathed. And she'd almost broken into *Country Roads*. It was obvious that this was the area the song was written about.

But now, as she faced the lodge and the reality of what she'd done, Brandy sat in the car for a moment, getting her bearings before opening the door and stepping out. She was used to business suits on days she was in the office. When she interacted with people, professional clothing was like armor—people would take her seriously.

Sometimes she did manage business casual. And she wore sweatpants and bunny slippers when she worked from home. But this new job? It was all foreign.

She had on fresh hiking boots and shorts. She would never have met a new boss like this.

But this was where she'd found a place to take her wayward soul. She had to make it work.

It had taken just two weeks to realize she couldn't stay in Los Angeles. She was supposed to be on her honeymoon for the first week. Her mother had tried to console her, had invited her to family dinners and not understood when Brandy said *absolutely not.*

Everything had been ruined, not just the wedding, but the very foundation on which she had built her life. Everything she'd thought would remain steady had crumbled in that one moment.

She still had flashbacks to going numb as she heard the words just beyond the door. She'd heard about these things happening on wedding days but had never believed it would ever happen to her. She'd never have believed Theo would do something like that. And certainly not—

Brandy cut the thought off before it could form.

She could still feel the tulle of her dress against the palms of her hands as she grabbed it in her terror, bunching it in tight angry fists as she fled down the long hallway. She hadn't cried then. She had still been too stunned.

She'd whiled away four days doing nothing. Then she tried to handle the cleanup. She returned presents, wrote the same horrible thank you note by hand over and over. She explained nothing.

Sometimes she found herself randomly livid, because she was supposed to be on the beach. Sometimes she was frantically working, scrambling to get all the money refunded—specifically into her own bank account. She'd managed to siphon about half of it back and she'd kept all of it.

At one point though, Theo had said if she was going to get the money back, she at least needed to split it with him. Brandy had put a quick, sharp end to that.

The man had no room to complain about anything. She'd been generous to stay silent on the facts and that should have been more than enough for him.

But when she'd gone back to work, everyone congratulated her. They talked about how she'd managed to not get sunburned, and she'd had to tell them all. The same shit all over again. There was no escaping it. When they asked what happened, she said only, "It didn't work out."

That was an understatement, and she should have been able to smear that man across the walls. But she couldn't. And she hated that, too.

It had been Bethany, standing in her office doorway, her arms full of files and three different tablets, who'd said, "Be careful coming back before you're ready. This job can drain you. It's good work, but you have to bring a full well and you don't have it right now, girl."

Bethany had been right. At the end of three days, Brandy had pulled out the penny and started searching for what she could do with it. She'd applied to a few jobs totally unlike this one.

She hadn't needed to cash in the penny, but she had taken a six month leave of absence from her job.

Now she was here of all places. No one came out to greet her and she was glad, because she had no idea what the hell she was doing.

The two workers painting the porch barely even looked at her. Neither of them was Roz. With yet another deep breath, she opened the car door and stepped out into her new life.

Then someone came around the corner. He actually looked

at her, this man with black hair that was just a little too long. He questioned her presence with sharp blue eyes. Tall and lean, he wore jeans and an old gray T shirt that had clearly seen some heavy work today. Dark smears streaked the front of it, yellow work gloves hung loose around his wrists as he stepped forward and said, "You must be the new dog trainer."

Brandy almost laughed.

CHAPTER FIVE

The firelight made the bright red of her hair into a soft glow. Ash tried not to feel the same gut punch he'd felt when she climbed out of that ridiculous little car earlier, but it was still there.

He ignored it. There was no sense in feeling anything for a co-worker. Not at a new job. Not at one that was taking everything to stay afloat like this place seemed to be.

The little car was like the woman: beautiful and curved in all the right spots, but totally out of place here. He'd thought she might be as ridiculous as the car, but a day and a half later, she'd proved herself useful at least.

Then again, she'd arrived to a lodge with two weeks of work on it. It looked better than it had when he'd first seen it—much better. She hadn't dealt with the grime on the windows or the cobwebs across her cabin railing. The front porch of the lodge had been shored up before she even arrived, the new pillar in place and a fresh coat of paint already going on. Brandy had arrived to a place on the upswing.

He had not.

It was definitely better now. The property inspector—whom

Roz had diligently worked with and trusted before she signed the papers—said the place had "good bones." Ash wouldn't have known what that was, but he did now.

The floors hadn't fallen through. The first crew had cleared the animals. The second had removed the rotting debris around the place and hauled it away in a dumpster. The third crew disinfected and scrubbed all of it.

He'd seen the hardwood floors look like a place he might want to take his shoes off for the first time just hours before Brandy had arrived. She had good timing, he would give her that.

Ash was almost surprised—but grateful—that he was still here, that any of them were. Roz had renegotiated the deal, closing escrow a week later, and bluffing her heart out to get the money to fix it up.

He got the impression that this might be a bit of a shoestring dream. He didn't ask.

He'd only just come back from the hotel in Charlottesville, where Roz had put him up for a week. Even with all the paid cleaners, he and Roz had put in their fair share. Her because it was hers. Him because he had nothing better to do.

The two of them had wrenched open most all the windows. They'd climbed ladders and brushed the leaves out of the gutters. They'd repaired and replaced the loose floorboards on the little front porches on the cabins themselves.

Not what he'd been hired for, but he didn't have anywhere else to go.

Yesterday, just as he'd been repeating to himself that he wasn't going to let the redhead get to him, Roz had burst in. All smiles and warm greetings, she'd then asked *him* to show Brandy to her room. He'd looked the new girl up and down, all freckles and red curls, and imagined her disappointment at the cabin.

But it never came to pass. In fact, her shiny, hard sided

luggage had sat down right next to the door with a little bit of a thump. She'd looked around the small singular room with the tiny, attached bathroom. And declared it *perfect*.

Not what he'd expected.

Now, she sat around the fire with him and Roz. Her jeans shorts were short enough he could see where her ass was directly on the wood. That couldn't feel good. But she smiled and laughed and ate s'mores.

"Did you finally get unpacked?" Roz asked her.

"Yes!" then she faltered. "Mostly."

He'd put her to work yesterday as soon as she set down her luggage. He'd seen the jean shorts that she was wearing might have been old friends, but her boots didn't have a single scuff on them. Her work gloves had come with tags.

Now he offered her a tight smile from across the fire. He was being an ass to her, but that was better than asking her out. Better than if he got attached and she left. She was only here for six months anyway. How many times had she told him that?

"No!" she yelped out. "No! No!" as she pulled back the long marshmallow fork that Roz had bought for them.

Brandy blew on the flames as if that would save her marshmallow. "No!"

But it was black already, and one little orange flame kept popping back up. She blew on it angrily two more times before it finally stayed dead. Then she eyed the charred piece angrily. An irritating growl fell out of her lush pink lips.

Again, he felt his gut tighten. Nope. Not good, not for a coworker. Not for someone he was technically higher ranked than. Though Roz was his boss, he'd been hired to be second in command and have jurisdiction over animal decisions. Right now, though, the only animals here were Shadow and Astra, Roz's personal search and rescue dogs.

One side of Brandy's mouth quirked, her brows pulling together. "Who wants a dead marshmallow?"

She held the tip of the fork toward Roz, then him.

He'd already learned that she liked her marshmallows golden toasted, and that she wouldn't even touch it once the black char had set in.

"Here," he held out the handle of his own fork. "I just got started. Trade me."

He should at least be nice around the fire. He hadn't been before. Plus, there were only three of them here. Roz had built the fire pit herself with the intent that it was a place they could relax. There was enough space between the three of them to make it clear that the boss intended for there to be more people around the pit than just them. But when?

He didn't know.

"Thank you," Brandy smiled at him as she awkwardly slid closer to him to trade the forks.

He smiled back at her even as he thought, *Oh, dear God do not let her get splinters in her ass.* He might be a trained doctor, but he was a vet and Roz would have to take care of that.

Before he even finished the thought, she was back in place, carefully holding the new marshmallow at the very tips of the licking flames.

Pushing the fork into the fire, he caught her reject-mallow on fire on purpose. Then he lifted his beer as he watched it burn. Brandy looked at him like he was nuts and he wanted to tell her to keep her eyes on her own sugar.

He would just be a friendly coworker. Beer was not the best mix with s'mores, but he wasn't going to be the one to tell Roz that. She'd carefully asked what each of them liked and bought it.

Brandy had gone for a bottle of some hard fruit juice mix. Roz simply had a high-end soda. He noticed but didn't ask questions.

"I'm so glad the two of you are here!" Roz held her bottle up.

They sat on three corners of the fire, unable to clink the

bottles but metaphorically they held them in a jaunty *cheers*. Brandy's smile reminded him that she hadn't seen the worst of it.

"This is not the start I had hoped to get off to," Roz told them. "But I appreciate your effort and we'll get there."

Ash understood. It had been just him and Roz for almost two weeks. Unfortunately, a lot of what they'd gotten done was just demolition of the things that couldn't be fixed. They were only now close to actually starting work—work he'd thought he'd design and someone else would build.

"We've got plenty more to do tomorrow and we should probably all get to bed after this last s'more," Roz announced like a mother hen.

He almost protested that he was an adult and could make his own decisions. But he would have made the same one, so he kept it to himself.

"Amen!" Brandy pulled her perfectly roasted puff off the end of her fork and sandwiched it between graham crackers and chocolate.

A minute later when she licked the chocolate off her lips, he hoped that Roz hadn't noticed him being a complete neanderthal.

"I need a shower and a good night's sleep," Brandy announced as she stood up and brushed off her ass.

No splinters. He smiled at her, as did Roz, who told her, "Tomorrow we'll see what we can do about putting your talents to work."

He wondered what Brandy's talents were . . .

CHAPTER SIX

"I don't understand," Brandy bit her tongue to keep from demanding that he just *tell her* what he wanted.

Good looking apparently didn't mean reasonable. He was hardheaded as hell. He wouldn't explain, he just said *no*.

She tried again, her jaw clenching, her fingers flexing on the T-stick she'd brought with her to test the soil. "If you use the natural curve of the land, you'll get a bigger area. Isn't that what you want? Space for them to run?"

"Yes, but every extra inch requires extra fencing, and we have a budget."

"I'm not proposing any extra budget. Maybe four or five feet of fencing but we'll save on posts if we do what I suggested." Exactly what she'd told him the first time. Her smile was forced, and she couldn't make it any more sincere.

What had she done deciding to work here? At least the view was gorgeous. He would be, too, if he wasn't such an ass. Constantly dismissing her, always with the short answers, and now with the plain *no*.

"How is the area you're proposing not going to require extra fencing?" He asked it as if she were a kindergartener trying to explain how she was going to build her house out of candy.

"It does require extra fencing. I said that." She breathed in through her nose in a failing effort to stay calm. "But we can save on *materials* if we push back to the existing tree line and make use of the trees that are already naturally here. Look."

"So, you think dogs won't just run past the trees?" He looked at her as if she were dumb and she gave up.

"Yes, I think dogs are afraid of trees and understand that when you tell them to stay somewhere they just will!" Her sarcasm even bit her, but she was so over his bullshit. "In fact, I don't know why we are even building a fence at all! Just tell the dogs not to run off! I'm sure you're such a fantastic vet they'll just listen."

She almost called him "the asshole whisperer" but managed to click her teeth together before that came out.

He now looked at her as if to say, "Are you done?"

Yeah, she was about to be done. Maybe she could work with Roz. But Brandy tried one more time. "They're clearly established trees. We'll need to test each of them to see if they're sturdy enough, but my guess is that most of them will pass. If you do a chain link, it will save a ton of money. And then you can have almost double the space you originally proposed."

"If we do a chain link, some of the dogs will climb it. They are too expensive. Roz can't afford to lose a dog."

"We can't go out and fetch the dog back?" *Dogs would climb eight foot fences?* But he was a vet. Or maybe he was dicking with her.

"Not with all the wilderness out there." He waved a hand and she understood.

"Big cats. Gotcha."

"Coywolves," he told her.

"What's that?" Was he just telling her crap and hoping she'd believe it? He'd been curt enough since she arrived to think he was either grumpy or just a plain ass. She hadn't decided which yet.

"Coyotes crossed with wolves. All the predatory skills of wolves with the willingness to invade human spaces of coyotes."

That did not sound good. She would check to see if he was lying and if he wasn't she'd watch herself on hikes . . . if she ever got to take one.

"And you're telling me dogs will climb eight-foot-high chain link?"

"Most won't. Most people can put that fencing in their backyard and their dog will be fine. But every once in a while you get a dog who will just go right up and over it."

"Do they climb down the other side?" He had to be shitting her. She should be working but she couldn't do anything if he didn't agree to the fencing.

"Most of them will jump," he said, "though I've seen more than one climb down. But if it only works for *most dogs*, we'll have so many dogs through here—" He waved his hand at the area he wouldn't let her fence. "That we'll lose a few."

He still held the shovel he'd brought along at her suggestion, one arm leaning on it, the other gesturing sharply into the trees. He was trying not to show it, but he was clearly mad at her.

She didn't understand. He was being obstinate. She was trying to help.

"Then we don't use chain link. We come up with some other kind of fencing that will keep the dogs in."

"I don't know why you think you can do it for that money. We have a budget!"

"I'm sorry." Initially she meant the apology but, as soon as the words were out, they were immediately followed by, "I didn't realize you were the dog run whisperer."

"I'm literally a *veterinarian*." His frustration vented at last. Ash leaned forward on the shovel, his eyes opening wide as if to ask *what could she possibly do to counter that?*

24

"I'm literally a *civil engineer!*" she tossed back. "So, you might know the dogs, but I know the fencing materials and how to best use the land."

She crossed her arms and stared at him. One hip cocked out on its own, she was so mad. She waited for his damn response, grateful today's shorts were more utilitarian than cute. But her hair was up in a ponytail, wild curls having escaped around her face with the heat of the work, even though the day itself was the perfect temperature. She crossed her arms and wished again that she had smaller boobs. It would have hopefully made him take her more seriously.

Instead, he seemed to absorb it in a slow-motion shock. "You're what?"

"A cih-vil en-gine-eer." She enunciated each syllable in case he had trouble with the big words.

"You're a dog trainer," he said as if to correct her.

"I am now." She'd applied for the job on a whim. She'd applied for a handful of them, but this one had seemed interesting and different enough.

Bethany had been right. The burnout was real, and it was harsh. It had come on so quickly after the-wedding-that-wasn't that she'd not even realized her own well had been shot full of holes and drained dry.

The air hung heavy and hot between them for a moment as they stared at each other with this newfound information.

Finally, he asked, "What did you do before you came here?"

She almost shrugged, letting go of her belligerent stance and the belligerence itself. Then she gave him one of the simpler answers. "You know those black balls they put on the surface of Lake Mead to help absorb heat and prevent water loss?"

He shook his head. Of course, he didn't.

"There's been a metric ton of documentaries about it." He still shook his head. If he'd seen one, he'd know what she was talking about.

25

"Well, we do that, among other things. I've been upgrading and implementing similar systems in reservoirs around the country. We've been doing irrigation projects to help design systems that will make farmers more efficient. Members of my team were studying long grasses and root systems to help put the prairies back together." As she recited it all, she realized it was a cool job. She really did like it, and she would go back when she was ready to forget all about Theo and enjoy the work again.

But the look on Ash's face told her he felt justified in his analysis. There were no long grasses at play here. No reservoirs to save from evaporation. Just a dog run.

One that she could build better. But it wouldn't happen because this absolute meathead wouldn't listen, gorgeous blue eyes or not. But she wasn't giving up.

Brandy stared him down and waited for him to crack.

CHAPTER SEVEN

Brandy tattled to Roz at dinner that night. There hadn't been another bonfire though Roz had proposed having them twice a week. But there were still only the three of them here. Five if you counted Shadow and Astra. Not at all the bustling dog training facility Brandy had thought she'd be working at.

So not only was she literally building fences, she'd spent her third day not getting as far as they had hoped. And it was entirely Ash Cooper's fault.

She'd gone back to her cabin and taken a shower in the tiny square stall. The water pressure was good, and it got hot quickly, so she counted that as a win. As much as she would have loved a long luxurious bath in the huge clawfoot tub in the church, she had not been dressed for it that day. As she dried off, she promised herself one day she would buy her own condo or maybe even a house with a huge soaking tub.

One day soon.

One day after her six-month tenure here was over and she decided what she wanted to do with her life since it wouldn't include Theo or children or the gorgeous house off Chester's Bluff Road.

In fact, she wasn't sure now if her future would ever include those kinds of things. Maybe a lover here or there when she was ready. But certainly not a husband, not a confidant, since her ability to choose who to trust was clearly so very bad.

So, she would buy her home on her own. No compromises this time. She would make sure that her future house had more than just this tiny square shower with one singular dish for a bar of soap. Her shampoo sat on the floor at her feet, and she'd mentally added a little suction-mount shower shelf to her growing list of things she needed to get when she got into Charlottesville this weekend.

She sat at the dinner table now thinking about the business suit, the nice skirt, and the high-end slacks in the cabin closet. She'd brought two pairs of heels. After two full days here, she found it laughable that she'd even packed them. When was she ever going to need that stuff?

Roz and Ash kept up a relatively steady conversation, mostly about the to-do list around the place. Brandy had quietly eaten bite after bite of an excellent chicken tikka masala and garlic roasted green beans. When had Roz had time to make this?

"How far did you get with the dog run today?"

Brandy snapped to attention as Ash was opening his mouth. She swallowed a green bean whole just to get in front of him. "Nowhere."

"Nothing?" Roz's fork paused mid-air and she looked at Brandy as if to say she couldn't be serious. Unfortunately, she could.

She hated this. She loved being in charge of her own team. She listened to them! And this ass . . . "He won't even consider any other fence designs I've given him. I can make the run twice the size, which is what I thought you wanted—space!"

"That's right." Roz turned to look at Ash who briefly sent a curse Brandy's direction with only the glance of his eyes.

Well, screw him. Good looking men needed to learn to compromise.

"It's my project. I'm responsible for it and we need something the dogs can't climb over." He turned to Brandy, "Everything you've shown me doesn't work."

"Then I'll keep showing you more until one of them does. Or you can admit . . ." She stopped herself right before she smacked the fork down onto the table. It would have splattered that wonderful red sauce everywhere. She tried to calm down. "You can admit that some of these are probably pretty good. With just a little modification or input from you, they would work well. And for a really good price, too."

Roz looked back and forth between them. Her eyes darting one way then another, and Brandy could almost hear the word forming on her lips, *children*.

Before it could come out, she turned to her new boss and said, "I'm sorry. I really am. And thank you, this meal is wonderful. I'm grateful you took the time to cook this for us!"

Roz started to smile ever so slightly. She gestured with her knife across the table. "Ash made it. It was his turn."

Brandy had to work to keep her mouth from falling open. It was his night? She wasn't on dinner duty until the weekend. But now she was concerned. The man had made chicken tikka masala? Didn't that have to simmer all day?

Turning, she looked at him, trying to keep her expression neutral. She did *not* want to give him the praise but knew she needed to. "It's excellent. And I'm impressed."

He shook his head. "Don't be. It's rice and chicken and the sauce is from a jar."

"A jar?" She would need that name.

"I tried a lot of them. I found my favorite. I didn't have time to put much effort into dinner."

There was something in the tone that made her think he was blaming her for that. Still, the dinner bar was higher than she wanted it to be. Especially since she had been considering mac and cheese as her own offering.

Roz was ready to turn back to what was important. She looked square at each of them. "After dinner you show me these fences, you two."

Fuck, Brandy thought she was a grown ass woman hired to do a job and she was already having to get mediated after just two days. But she nodded as agreeably as she could. She probably deserved this.

Then again, Ash Cooper did, too.

The sour twist to his mouth only made her feel a little ping of delight. *Good. Let him suffer.*

Roz was opening her mouth to say something else when Shadow and Astra began barking furiously from the living room. The three turned to look at each other to see if anyone else had a clue.

It wasn't the first time the wildlife around here had come a bit too near the house and set the dogs off. The creatures seemed to have gotten used to the idea of not having people in the house and had moved in a little closer than was comfortable. It would be a while before the boundaries moved all the way back out.

Roz called out their names, "It's okay, you can stop barking."

Brandy was wondering if that actually worked—she'd had dogs and worked with them in the past, but Roz had hired her saying she would train Brandy.

It worked for all of ten seconds before they started in again.

"I hear a car." Ash was already on his feet, curiosity coloring his expression for once.

Roz's face lit up. "Oh, I hope so!" Then she was on her feet behind him, already halfway into the grand room at the front of the lodge.

Brandy could only trail along, confused. It was almost eight. They hadn't started eating until seven-thirty. She got the impression that dinners ran relatively late around here. They tried to take advantage of the daylight to do the work.

But her sore muscles wouldn't hop up quite as fast as the other two had. Her work had been mental up until this job and the physical labor was more than she was used to. Brandy estimated it would be another good four or five days before she fully settled into it.

Still, she followed the other two out toward the front of the great lodge, where she now heard a deep voice at the front door. Murmurs of pleasant but slightly formal greetings followed from Roz and Ash.

As excited as they'd been to hop up, Brandy would have expected more ringing endorsement at the door. But this seemed relatively reserved.

She was in the doorway before she knew it. Roz must have heard her approach. Shadow and Astra paid her no attention, crowding around the feet of the new guy, sniffing at him.

Turning to face Brandy, Roz waved one hand at him. "Brandy, this is Beck."

As she stepped out of the way and revealed their newcomer, Brandy got her first glimpse of him.

She was not at all prepared for the man she saw.

CHAPTER EIGHT

"You've gotten here just in time . . . for dinner," Roz told him, wondering if her voice shook a little.

She was afraid that she sounded a little afraid. Tattoos crawled up his arms in black ink, only very occasionally splashed with color. At the neck of his T shirt, more ink peeked around and arced up his neck. Across his knuckles, letters marched, but she didn't stop to read them. She didn't have to stop to notice that they were blurred, and almost blue—prison tattoos.

She'd known he had a record when she hired him.

She just didn't remember all the ink.

When she'd hopped on the video call with him, she'd not seen it. She did remember the eyes so dark they were almost black. But he looked . . . different.

It took her a moment to place what it was. Clearly, her filters were off. She had been raised a genteel Southern woman two states south of here. So, it was absolutely her own fault when she raised a finger and pointed at his head. "You . . ."

"Grew some hair. Yes, ma'am," He offered a chagrinned look,

running his hand over it as if he wasn't quite sure how he liked it.

Yes, she thought, that was why he looked different. She could only hope that he believed that was why she had been staring. She tried again, "Ash made us dinner."

The vet had made his introductions and was already heading toward the back of the building, back toward the dining room. Nothing about him said *veterinarian* right now, though. No scrubs, no stethoscope, no kittens in his pocket.

Brandy had lingered in the doorway a little longer. She'd said her hellos and exchanged basic pleasantries, her stance somehow completely neutral to their visitor.

Roz should have done that, too. "Brandy is also a dog trainer."

"Hardly," Brandy said, and Roz could tell she wanted to snort at the idea. "I got hired for that position. But I need to be trained to be a trainer."

"She'll actually be working under you," Roz said, wondering if maybe she should have warned Brandy upfront that the head trainer had learned his skills in prison and honed them in a parolee halfway house. If she did, she should also tell Brandy that he had a master's in World Literature. That, like the ink, was something he'd gotten in prison.

She turned back to Beck, too flustered to be the one in charge and she tried again. "If you want to eat with us, just leave your bag by the door, we'll get it in a little bit."

She heard the catch that still lingered in her voice, the stutter that found space between the words, and she wondered what had happened to her.

Then again, it was all easily explainable. She'd cut ties with everything from her past. She'd picked Shadow and Astra out of a shelter she'd passed on the way here, recognizing them as highly trained specimens. They were very valuable dogs, approximately two to three years old each.

They must have been lost or something. Whoever had worked with them originally would never have surrendered them, not knowingly. She'd adopted them on the spot and she'd come here to the place she'd sunk every last bit of savings she had into.

She'd hopes of starting over.

Finding it in shambles and having to renegotiate her dream had not been easy. But she kept reminding herself that New Roz could do this. None of these people had known Old Roz. None of them had any reason to disrespect her or disbelieve her. And she had every intention of keeping it that way.

She'd debated for several weeks now, if she should tell them that she was robbing Peter to pay Paul on this one or if she should fake it until she made it. She hadn't decided. She had simply been vague the whole time. Probably not a good look.

Having left his bag by the door and leaned down quickly to make friends with the dogs, Benjamin Becker—*Beck* as he told them to call him—looked up and began to follow Ash across the wide room. He trailed the others toward the dining room.

Roz hung back watching. Though both men were in jeans and T shirts, the two could not have been more different. Ash was tall and lean, his skill one of fine tuning. He looked like a runner, and there was something just a little aristocratic, or maybe just aloof about him.

Beck was shorter, definitely a kid of the streets and thick with muscle—the kind that came from weights and maybe fights.

Brandy was already calling out over her shoulder, "Shall I get you a plate, Beck? We have chicken tikka masala and garlic green beans over rice."

"It sounds wonderful," he said, and Roz couldn't help but wonder what kind of food he'd been eating before now.

She watched as he followed Brandy into the kitchen. From the clinks and the noises, she could hear them serving up a plate for him and grabbing a drink. Ash made himself at home back at the table, digging his fork back into the last of his food, though he was the only one sitting there now.

After a bite, he looked up at her. Had she paused in the doorway? Was she making too much of this?

Ash had been here the first afternoon she'd arrived, and there had been just the two of them for a while. Then Brandy had joined them, making three and it had felt easier to her. More right.

Now with Beck here, there were four. How many more people could she put in place as pillars of her dream before she fucked up and picked the wrong one?

Just like before . . .

CHAPTER NINE

"She doesn't know anything about dogs," Ash told Roz.

Roz had set up weekly check-ins between her and him. She was probably going to do it with Brandy and Beck too, so it wasn't anything special. And Brandy would probably complain to Roz about him, if she hadn't already.

"She's learning," Roz said.

"She's learning with Shadow and Astra, who are obviously very well trained already."

"And that's how you learn," Roz reiterated to him. She didn't quite have the tone of suggesting that he was being stupid, but it was clearly a reminder.

"True, but she's one of the first that you hired. Wouldn't you want her to know more?"

"I had all these weird options," Roz told him, putting her hands flat on the desk in front of her. He appreciated that she kept a semi-formal office though semi-formal was about as much as any place dealing with animals got. Sure enough, two dog beds were aligned along the wall under the window. And the two large dogs were snoring through his meeting. If he wasn't a vet—if he wasn't already used to this—he might have found it odd or off putting.

"You're just starting out," he tried again. "I would have thought you would want someone who'd be able to train downstream."

"True and that's who I had first, but she quit at the last minute." Roz sighed and looked out the window.

With the grime gone the view was beautiful. An eagle caught a draft in the distance and if he believed in any kind of god Ash might have thought it a sign.

"I only had a handful of applications for people who could do the work and start in the short period of time that I had to fill that vacancy." This time she looked at him as if she were confessing something. "I'll be honest, the whole thing seemed like a sign."

Ash held his tongue from saying in response that he should be honest too, and that running a business on *signs* probably wasn't a good way to make money.

Though maybe Roz was better at reading signs than he gave her credit for, because she immediately said, "I'm not in this to make money."

His heart clenched. He'd been here before and it didn't end well. "But if we don't make money, how do we survive?"

"I'm in it to make enough to pay all our salaries, to keep all the dogs in good comfort, and hopefully train more and more, but I'm not in it for massive profit, not here to get rich or to pay off any shareholders. It's just about making this place run."

"That's fair." And no different than his paycheck would look anywhere else. Veterinarians could own their own practice and actually make pretty good money. Or they could work at clinics or in zoos or rescues. There were all kinds of salary levels. His here was pretty decent for a rescue, but the digits on his paycheck alone made it clear that he wasn't here to get rich either.

Roz had told him that she wanted to pay enough to attract the best people. He'd been proud to be on that list. But the addition of Brandy Blackwell was making him wonder what Roz considered the *best people*. As he looked up at her again, trying to formulate how to ask exactly that, she once again seemed to read his mind.

"She wanted to change her life." There was a slight pause, a slight softening of tone. "And I'm here for that."

Ash had to wonder if maybe Brandy was the first rescue the place was taking in. It would explain a lot. But Roz was speaking again.

"And I saw that she was a civil engineer. I knew—even when I believed this place was in much better shape than it was—that we would have a lot of work to do. It had kennels for dogs, but it was by no means set up as a training facility. The ones here were for the dogs that came with guests that stayed for a handful of nights. Not to live and work and train here."

He understood. The kind of training she was talking about would require more things to be built. More of everything.

"We both knew it wasn't ready to be the kind of operation we're taking on." She paused again, "And not the kind I'm considering growing into."

He'd heard it before: Initially, they would train emotional support animals and seeing eye dogs, dogs for people with wheelchairs, for deaf people, those who had medical conditions who needed alerts. After that—if Roz had her way—search dogs, rescue dogs, and cadaver dogs. Even bomb and accelerant sniffing dogs.

It occurred to him then that maybe he had things wrong. "Why am I second in command?" He was a veterinarian. He was here to help take care of the animals. But, given her broader goals, the top people should truly be the trainers. "Why not Beck?"

Roz merely pressed her lips together and the lull hung

between them. When she finally did speak, she said, "I know my decisions aren't always clear. I'll try to make them clear whenever I can. Sometimes I'm going by my gut. Sometimes, like with Brandy, I've lost the person I expected and had to scramble to find a replacement. But I will say having a civil engineer here has already helped."

She paused and he waited for her to sing Brandy's praises. He should stop complaining because Roz adored her and her ideas.

"Having a dog trainer would help us get our inaugural class on their feet. But we already have Beck for that. Brandy doubled the size of our dog run for an extra three hundred dollars in supplies."

He'd conceded that to Brandy already. And to Roz.

They'd use her chain link idea. And, as she'd promised, she'd managed to enclose the entire space for the original price. How she'd not had any errors or gone over budget with any surprise costs was beyond him.

Given the tree's thickness and their root systems, Brandy had pointed out that the trees could be further apart than any post that they might sink. And that had been the bulk of her massive savings. The extra money had gone to the way she enclosed the fence at his request so the climbers couldn't get out. She'd even made it attractive.

Damn her.

She'd painted it a soft cream and used black bolts. The non-tree posts had been wooden six-by-sixes rather than metal ones. She'd pointed out that any metal cheap enough for their needs would be sturdy only until something very heavy hit it, then it could fold like paper.

The fence was now capped with a painted-to-match two-by-six rim around the entire top. So, if a dog climbed it, he wouldn't be able to get over the lip. It was smart. In the end, Ash had been forced to admit it.

Now he nodded at Roz as she said, "That fence that Brandy built? That will already improve Jade River Sanctuary for its entire life."

Whatever Ash thought about her methods, Roz was the boss. She signed his paychecks, and she decided that Brandy Blackwell was a good investment.

So, Ash would need to make her into one.

CHAPTER TEN

"Why do I need to know this?" Brandy asked. Her brain was full, and Ash wasn't making it any easier.

It didn't matter if his ass looked great in those jeans, her eyes were crossing. Could she not just do some math? Math she understood, but she was struggling with American Bulldogs versus French. The shared origins of Irish Wolfhounds and Great Danes.

"Because," he said, "you need to be able to recognize the breeds in a dog. That way, when you work with Beck and he tells you a dog is a certain breed, you have a better idea of how they're going to respond."

Weren't they all just dogs? Maybe she was truly in the wrong job. Maybe she should have gone off and been somebody's nanny for six months. But no, she wouldn't have loved that.

While she could tell Ash wasn't impressed with her utter lack of knowledge, she loved Shadow and Astra. She loved dogs in general. So, she sucked it up.

She didn't know if he was pleased or not that she brought a notebook and took copious notes as she sat at the desk like his lone student.

Brandy wrote down everything she could, trying to absorb every last bit. She'd be a freaking veterinarian herself by the time she left here. But for now, she looked at the scramble on the page. She would have to organize it and really learn it this evening. Because Ash would start tomorrow as if she already knew these things, despite the fact that his topics wandered all over the place. He did too. Sometimes he stood at the front of the room and sketched out a few things—hideously—on the whiteboard, as though he were a teacher. Then, other times, he sat opposite from her, pointing at different things in a book.

When he did that, she could smell him, and she could start to feel just enough to let her know that Theo hadn't fully broken her.

But she quashed it then. There was no room for anything like that here. She was too raw. Despite his raw good looks, Ash Cooper was her last choice.

Roz had told her that this room would later be used as a classroom. That as people were matched with service dogs, they would need to learn to work with their companion. They would come and stay in the bedrooms and study in this classroom—all in the main lodge. Brandy couldn't wait to see it full.

But they were still doing some of the work on the lodge rooms, making sure at least half of the rooms were fully ADA compliant. That was a huge undertaking, given the fact that the lodge had previously been used for vacationers and only had the one room that was wheelchair accessible.

It would be a while before the people came. They currently had no service dogs in training yet. Roz was just planning ahead.

One of the rooms was getting fitted today with blinking lights tied to the smoke alarm and various noises around the lodge. It would also have an alarm clock that flashed and vibrated and so on.

Brandy might not understand all the dog breeds and

temperaments that Ash was throwing at her. But she was helping Roz design the rooms. As for the dogs, she would learn to the best of her ability, because the work felt important.

They went for another hour, her mind turning to mush. The textbook Ash used was old and looked like it had been bought from a secondhand shop. Or maybe it was simply one he'd brought with him from his veterinary school days.

"Can I take it with me?" she asked when he closed it.

He seemed surprised. But it didn't matter to her that she was the only student in his class. She had grown up labeled 'gifted' and she'd never lost the drive to excel.

"Sure." He pushed it over to her and checked the time before adding, "It's a good stopping point for today."

Thank God, she thought, though she nodded at him like she could easily go another hour or five. She was such a liar.

When he didn't press it, she grabbed up the book and her notes and scrambled out of there before he could say anything else.

She headed back to her cabin. Just getting outside and in the sun for a moment perked her up. She would spend the early afternoon with Roz or whoever Roz wanted her to work with. They would take care of whatever needed building or cleaning or scrubbing or planning.

She had gotten blisters on her hands from clearing underbrush along some of the trails. She had refused to complain. She didn't want Beck to think she couldn't handle it, and she wouldn't give Ash the satisfaction of seeing her in pain.

As she'd worked, feeling the burn with each swing, she promised herself that, one of these days when she had free time, she would go for a run. She would put on her sneakers and her playlist and take to one of the trails, *blessedly alone* in the daytime.

Right now, her entire life was in stark contrast. She was always alone in her cabin. No one else even set foot in there.

She had no dinner guests. No one moved her things. It was empty except for her. Sometimes it was wonderful, and sometimes lonely. And always not at all the life she had expected.

She should have been decorating the new house now. She'd planned on being a wife. They'd discussed how many months they would wait before they pulled the goalie and started trying to have a baby. Though they hadn't made a final decision, the number of months they were talking about would all fit on one hand.

And now . . .

Burning rage bubbled up just thinking about it. How far along was she? Did anyone in her family even know? They would soon, even if they didn't understand why Brandy had left. It would be too much to get updates, to hear just how excited they were. She hadn't told them the truth. *Would Sammy?*

Tamping down the anger and the pain it covered were hard, but necessary. She needed a sandwich and she needed to function. She told herself she was fine, and she opened the adorable half-size fridge Roz had put in her cabin. It was red with a matching microwave, a little bit retro looking. The coffee pot was the same. Not so the two-part burner, though it too was new.

Brandy contemplated grilled cheese and a can of soup. But the day was getting warm, and she was going to go out and work. She settled for cold cuts and cheese on an artisan bread that she'd found in Charlottesville. She ate it alone in her room, the little AC chugging though the day wasn't too warm, and she contemplated her next turn to cook dinner.

She'd stepped up her game and made apple stuffed pork chops, only to find Roz serving mac and cheese the next night. *Good.* The lower bar was better.

When she finished, she consulted with Roz on the lodge

rooms and they met up with both Beck and Ash, where all three of them argued about the best construction for the kennels.

Then she headed off with Beck for more lessons in which she pretend-trained Shadow and Astra.

"Use a lower voice," he kept saying, until she was speaking in tones so guttural it was laughable. But Shadow and Astra listened to her.

"Now, the same run, but just with hand signals."

It was important, she knew, that all the dogs be trained multimodally. So, with a wave of her hand, palm open, down at her side, Astra heeled.

Brandy snapped and put one finger out. Astra sat.

Brandy was proud of herself, though obviously the dog already knew this. Beck had made it clear that they were training the dogs, but they would also be training the dog owners. Without consistent reinforcement, any training would eventually fade.

At last, he said, "Let's call it. You did good work today."

Better than Ash ever said, she grumbled in her own head, though outwardly she smiled at the praise. She was grateful that she was not on duty for dinner, and she was free until eight a.m. tomorrow when she would start all over again.

Could she really do this for six whole months?

Brandy was thinking about a walk, or heading back to her cabin for a shower, when Beck stopped her at the doorway. "Are you ready for tomorrow?"

"What's tomorrow?" She didn't even know.

CHAPTER ELEVEN

The ride had been slightly awkward. Charlottesville wasn't close.

Roz had been at the wheel of the big van that was already fitted with kennels in the back. As Roz had ushered them all into the vehicle, Brandy slid easily into the back seat. The hierarchy was clear for her, but there had been a moment when Ash and Beck had quietly sized each other up, figuring out who got the front seat and who got the back.

Ash wound up conceding the front to Beck in a moment that made Brandy wonder if he really thought Beck should be in charge. But then Roz was bouncing the big vehicle down the drive. "Okay, tell me if the seats are comfortable, if there's anything you think of that needs to be fixed or improved. This is a test drive."

Brandy looked out the window thinking that everyone had seemed to know where they were going except her. It seemed to be a joke, not to let the new girl in on it, even though Beck was technically the new kid.

Roz had pulled up first to a restaurant, the large hulking

vehicle out of place in a parking lot full of family SUVs and the occasional electric car. "Lunch!"

Both Beck and Ash seemed ready for it.

"I'm glad to eat something none of us had to cook for ourselves." Ash looked ready to enjoy the meal, though they were all a bit underdressed for the place.

Brandy didn't say anything, just trailed along, wondering if this was it. If they'd driven all the way out here for a lunch she might have worn a skirt to, and definitely not her boots, had she been given any kind of warning.

"We definitely need something that isn't drive thru." Roz held the door, ushering them in.

It wasn't high end, but it was a nice sit-down meal with service and hot food. Though Brandy had gotten the impression that Roz was running the place at the absolute edge of what she could afford, the boss had paid for all of them and allowed no argument.

"You're my employees. This is a business lunch. I'll write it off." She said it with a smile. But Brandy understood at least enough about write offs to know that it didn't negate the cost.

When she climbed back into the van, she was happy and full. The meal had been wonderful, and the group had gotten along relatively well. They still sometimes knitpicked each other's ideas over dinner, the four of them pushing and pulling until someone caved or Roz declared a winner.

It was nice to just have casual conversation, even if the truce had been declared only while they were in public. Still, no one had told her where they were going, and she wasn't willing to admit defeat and ask.

When they pulled up in front of the Albemarle County Animal Shelter, she shouldn't have been surprised. But she was.

Brandy was unbuckling her seat belt and climbing out before even asking, "Are we getting our first batch of incoming trainees?"

Roz had called out "Yes!" to her back.

"How many?" Brandy questioned back, but before anyone could even say anything she was at the shelter door, opening it and stepping inside.

The long, cream-colored building greeted her, making her feel at home with the distant sound of animals moving around. The smell, though clean, was definitely a place with pets. The heavy mood hit her, as it often did, of wanting to save them all.

"Five dogs," Ash told her. His breath sent a shiver down the back of her neck. By his tone, he was just as excited about getting their inaugural class as she was.

Had he been that close behind her? Turning around, she almost bumped full into him. Sucking in a quick breath, she stepped back. "What kinds?"

She'd been paying attention and she believed she knew what to look for in the dogs.

It was Roz that answered. "My goal with the first batch is basically one of each. One small emotional support, one hearing dog, one seeing eye dog, one wheelchair support and one medical alert."

"Is that going to be too many different things to train at once?" Brandy asked.

"Definitely." But Roz smiled and almost laughed. "I'm bringing in two new trainers in the next couple of days."

Five dogs, five of them, plus Roz, Brandy thought. They could do it.

Beck joined in. "We'll all participate in the training of all five dogs. If one type of support dog appears much easier to train or more profitable, that will help us decide where to gear the next incoming class."

Brandy loved that the team only spoke of the dogs as though they were students. Graduates. Incoming classes. But she was ready to leave the lobby and see the options. She would have run into the back with the kennels, but she managed to act like an adult. Barely.

Roz approached the front desk, explaining who she was and that an agreement had already been made.

Once she had everything settled, Ash looked to Beck. "Alright, let's see what they've got."

What if there weren't five good candidates here? Brandy knew she would take more than that if she could. Though Ash and Beck clearly respected each other's decisions regarding the incoming class, they still clearly didn't quite know where they stood with each other.

They were coming at the same thing from very different angles, she understood. So, while Brandy had wished to be included in the decision, maybe she should just trail along for now.

She watched as Ash walked up and down the line. Dogs barked at him and some cowered in the back, and some came up to the fence begging to be petted.

"What are you looking for?" She asked Beck, who was right beside her, but it was Ash who answered, a smile on his face.

Holy shit. The man was gorgeous when he was actually happy. And damn, he had looked good enough when he was irritated at having to work with her.

"We need dogs that respond but aren't overly excitable. No obvious bad behaviors. They need to react equally well to all of us, because we don't know who they're going to end up with in the future."

"If we get a dog who is, say, afraid of men, we can't take him or her?" Brandy asked.

"It depends on how afraid and what kind of behaviors they exhibit when doing it. Some of it we should be able to work around."

It made her feel better that something like that wouldn't

necessarily keep a dog out of their program and on track to a better life.

Beck turned and looked at Ash and something passed between the two of them. But it was Ash who turned again to Brandy, and said, "Go ahead. Look up and down the aisle. Pick out seven or eight that you think we should take the first five from."

Shocked that the preliminary task had been given to her, Brandy looked to Beck and then to Roz, as both of them nodded. Well hell, it was time to put all her new skills to work, and she didn't want to examine why it was so important to make them all proud. She couldn't hide the smile when she looked back at Ash.

CHAPTER TWELVE

I t wasn't surprising to Ash that Brandy had helped get the dogs calmly out of the van and was now taking personal moments to get face time with each.

All four of them had worked on getting the first class used to the area and settled. It was a big change. Adoption was happy, but for these guys, it wasn't quite the same.

Jade River Sanctuary wasn't forever for them, but it was a promise of forever. It was a chance to be a working dog with responsibilities and all the benefits that came with that.

They'd been given time in the dog run. Ash had thrown the ball for each of them, both just to play and to see how well they fetched it. They'd been given their first round of food—food that Roz had bought to match what the shelter was offering. There were enough changes already today, anything the team could hold steady was a good thing.

As Brandy moved from the end of the line, leaving the largest in the furthest kennel, she started to return to the dog closest to him, to start all over.

"Let's let them rest and get used to their new homes," he told her, watching her disappointment and wondering if it was with him. "We'll give them an hour or two."

He'd sent everyone else off to their cabins and settled in nearby with a good book. He'd already convinced Roz that there should be no construction today, no lodge improvements, no lawn mowing. Nothing that would startle a dog or make it irritated. He sat in one of the Adirondack chairs that she'd had added to the wide back porch and read his book as he watched over his new charges.

It had felt weird to be here and have no things to take care of. When Brandy walked back past him, he saw it was almost exactly the hour and thirty minute mark. Her long legs ate up the ground, and he tried not to admire the way she moved, the freckles that marked all the exposed skin. Would they dance down her spine, too?

He reminded himself he didn't need to know.

She didn't even see him. So he stayed still like a rabbit, watching as she took each dog out, carefully talked them into a leash, then walked them around the compound. She handed out copious milk bones and ear scratches.

When she disappeared with the second one, asking the pup if he wanted to keep his shelter name or have a new one, Ash stood up. He could only play the watching game for so long or it was creepy. What if Roz saw him? What if Brandy spotted him and jumped?

He headed to the third kennel and knelt down to coax the dog out. That was unnecessary, as the little dude bolted out and jumped up to lick his face. There was a reason he was a veterinarian. Dogs didn't judge. Dogs were grateful for any help that was given, and they recognized all of it, even when things didn't work out.

He was never the scapegoat for a dog or a cat. Only for the owners.

Something about the way Brandy interacted with everyone

told Ash that she didn't understand what it was to be the one who was always wrong.

While he wasn't always right when it came to veterinary medicine, at least it played out reasonably. His right decisions were rewarded. His wrong ones fixed whenever possible.

He was starting down the path only to see Brandy returning. She looked up at him and smiled slightly but didn't ask if what she was doing was okay. Her smile reminded him that he'd said "one to two hours" so here she was.

After he took the last dog out walking around the compound, getting him used to being on the leash, and getting him used to lots of compliments and treats for good behavior, he brought the dog to the kennel where the others waited.

The little guy rolled over, requesting a belly rub. A very good sign, Ash thought. He definitely gave the belly rub.

Involved in the task of praising the dog, he didn't hear that Brandy had come up behind him.

"What's next?" she asked.

"Baths. Flea treatments." He waited for her to object. As usual she didn't. He should have stopped waiting for her to tap out a while ago. "Then we'll do wellness checks."

"More than what you did at the shelter?"

Ash only nodded and didn't add that if certain medical tests came back positive, the dog would have to go back. Brandy wouldn't care what the treatments cost or how long they took. He understood that about her already. She'd made her choice, and she was going to be loyal.

Maybe he should give her more credit for that. Even if he would have to explain that Jade River Sanctuary couldn't afford that. Or that they could rescue more dogs if they made smart choices. But he didn't.

Brandy grinned at him, all red hair and freckles, her wide mouth lush and happy. She was stunning when she smiled like that. And he shouldn't think about it, but he did.

It wasn't that she was unhappy, usually. It was that she was busy concentrating. When she wasn't concentrating, when she wasn't actively being entertained, he saw something creep in at the edges. He had to admit that he was curious what it was, even though it wasn't his place to ask. And he wouldn't ask, because Lord knew he didn't want to tell anyone about his own past.

It was complicated and ugly, and he refused to be judged for it ever again.

He reminded himself that Brandy had done well with the initial picks on the dogs. Though she'd chosen eight and they'd brought back five, the other three choices weren't bad options, they just didn't pass more than the initial tests. They would make good family pets for someone.

"You did good picking these guys." He told her because she needed to be told. Withholding praise was almost as bad as random outbursts or unpredictable responses. He was opening his mouth to say more when she beamed at him.

His words lit her up in a way he hadn't expected. He'd thought she was pretty before, but this had nothing to do with that and everything to do with the heat that shot through him in a way he wasn't prepared to deal with. A way he shouldn't be feeling.

CHAPTER THIRTEEN

"Do we use the shelter names or just pick out new names?" Brandy asked as the dogs were all lined up after baths.

Ash and Beck had each taken charge of bathing one dog. Brandy and Roz had flitted between them, fetching soap, or creams. They held faces and made soothing noises, then administered towel rubs after.

Ash had been pleased to see that Beck had a professional and firm grip on the dog he bathed. Then again, he'd come highly recommended. Maybe Ash had just doubted what training Beck had been given in prison.

Damn, he had to stop doubting everyone around him.

Was he becoming *her*?

Always thinking everyone was wrong or not good enough?

The thought alone was horrific to him. He reminded himself that people floated toward what they knew. She was what he knew. He would catch himself being an asshole and change it.

He picked something good to look at. Brandy and Roz were tipping their heads back and forth as they tried to decide about names.

There were so many things Brandy needed to work on here that she didn't know yet, but he was done being upset that Roz had hired someone without the knowledge he expected. She had other skills, and the sanctuary needed her. She dove into the work, trimming nails expertly after quick instruction. He'd told her once how to grab the scruff of the neck and hold on to an uncollared dog. She'd not needed to be told again. She'd sized their collars accurately without his help at all.

He was opening his mouth to answer her question but Beck beat him to it. "When we fostered, we usually gave them names that belong to a certain group. Once it was named after different kinds of chips. One litter was potatoes."

"Potatoes?" Roz asked, clearly confused.

"Yeah," Beck actually looked pleased to be telling the story. "Spud, Yam, and the littlest one was Tater Tot."

By the look on Brandy's face, Ash knew exactly how adorable she thought the name Tater Tot was. She took only a moment to come up with her own proposal. "We can name the next groups after potatoes or restaurants or superheroes, but how about we name these guys after famous firsts?"

Ash had no objections. There would be so many dogs trained here that any name he wanted to use would eventually get used. He'd seen some good ones in the shelter and in the clinic, too. But he was wondering where she was going with this.

"How about Sidney Poitier?" She knelt down in front of a regal looking black lab/pit mix, and Ash had to admit the young pup seemed to like both Brandy and the name.

She turned to the smallest of the dogs. "Buzz Aldrin."

Beck was grinning. "I like it. What else?"

"Marie Curie!" Roz christened the female at the middle of the group.

Then Brandy added, "Katherine Switzer and Tensing Norgay!"

Ash was confused. "I get Sidney, Buzz, and Marie but . . .?"

"Katherine Switzer was the first woman to run the marathon," Beck added, and Brandy beamed at him.

That shouldn't have made Ash jealous. It was stupid. He didn't fall for coworkers—he shouldn't, and he wouldn't. But his lips pressed flat as he tried to smile back.

"But I don't know the last one," Beck admitted, running his hand over the hair that Roz had said was new.

"Tensing Norgay guided Sir Edmund Hillary to the top of Everest. Hillary has long been called the first, but I think Norgay here deserves the real credit." She scratched at the last dog's ears, a mid-sized beauty who was going to get a decent bit bigger, he was so young still.

They'd fed the dogs, taken them for one last walk and let them settle in overnight. Ash had, of course, come out and checked on them at two a.m. not surprised to find that they all seemed quite content. Maybe, finally, so was he. Roz had built a haven out of the trash heap he'd first seen.

He'd headed right back to his cabin upon seeing that everything was as it should be. But in the morning, someone else had come out before the start of work, too. Each kennel had a little hand-painted name tag over it when he arrived. *Brandy.*

Her knowledge of the process of training dogs had been limited to the standard stuff someone who'd grown up with dogs knew. But as he told and showed her what to do, she simply dove in. She'd actually cheered when all the medical tests came out with good results, giving each dog a treat and praising them for being so healthy.

The work here had shifted, and he could feel it in his bones.

Though there were still things to build and design and add to Jade River Sanctuary, this was what the work should be. The next two days had gone by without a hitch.

Work had resumed on the interior rooms. There was now a regular schedule to train the dogs, with all four of them rotating through. True to her promise, Roz delivered two new employees: Casey and Lynzee.

Casey was only in for the rest of the summer—a short stay. He had an undergraduate biology degree in hand and was on his way to veterinary school. He'd surprised Ash with his knowledge until he mentioned that his mother was a veterinarian. He'd basically grown up in the clinic. He was going to do well.

The other hire must have been one of Roz's "signs." Lynzee was grumpy, arms often folded, answers doled out in dry, monosyllabic tones. On her second day, Ash had learned that she just graduated high school. Barely. She'd graduated from the school that Albemarle county sent kids to after they'd been expelled from more than one of the others. She didn't just have a chip on her shoulder, she had the entire woodblock. He didn't need another rescue, what they needed was another trainer. Still, he felt for the girl.

Brandy, somehow, for all her shiny stability and seemingly easy past, managed to be the only one that Lynzee would actually talk to, at least in anything resembling a full sentence. Ash decided to be pleased that when he gave her an instruction, she often simply said, *okay*, and then did it. At least, she tended to execute the tasks reasonably well.

Brandy managed to fit in with the new hires. Despite being noticeably older than either of them, she was in the same boat a lot for learning what to do as far as being a trainer was concerned.

And Ash—though he hadn't admitted it specifically—had learned to concede to her when it came to building materials, construction sites, and how they could get the most out of their money for things that would be sturdy enough to hold up to the larger dogs.

Maybe Roz hadn't been wrong. Maybe it had been very wise to hire a civil engineer. He wasn't quite ready yet to concede that it was a "sign" though. Still, he needed to tell Brandy that she was fitting in. More than just the occasional "you did that task correctly."

Somewhere over the course of the week, he'd quit snapping at her for not being what he'd expected. He grudgingly accepted that she needed training in certain areas, and that he should listen to her about others.

He watched as she rubbed Sidney's head, scratched him behind the ears, and unsnapped the leash, pointing him into the kennel. Though Sidney could have bolted into the distance, he listened to Brandy. Whatever Beck had taught her about being an authority with the dogs, it had worked. Ash had seen the change.

Leash still in her hand, jean shorts still showing off her long curvy legs, hiking boots now with legit scuffs, she smiled at him. The grin at her happiness with the dog turned tentative as she looked at him, as if to ask if she'd done it right.

He should have said *good work* and headed off. He should have done any number of things except what he did.

But he heard the words falling out of his mouth. "I'm off tomorrow and I saw that you were, too. Do you want to go grab a coffee with me?"

CHAPTER FOURTEEN

"Are we going past the turn?" Brandy asked as she reached out to brace against the dash. She was used to Theo taking his turns hard, but Ash didn't throw her around.

She shouldn't have reached out, and she shouldn't have asked. They were clearly driving right past the turn into town and heading up the mountain road. "Where are we going?"

"There's a really great cafe in Charlottesville." He grinned at her, one hand casually on the wheel, the other elbow down on the armrest between them.

Just looking at him, she would have thought he was a sports car kind of guy—like Theo—but here in the big SUV she could see him with dogs and cats all around.

She'd gotten used to checking the seats for fur before she climbed in. Definitely not something from her old life, her regular wardrobe wouldn't have survived the past few weeks.

Being at the sanctuary was like stepping out of time. She had minimal connection to her old life, just the way she wanted it. Bethany had emailed, checking on her. Brandy had emailed back, assuring her work friend that she was A) having the time of her life and B) definitely coming back when the job was done.

Of course, she'd heard nothing from Sammy. Nothing from Theo either, though she'd been clear to Theo that she wanted to never speak to him again. Her mother, of course, checked in all the time. She always brought up Theo and asked *what was Brandy going to do about it?* As if this were her own fault.

Some days she thought it was. It was definitely her fault for getting all the way to the church and the white dress. She gave her mother only vague answers, knowing that telling the whole truth would destroy both of them.

Now, she pushed thoughts of her old life out of the way. She would only be here for a while. Apparently, Ash wasn't just taking her to the coffee shop in Jade River Valley. This was going to be quite the drive.

She was opening her mouth in an attempt at small talk, wondering what was appropriate to say to the boss on the way to a coffee shop, when Ash beat her to it.

"So, do you like being a civil engineer? Do you think you'll go back to it?"

"I'll definitely go back," she said. "Honestly, I love it. I get to design and create things. I'm in charge of a team. Since I've been in charge, we've had seven small projects and five big ones come to full completion. In two cases, we weren't able to do quite as much as we had originally thought, but in the other three we did more."

"You sound passionate about it."

She was. But she only shrugged. She couldn't help that she loved the work. She was only gone because . . .

"So why are you here? Taking a job well beneath your paygrade in an area that you don't really have a skill set in."

She turned to face him and raised an eyebrow. He only glanced at her, mostly keeping his eyes on the winding road flanked by lush green trees.

But she couldn't say he was absolutely wrong about that.

"Did you need a break from your very nice life designing things to make people's lives better?"

"Not that part," she shook her head, breathing in the warm mountain air. It definitely did a body good. "The work is a lot. Nothing ever goes according to plan. You go to work in a local place that needs something, so there's a lot of travel. You first have to assess the situation and figure out all the specifics of that job—no two are completely alike. Then you see what they need and what kind of resources they have to cover the work."

She looked out the window. She missed it. She missed her friends at the office, she missed the travel, and the nice apartment with the mist shower and the double french doors into her bedroom. But she hadn't been able to stay.

Looking back at Ash, she could see he was waiting for more, so she told him. "And then sometimes they get mad at the way that you handle it. I just needed a break from the stress."

This time she laughed though, for all she'd said, she'd basically lied. That was the stress she thrived on, not the actual problem.

Turning and looking out the window, she slid her sunglasses down from the top of her head. The sun was out, and the day was gorgeous. She was looking forward to sitting on the patio with a coffee and a pastry and not needing to be in charge of any furry creatures for a while.

She still wasn't sure why Ash had invited her along. Was he going to tell her to stay in her lane? Suggest that she shouldn't be at Jade River Sanctuary? That she should move out so they could hire a real dog trainer?

The temperature wasn't quite as warm today as it had been. She'd also been doing manual labor most days on the job, getting hot and sweaty. Today was her day off, so she'd worn jeans. A fact she was grateful for now as she rubbed her palms down the front of her legs and wondered if he noticed.

When he didn't push, she returned the favor of asking a

softball question. "What made you decide to get in on the ground floor of the Sanctuary?"

He paused for a while, taking several deep breaths. Enough to make her wonder what he had to think about. Did he regret it?

"Lots of reasons. Roz is definitely one of them."

"Agreed," Brandy smiled at him. She could be nice. "She practically persuaded me into this job."

At those words, Ash's eyebrows rose toward his hairline.

Had he thought she'd pushed her way in? Begged Roz for a chance to come work at the sanctuary? Yes, she'd wanted a temporary job far from home, but Roz had pushed her to take it.

"What did Roz tell you to get you to come?" she asked him, not saying any more. Let him think what he wanted. She wasn't going anywhere.

"She said I'd get to be the solo vet. That I'd get to help grow the program. And, because we were small, I'd have my hands in all aspects of it. It sounded like a good challenge and a nice change of scenery." He waved his hands at the beauty of the mountains all around them.

"Tired of giving Parvo shots and dental cleanings?" Brandy asked.

He laughed, but it was a rough sound. When he shook his head, his gaze darted out the window.

There was a story there.

"Did you not like working in a vet clinic?"

"I did, but I bounced from clinic to clinic. Never stayed at one place too long. Apparently, I'm super picky about who I work for."

Brandy offered a tight smile, instead of voicing the word *shocking* with as much sarcasm as she felt.

"What did they do wrong?" She was dying to know how snobby he could be about vet work, though she had to admit she hadn't seen any red flags in his work with the animals.

"One of the vets was prescribing probiotics and supplements instead of dewormers and vaccinations."

"No woo woo. Got it."

He almost grinned at that. Almost. "Another was overcharging the patients. I'm not sure how I felt about that, the neighborhood could afford it. But I found I didn't like working with vain, uptight people who were just as vain about their pets and made them just as uptight as their humans."

"Yuck."

"Yeah, then I found someone, and he was wonderful. An older vet, doing all the right kind of work, taking care of his patients, helping the families who couldn't pay so their animals stayed safe. He did farm and big animal work."

They came to a full stop at a T in the road, and it felt weird to go from a high speed all the way down to a stop. Almost like the conversation, but Ash took the turn smoothly. He was probably used to driving dogs around and Brandy decided she should be grateful that he thought dogs should be cared for and that he'd give her the same consideration.

"So why didn't you stay there?" Brandy asked, hoping he didn't read into it, *Why did you come here to pester us?*"

"He got sick one day and then he stayed sick. I took over more and more of the practice. Added his duties to mine, when I looked at getting paid for all the extra hours, I found out the truth about the clinic."

CHAPTER FIFTEEN

Ash pulled into a space and put the car in park, glad that it should stop Brandy's questions. She was still pressuring him about the clinic, but he climbed out and led the way.

He had no idea how this was going. He hadn't even really meant to ask her out, it had simply fallen from his lips, and he hadn't taken it back.

"Right here." He pointed, realizing the polite thing to do would have been to get her door. But she was faster than he would have been, and he would guess she was more of the *I can get my own door* type.

The tables were under a little pergola with vines growing up and over the top. They crossed the lot in silence, and he was grateful. He didn't like spilling other people's secrets.

This time, Ash did hold the door for her, and kept watch as she passed him. The jeans hugged every curve of her, and he understood why his mouth had asked her out even if his brain had said no.

For a moment, he realized he liked being alone with her, without having a task that wasn't going well or having her be oppositional. It felt like he finally had her to himself and he liked this Brandy. He liked the passion for engineering when it wasn't telling him he didn't know what he was talking about.

She stopped short of the counter, her eyes up at the menu on the wall.

He grinned. "We should get food, too. They have excellent grilled sandwiches, and the coffee is wonderful."

"You know the area?" she asked, and he just laughed.

"I know the mountains." He'd grown up a few hours south of here. "But I don't know Charlottesville. I just happened to find this place when I was staying here."

She seemed to take that as a good enough answer—which he never knew if she would. Brandy ordered a sandwich with a side of chips and a large frothy coffee and when she pulled out her card to pay for it, he pushed his hand out to stop her.

He offered up something he'd learned from an ex-girlfriend. "I invited, I pay. If you invite me, you pay."

"Fair enough."

At least that was easy. Ash had learned too many habits he disliked, first from early high school and then college girlfriends who insisted that the manly thing to do was to pay for everything. It had been Rena, much later, with her equity and independence who'd set him free and made it sound so reasonable. She'd said, "I won't invite you anywhere I can't afford. And you shouldn't invite me anywhere you can't afford. And I shouldn't invite you somewhere not knowing if you can afford it or if it's what you want to spend your money on."

He didn't still have Rena, but he still had that.

He paid for the order and was handed an old-fashioned metal stand with a plastic number on the top. He led Brandy outside to where the sun came in through the vines and colored flowers cast diamonds all around them. Though the parking lot was just on the other side, it still felt secluded, and the patio was only sparsely populated.

He headed toward the corner. "Is this good?"

Far away from everyone else for a moment, he would stay here surrounded by greenery with Brandy's attention on him, even if she didn't seem quite all the way open yet.

He sat down but didn't know what to say. She fidgeted with the stand, moving the plastic number until it was perfectly upright.

"So, what happened? What did you find out about the clinic?"

He should have known she wouldn't let it go. "The problem is that it's not mine to tell." Ash sighed. Still, she was never going to meet the man, he was a good while gone. "I don't think you'll have enough information to tell anyone, but all the wonderful work he did, it didn't pay."

"That was surprising to you?" she asked, not accusing but almost as if *how had he not known that?*

It was a fair question. "Well, if you own your own clinic, you can make a really good living. With all the charity, I wasn't surprised that he wasn't rich, but it was a shock to learn that it didn't even pay our salaries. I don't know if he was a terrible businessman or just so soft hearted that he would do anything for anyone. He was barely covering supplies. The place was upside down and underwater and every other bad financial term you can think of."

Her expression had moved to sympathy and Ash wasn't sure if he wanted that either. "What did you do?"

"I stayed on. I let him pay me and didn't let him know that I'd seen the records, the overdue mortgage or even his hospital bills." Ash still didn't know if it had been the right decision, and he wasn't sure if telling Brandy was right either. But it did feel good to finally share it with someone. "I kept working until he died so that he didn't have to see the place fold."

"Ouch."

"It was hard. It was the one place that I really thought was well run, the way I would have wanted to do it. I guess I was really stupid." What a wonderful thing to tell a woman. He'd finally admitted to himself that he wanted to impress her and then he told her this.

"Are you afraid you'll become him?"

He almost rotely answered 'no,' but it hit him. Hell, she was right. "Maybe."

"Well, we've all been stupid about things that should have been obvious." Something about the tone in her voice made him think she could put her finger on one specific thing. "Then you came here?"

Shaking his head, Ash admitted. "He passed almost two years ago."

Just then, the server showed up, setting a wide, white mug of hot coffee in front of him and the cold, frothy drink with whipped cream and chocolate sauce in front of her.

"That's all sugar," he commented.

She shrugged at him as if to say his opinion didn't matter to her at all.

She peeled the straw and took her first sip. It made her happy. That was clear. Why was her giving him the politest 'fuck you' ever so sexy?

He sipped the strong, bitter flavor that invaded every sense and tried to steer the conversation back onto less sad ground. "I helped a friend open a veterinary clinic and shelter in Nebraska—"

"You weren't near the floods, were you?"

If only she knew. "Don't ask."

She tipped her head, her gaze sharpening at him, as if to say *tell me more*. But nearly dying and lying to the first responders because he couldn't stand to watch a dog die because a human hadn't done their job wasn't anything he'd wanted to tell her about. He didn't want to admit that he'd been frantic, and they'd all been scared. He'd been afraid more than once that he was going to wash away at any moment. More than that, he watched the firefighters who came to rescue the dogs almost get washed away. If it hadn't ended well, he would never have forgiven himself.

It was nothing he wanted to relive.

"So, what did you want to talk about?" Brandy asked, her tone open, the cold drink cradled between her hands, her words punctuated with sips.

"Anything," he shrugged. "Whatever comes."

Over her shoulder he spotted the server with white plates and thick sandwiches. Brandy's was overflowing with grilled peppers, cheese, and spinach and she smiled as it was set down in front of her. She'd ditched the side salad for chips, and he was glad she ordered what she liked.

They were silent for a moment, each of them taking a first bite, the crunch of the sandwich always a delight. When he finished chewing, he looked up to find her watching him.

"If you didn't have anything that we needed to discuss away from the sanctuary, then why are we here?"

"I asked and you said yes." For a moment, he was flummoxed. *What was she even saying?*

Then he swallowed hard. He was here across the table from the beautiful redhead, freckles scattered across her nose in the sunlight, iced coffee making her smile, but her hazel eyes were confused because, once again, he'd been an idiot.

She didn't even know that he'd asked her on a date.

CHAPTER SIXTEEN

"**B**ut you don't even like me." *How could he have?* She was so confused!

Brandy set her sandwich back down. How was she supposed to eat when he said that? She was stuck forty-five minutes away from anything on a date she hadn't realized she'd agreed to!

"A date? You're my boss! We can't date!" she protested. As she grasped for straws it seemed the most polite and most damning way to get out of it.

"I'm not your boss," he replied immediately. "I work for Roz and so do you. We all work for Roz."

"Maybe I just thought you were my boss because you're bossy."

Maybe she shouldn't have said that. Maybe he shouldn't have asked her out! Did that mean he was interested in her? In that way?

He was fumbling for his next words, and she wasn't mean enough to let him suffer, but she wasn't a fan of rote politeness either. She very much preferred honesty, which might be why the whole thing with Theo and Sammy had hit so hard.

"You've been an ass to me at every turn!" She wanted to eat the sandwich. It was really good. She wanted to drink the coffee. She had been prepared for him to tell her that she was doing a shit job or to maybe even say she was doing a good job and tell her she got a sandwich for learning how to stay on her side of the fence. For finally getting Buzz to lay and stay where he was put until he was told to get up.

But she couldn't even enjoy the sandwich now and it was a damn good sandwich. It was going to sit here and get cold while she untangled this complicated man.

His hands stilled. "Yeah, I'm sorry about that."

She gave him half a beat and when he didn't fill it, she did. "*That's it?* You're an ass and you're sorry about it?"

If she had something that would work, she would have pulled the napkin off her lap and thrown it dramatically onto the table—but it was paper and would have ruined the moment. She could scoot the metal chair back with a screech against the slate tiles and storm out. But what would she do once she hit the parking lot? Her lunch was right here on the table, and she had no ride home.

It surprised her that she thought of the tiny cabin with the tiny cluster of cabinets that passed for a kitchen, and the one bed, and the tiny shower as *home*. But it did feel like it now.

Her lips pressed together as she looked to Ash. Was it all his fault? Or was she overreacting? She could pinpoint the *exact* moment when she'd lost all patience with asshole men telling her they were sorry.

She stared at him, unwilling to tell him that she forgave him or that she was going to let it slide.

"It's not an excuse," he said, his hands splaying out like a blackjack dealer showing he had nothing to hide. Ash's long fingers were work rough, but still the kind of hands her mom had always told her belonged to an artist. The same long fingers that Brandy had admired in Theo until she learned—far too late —that the only thing Theo was artful at was lying.

Either that or she was just a fucking idiot. Brandy had to admit it was also a possibility, but Ash was offering more, and since she might have misread things—hell, she clearly had as she was on a date that she had thought might be him asking her to leave the sanctuary!—she listened.

"I got here about two weeks before you did. I thought we were going to have a couple of days of work to get the place ready and then we'd get the inaugural class of dogs in. I thought the work would be as a *vet.*" He sucked in some air and looked up at the flowers overhead. "But then our initial trainer, whose job you got, canceled on Roz at the last moment. And it was just the two of us."

Still not a good reason for being a complete dick.

She was not in a good enough place to be gracious. Women weren't allowed to be complete assholes just because something had gone wrong. She'd been screwed and she didn't think she was a complete dick to him. And she was dealing with her mother suggesting she forgive Theo his "indiscretion." She said things like "but you love him" and "when will that kind of love come around again?" If she was lucky, never. But there was more to it than just that Theo had been sticking his dick in another woman. A lot more.

Brandy was more than tired of excusing men for their bullshit. They needed to grow up and learn how to handle problems like an adult. She didn't say so, but she was confident her stare held every last bit of it. Consciously, she picked up the sandwich and took another bite, determined not to let him ruin the food along with her mood.

"You didn't see the place. It was a . . . *mess* doesn't cover it. There was a huge spider—" He held up his fingers in a circle, indicating the size of it. "—right across the whole front porch.

The front window in the lodge was broken. Roz and I made a bet as to whether it was raccoons or snakes inside—"

"What?" Brandy set the damn sandwich down again.

"No worries, it was possums."

"There were possums *inside* the lodge?"

"And the cabins were just as bad. She put me in a hotel in Charlottesville and I commuted for a week. We had to hire a company to come clean the trash that was just piled up by the side of the building."

She took another bite, admitting that the sandwich might be tasty, but so was the gossip. "She hadn't prepared you for any of that?"

He laughed, a harsh rude bark. "She hadn't seen it until I did. She wanted to try to fix it. So, while she re-negotiated the whole sale, I became a day-laborer. She helped, but we did all that work. No dogs to train. Not sure if the place was going to go belly up before we even got started."

Something in his tone made her link it back to the words about how he bounced around before he got here. He'd been in Nebraska when it flooded. That was months ago. What had he done since? He hadn't said.

"Then after two weeks of manual labor, which I'm not against but not really what I was hired for, you show up."

"With no ability to train dogs," Brandy filled in.

This time he offered a wry grin. "And to top it off, you told me everything I wanted to build was wrong, and how I could do it better."

He wasn't wrong about that. She hadn't been the best about it. She had her own past hanging over her. He might have bounced around, but she'd practically crawled out of the bathtub in the church and into this job.

"About that . . ." She owed him at least a little. Not full forgiveness, but something. "You pushed me, and I pushed back."

"It was fair. I deserved it."

"I needed the win," she admitted and that was as close as she was going to get to saying anything.

She'd needed something to go right. Something she said and believed to work the way she wanted. Because, while she could see Theo for what he was, his betrayal had not been the sharpest knife to go through her heart.

CHAPTER SEVENTEEN

"No, they don't really get a day off," Roz told Lynzee. "Not working dogs."

Ash and Brandy had their day off today—Roz knew she couldn't make her people into working dogs. So far, she liked all of them, and she hoped that didn't become a problem.

She walked the trail, trying to let the fresh air clear her head from everything that wanted to clutter in. But Lynzee was in front of her clomping along as though a hike was the worst thing in the world. Roz feared the girl would have blisters, given that her boots were cheap goth things and not made for trails.

That was a problem for another day.

Her mind turned to her two absent workers. Roz hadn't seen anything happen between her vet and her trainer/engineer, but she wasn't stupid. Neither of them was here at the compound and only one car was gone. An interesting development.

She had staggered everyone's days off on purpose—the dogs needed staff present at all times, it was impossible to simply close shop unless she was between classes. So that meant she and Beck were here with the two newbies. Beck, of course, had two dogs on leashes, the rest of them had only one.

"It's not that they don't get a day off," he jumped in. Quickly he seemed to stop himself, his eyes darting sideways to her, almost as if to ask if he could answer the question.

She tried to answer not only with her voice but with her expression. Curie pulled on the leash right then, saving her. He should talk, he should establish himself as the leader here. He was the most knowledgeable and she would follow his lead herself if he said she was doing something wrong. She might be the boss, but she'd learned a few things about good leadership along the way.

Beck continued. "We're out for a walk in the woods. We're having a good time. We'll go back and we'll let them play in the fenced area, we'll throw the ball, do all of that but you're training them all the time."

Lynzee, three steps ahead on the path, was letting Sidney pull the leash a little too hard. Roz could tell Beck was biting his tongue not to correct her.

She said it herself. "What happens when Sidney is in a home and his owner has a seizure? What if he's taking his day off?"

Lynzee didn't answer that. Because it was a fair question that made a very valid point. Something they all had to keep in mind as they trained the dogs.

Beck added, "So when he tugs the leash, you have to correct it. He's getting wheelchair trained. We can't assume his person will have the strength to correct him. You're the leader right now, but before Sidney goes to his forever home, he has to be capable of being the leader."

"Okay. I can do that," Lynzee said, more cheerfully than anything she'd answered before. She looked over her shoulder at Beck, a small smile on her lips. "That makes sense."

Where had that smile come from? Roz tried to hide her surprise as Lynzee looked back ahead at the trail, taking a firmer hand with Sidney now. Her ponytail bobbing as she worked. Roz got a feeling that the perky hairstyle was just a concession to the heat and not really a choice.

All she'd usually gotten from the youngest team member was an eye roll.

Casey was bringing up the rear of the little hiking group, quiet enough that they only heard the occasional voice command between him and Buzz.

Beck was working on keeping pace right beside Roz, the trail was wide but barely enough for two of them and three dogs. His shoulder brushed hers occasionally and she tried to ignore the sensation.

"How far does this trail go?" he asked.

She almost laughed. "I don't know. I've never been on it."

"We have no idea what we'll encounter?" He seemed a bit too concerned, but she thought it was cute. It was good that he was always looking out for the dogs, though.

"I mean, I've taken several of the other paths, and I haven't seen bobcats, black bears, or vipers."

"I don't think we have vipers up here. We do have rattlesnakes and water moccasins though."

"No water moccasins on the trail," Roz grinned at him. "The water's down there."

She pointed down the hill, only to have Beck shake his head and point in the other direction. *Shit*, they were on the other side of the peak from the Jade River.

They'd only gone a few more steps when he turned to look at her a little bit too seriously. "You need to learn which direction you're headed. You should always know where you are on these mountains."

Roz shrugged at him.

She needed to learn how to deal with Lynzee. She needed to learn the accounting software. She needed to figure out how to be more forceful with her lawyer in getting the things that they needed, getting established as a nonprofit.

Which direction she was going while following a well-worn path was not high on her list.

"No, really," he emphasized, "You live up here. You're going to take dogs on hikes up here. Hell, you might even come out here for a walk on your own. What if you get lost?"

She was starting to shrug him off again when she felt his fingers wrap softly around her free wrist.

She turned to look at him. *How did he have a free hand?* He was walking both the dogs, but he'd managed to put both leashes into his right hand, the consummate pro.

Looking down, she thought as if she might examine the contact, it felt so foreign for a man to touch her softly. Instead, she watched him yank his hand back, as if maybe he'd been too familiar.

Her eyes focused on his skin. The letters across his knuckles were faint. Had she thought they were more prominent before or was she simply getting used to them? Maybe they were aging, and the ink was bleeding. It wasn't professional work.

Consciously she decided to ignore the touch. She couldn't afford it and mostly she was just glad that her reaction was relatively this side of normal. She focused ahead on the path.

As much as Lynzee's petulance bothered her, Roz knew that she had once been a Lynzee herself. She wanted to say she had turned out okay, but it had taken far too long and with far too much heartache. If there was anything she could do to speed that process up for anyone else, she would. Lynzee was just going to have to suck it up and take Roz's good intentions.

"What if you get lost out here?" Beck repeated, not looking at her, deftly handling the two leashes, somehow not letting his two charges get tangled.

"You would come find me." She smiled at him. Initially she meant it to be a joke but realized as the words came out of her mouth that she was serious. *He would.*

His look was chiding again. "No, really? What if we can't find you? There's so much open space up here."

"That's the draw of the place," she answered back, having to remind herself that there were two other workers with them. Though Beck looked at her like she was the only one here, that wasn't the case.

"Don't let it be the downside, too." At least he quit giving her instructions and merely pointed toward their left. "That way is down the mountain. But the river is over there."

"Aye aye, captain." She saluted him and she mostly stayed silent for the walk back.

Lynzee, bless her heart, managed to chatter a little bit, asking Beck questions and absorbing the answers like a sponge.

At last, they looped all the way back. It was probably close to five miles by the time they were on Sanctuary grounds again. She and Beck left Lynzee and Casey with the five dogs and a series of toys in the open space that Ash and Brandy had built—once they'd stopped squabbling.

With what she hoped was a neutral expression, she motioned for Beck to follow her inside the lodge. Once she was in the back hallway, she closed the door behind her leaning on it with a heavy breath.

She focused on Beck. "I have to tell you something."

He leaned in, something in his eyes drawing her in, something that she wasn't sure should be there. She spoke quickly.

"In case you haven't noticed, Lynzee has a crush on you. You'll need to be careful there."

His expression dulled as he leaned back. This was not what he had been expecting from her and she wondered if she could live up to what he had been expecting.

And she knew that she couldn't, shouldn't.

CHAPTER EIGHTEEN

She slid her feet into her running shoes, stepped out onto the little front porch of the cabin, and pushed her earbuds in, finally shutting out the rest of the world.

No one was in sight and Brandy was moving before she even hit the trail. Deep breaths, shoulders relaxing, the tension she hadn't realized she was still carrying starting to drain away. She'd needed this for longer than she'd realized and wished she'd done it sooner.

Roz and Ash had planned their days off to be separate, so that everyone else could have two days in a row. Brandy hadn't argued.

Yesterday's "date" with Ash hadn't necessarily been relaxing. Hitting the trail was definitely what she needed.

Her feet moved along the path, her eyes darting left and right. Though mostly she watched the ground in front of her to make sure she didn't hit a root and face plant. Trying to breathe in through her nose and out through her mouth was a little too much, she was already working. Instead, she aimed to move her feet to the rhythm of the music.

Maybe she could let it all just take her away, but she wasn't very far down the path before her brain was churning again.

She had been tense on the ride out to Charlottesville, thinking that Ash was going to ask her to step away from the job—make space for a more qualified candidate. Then, she'd been even more tense, realizing that she was on a date she hadn't even known was a date!

When they'd finished eating, they'd reached some kind of a truce. That had helped, though at that point she was still just processing that he didn't hate her . . . that he maybe felt something entirely different.

She sucked in the mountain air. So different from Los Angeles. It really did feel cleaner. There were no cars, no people, no horns honking, no helicopters overhead, no freeways. And no palm trees lining the roads like party toothpicks. No tiny, glamorous starlets in the coffee shop making her feel like an Amazon.

Brandy's feet pounded on the trail. A root felt like it just popped up under the arch of one foot and her ankle rolled. She stumbled to a stop, waiting for a few beats before testing it. But she was fine, so she picked up the rhythm and kept going.

After they'd eaten, Ash had casually suggested they see the Fralin Museum of Art at the University campus. They were already close by and she had wanted to visit.

Still, the lines had been blurred. He'd been the perfect gentleman the whole time. Paying her way in, never telling her he didn't like what she said. Then again, she didn't suggest any materials or designs for the day, so that might have been it.

Ash's knowledge of art wasn't profound, but he managed to discuss the pieces like he knew what he was saying.

"Impressive for a veterinarian," she'd told him. Even now she could remember the feeling of the grin tugging at the sides of her lips.

He'd shrugged her off, then beelined across the room, sounding excited. "It's a Cassatt!"

"A what?" She'd had to move fast just to keep up.

"They have a Mary Cassatt. She painted women and children and her use of light is stunning."

"Okay, Mr. Art historian," Brandy had teased again.

This time he grinned. "I took the AP class in high school. I mean, I took every AP class in high school that I could get my hands on."

"You remember this from high school?" Did he really? She didn't think she remembered anything from high school and she'd been a good student, honors and everything.

He brushed it off again. "The teacher was really good."

Or really pretty, Brandy had thought. But even as she'd been looking at the picture, contemplating the light he'd commented on, his fingertips had slid across her palm. He'd gripped her hand so lightly and pulled her across the wide room.

"Look at this." He pointed out a marble statue of a veiled woman.

They'd stared at it for a few minutes together, marveling at how the artist had managed to make marble look see through. Somehow the stone captured the delicate ridges and bumps of what would have been a sheer veil.

Brandy had been awed enough that she hadn't quite realized Ash's fingertips were still pressed against her palm. Maybe he'd realized it, though. He'd then let go to touch her on the back, almost whispering, "There's more to see upstairs."

Then the light pressure had disappeared. It had been a smooth move if it had been intentional. What if it hadn't? What if he simply hadn't realized he was still holding her hand?

The music from one song faded, bringing her back to the mountain trail and the reminder that she was here to clear her head, not cloud it with ambiguous memories.

The next song took a couple of beats to get going as she jogged a little further. She came to a rise in the trail that opened to clear sky as the side of the mountain fell away at the edge of the rock.

As beautiful as it was, she wondered how dangerous it might be, too.

Stepping closer to the edge, Brandy leaned over and looked down. It was too far to survive. She stepped back—not an edge-of-the-cliff girl.

Would they train the dogs to pull their humans back from the ledge? Would they do exercises out here? She had no idea. This wasn't even the same trail they'd taken the other day.

She took off running again, trying to think about the dogs. Brandy didn't have to second guess their motives or overthink every interaction.

Roz had told her that once the dogs were sufficiently trained in the basics, they would begin prepping for real life. They'd have unique and individual exercises, depending on what service the dog would be trained for—things like turning light switches off and on, locating medications, and who knew what.

But to train them for everyday situations, they would have to bring the dogs to all kinds of normal places. In the car, into a coffee shop, to the veterinarian, to a movie, and more. Roz said that was the much more fun part of training.

Brandy offered to take the dogs shopping with her. Beck and Ash had both raised their eyebrows. Lynzee had smirked. Brandy didn't care. If she could shop on the clock, she'd take it.

She'd kept her mind off Ash for a bit. Good for her.

Checking the time, she saw she had maybe another twenty minutes before she'd have to turn around. She had no idea if this trail looped back to the sanctuary or how lost she could get herself.

She set the timer, and when it went off, she was once again

running into oblivion, thinking about Ash, even though she tried not to. Time to turn around . . . in more ways than one.

Though she was facing the other way, her thoughts were still on the same track. The date had to mean the man was attracted to her. Even just thinking about the brush of his fingers across her palm, or the splay of his hand on the small of her back, had her fighting tiny shivers at the memory.

Had she reacted the same way at his real touch? Or had she made it better in her memory?

It had been a while since she'd been touched. But when she thought about it, she thought about Theo. About the lies. About the other lies that made the cheating seem like nothing to really worry about.

She hated that she'd become a liar, too, because of all of this. But she wasn't going to be the one to break her mother's heart.

Or maybe, she just didn't want to hear her mother shift her attentions to Sammy. Theo had plunged the knife. Sammy had twisted it, hard. But if her mother decided that Sammy was the golden child, that would be like pulling the blade out and letting Brandy bleed to death.

She wasn't strong enough yet to risk it.

So she lied.

And she hated herself for it.

Wow, she'd found a subject that was even less relaxing to think about than Ash!

Brandy gave herself permission to let her thoughts wander all over the man.

Was she attracted to him? Absolutely.

Was it a good idea? Absolutely not.

Then again, what did she have to lose? It wasn't like she was a married woman, or even an engaged one.

Ash had told her he tried not to date coworkers, and so did she. But she was only here for a handful of months. How bad could things get?

She tried to imagine what that *maybe* would look like. She was on a full-scale fantasy romance when strong arms reached up from behind her, grabbing her, and dragging her off the trail.

Brandy screamed.

CHAPTER NINETEEN

Ash tried to be gentle. But she was still screaming, and he needed her to turn around and see that it was him before she threw an elbow and gave him a black eye or a cracked rib.

He tried to grab her shoulders without taking any hits and he was grateful when he managed to turn her around to face him.

She was stumbling, attempting to go down, and Ash wondered if she was trying to do the dead-weight thing, so her attacker couldn't pick her up. It was smart, even if it was making his job that much harder. But that was pretty much the point.

Once he had her facing him, he waved his hand in front of her face. Even then it took a moment to get her to focus.

When she did, her mouth fell open wide, her brows knit together in rage. Hard and fast, she shoved at him, and he stumbled back a few feet.

"Hey! Why the hell did you do that?" she yelled, taking a step forward.

Because he thought of her as curvy, and thought of some of her curves as generous, he'd not been thinking of her the right way. Now, when she shoved him, he realized she had the gravity to move him with real force. If she hadn't been so damn angry, it might have been hot.

"I yelled at you. I was trying to get your attention for half a mile," he countered. *Okay, that was an exaggeration*, but he had yelled at her. "I called out your name. When I realized you didn't hear me, I got closer. I called louder. Then I was right behind you, yelling for you, and you *still* didn't hear me! So, I tapped you—"

"You *grabbed* me and tried to *pull* me off the trail." The accusation rang harsh.

"*No*, I *tapped* you. Then you swerved to the side—" his hands flew up, fingers wide as if he had had no idea what was happening. "— I thought you were falling. So, I tried to catch you."

He emphasized each word, realizing now how she'd seen it . . . only too late. Had he understood she was scared out of her wits, he might have . . .

"You had no right!" She was still mad.

"Maybe not." He shrugged. "I'm sorry I scared you. I didn't mean to."

He bit at his tongue, not wanting to say anything to make her mad again. He could watch her visibly cooling down, some kind of control she exerted over herself. Something he figured he would do well to learn.

Brandy waved a hand up and down him. "Fine. What did you want?"

Good question.

"Well, first I wanted to say *hello* and let you know that I was on the trail behind you so that you didn't get startled—"

"Great going there." She crossed her arms and pressed her lips together. Her earbuds had been popped out and she held them in one clenched fist now.

He tried again. "Then I was trying to get your attention so

that you would know that you couldn't hear anything, and that you weren't paying any attention. And that's not safe."

"I was perfectly safe out here except for *you* trying to tackle me."

"I *tapped* you." He was getting angrier now. "And *no*, you're not perfectly safe out here."

"The only thing out here is *you*." She waved her hands sharply toward the wilderness on either side of them.

"That's not true. There are poisonous snakes and large cats and even bears up here."

"I'm sure I'm far too noisy for them to come near me."

"Well, you wouldn't know what was near you with those damn earbuds in! Would you run that way in the city?"

"Never!" She was mad again, but so was he. Brandy was still going. "But that's the beauty of being up here."

"I hate to break it to you." He put his hands on his hips, hating to burst her bubble, but he had the pin, and it was necessary. "But it's not. Do you know what the highest cause of deaths on hiking trails in the mountains is?"

She looked at him, one eyebrow up, arms crossed again. One hip cocked out as if to say she knew the answer and she'd had enough of him. She rattled off the options. "Hypothermia. Dehydration. Probably injury."

"Murder," he told her.

She just laughed. Those broad lush lips flew wide, revealing even teeth. Her eyes closed with the mirth. The little diamonds of sunlight filtering through the trees caught the freckles and lit up the red in her hair like fire.

She was beautiful when he was mad at her.

"I hate to break it to you. Murder actually ranks higher than hypothermia. It's the second leading cause of death on hiking trails."

That at least got her attention. "You're shitting me."

"Sadly, I'm not." He watched as it dawned on her. Then he felt like crap for saying it. *Bubble burst.*

She'd put both her earbuds in and gone running without paying attention. Thinking and feeling that she was safe. For once. And he'd been the ass that had broken it to her that she didn't even have that here.

Brandy shook her head and looked at him again. "For real?"

"Yes." He put his hands on his hips and paced off a tight circle.

"Not even mountain lions or bears?" She sounded incredulous. He had been too. He'd checked after he'd read that article before coming up here. He'd been looking for tips on what kinds of shoes to buy. He'd gotten more than he bargained for. Now, so had Brandy.

"It ranks higher than wild animals and injury."

"Well, crap." Her voice was soft even though she was sad and angry all at the same time. He wished he could . . . do something to comfort her. But she wasn't his.

They stared at each other for a moment, and he felt the weight of his failed date hanging between them. He was glad that she'd forgiven him for startling the shit out of her.

The topic of her untimely murder having sunk in, she sighed and changed the subject. "Were you on the way out or the way back?"

"Back."

"Did you leave before me? I didn't see you pass me." Though something about her expression told him she was now questioning whether he might have passed her on the trail, and she'd been that oblivious.

She hadn't. "I looped it. This trail also leaves from the east side of camp."

The cabins were on the west.

"Well, that's good to know. How long is it?"

"About five miles." She was already headed back the way

she'd come. He knew she hadn't passed him on the trail. He definitely would have noticed. "Do you want a running buddy?"

"We could walk," she offered, her tone solemn.

Damn, he would have loved to take her up on that: A few moments here in the woods, no one likely to walk up on them or interrupt, a chance to see how she felt.

He needed that because he still didn't know. But he wasn't going to get that today. "I can't walk."

"You look like you're doing pretty good to me." She motioned up and down him, letting her hand linger aimed at his running shoes.

"I meant I don't have time. This is your day off, but I'm only on my lunch break."

Ash started moving his feet as if to make himself do it. Because otherwise he wouldn't want to leave her out here.

"Fine," she said, "We'll run."

He motioned her to take the lead and she was several feet in front of him before he remembered that he, too, needed to move his feet and keep up.

He watched her ponytail bounce and enjoyed the lycra she was wearing and told himself he needed to figure this shit out. Because he wanted her.

Bad.

CHAPTER TWENTY

Ash heard his name and turned toward the back door of the lodge. He'd slowly grown used to the kind of space the Jade River Sanctuary afforded.

Even the vet clinic he had loved so much—the one the old man had started in a refurbished barn—did not have this kind of space. In fact, only the university, with its large animal clinic, and necropsy labs for zoo animals, had even begun to come close.

And there were only seven dogs here, two of which were Shadow and Astra who weren't training. So, seven dogs and six people, and two of them didn't live here. There were five more empty cabins, because Roz lived upstairs at the main lodge, not wanting to leave it unattended. Maybe she just didn't want to be too far away when the first graduating class integrated with their humans.

So now he had to holler back just to be heard across the distance. "Yes? What do you need?" He had to watch, too, in case the sound didn't travel well, and he needed body language clues.

"Beck and I are heading out for supplies," Roz yelled out.

Ash didn't even try, he simply held his hand over his head with a thumbs up, his eyes darting back to the dogs. Only two of them were in the yard, but they were often allowed to play in this space. They also had to understand that no matter where they were and what they were doing, commands must be followed and needs must be met.

But Roz's voice carried back across the air one more time. "Casey and Lynzee are off today. So, it's just you two."

"We're good!" he yelled as he smiled and waved, hoping she'd catch the clue to just go. He had this. It was going to be fine.

But he did wonder why he was here training the dogs with Brandy. At least one of them should have been replaced by Beck. The man knew what he was doing.

Ash understood *how* training worked. In fact, he'd done it with far more than just one dog, but not as a profession. His job as a vet was finding illness, diagnosing, fixing. Then again, he and Brandy weren't working on anything difficult today.

He faintly heard the click of the back door, then a few minutes later, the whirr of the engine from the front gravel lot. They would take Roz's SUV, as it would hold plenty of supplies. The van was full of crates that would get in the way when one was carting massive bags of dog food, Gallons of dietary supplements and tubs of treats.

Brandy caught his attention, giggling and turning in a circle her hands up in the air in a ridiculous dance. "Whooop! The boss is gone. I can do whatever I want."

Buzz followed along with her, bouncing around and yipping.

"Yeah, no," Ash told her, pointing toward the ground as if to give her a command.

Then he was quite pleased when both of the dogs immediately lay down. "Oh, good work, boys."

Brandy was already reaching into her pocket for the tiny training treats that they often used. They would phase those in and out. The dogs would learn to lay, sit, stay, and go on command whether they got a treat or not.

The two of them worked a little longer, but then sent the dogs off on their own. They had to not pay attention to them for a while and see if they would come immediately when summoned.

Ash turned to Brandy, thinking he was being cute. "Tell me a secret."

She laughed, an almost choked sound, and offered up. "I have a broken heart."

"Not like medically?" He tipped his head and looked at her. No, she didn't mean that. Then, without thinking, he added, "That's hardly a secret. What's a real one?"

"You first," she countered, still smiling at him.

"Okay. My mother has called me every week for the last six weeks, and I've ignored her." He wondered if it showed on his face, how good that felt.

It must have, because Brandy's immediate reply was, "You *ignored* your mother?"

"I have my reasons." *Thirty-seven years of reasons*, he thought. His second thought was often the same: why had it taken him this long to even begin to extricate himself from her?

He did okay though, he thought. He was still standing. The dogs ran around but periodically looked to him or Brandy as if checking in, waiting for his command to get back in line or sit.

He almost snapped his fingers to call them back, but then realized they would have to have an alternate command. Many people who needed support animals might not be able to snap their fingers. He didn't call the dogs back, not yet.

But he'd said it and he hadn't shivered or broken inside when Brandy's expression had suggested what a terrible person he was for not speaking to his own mother. He'd known that was coming and it was likely part of the reason he'd said it: to test himself.

In the past he had listened to the people who told him he'd regret it. That he was making a mistake. In the past he'd tried and tried again. But not this time. He was just glad that his own heart hadn't broken or cracked.

Looking back at Brandy he said, "It's your turn."

She nodded. "Two and a half weeks before I came here, I was standing in the church on my wedding day."

His mouth dropped open. Then he closed it. He'd known there was something in her past. The broken heart wasn't a surprise. It had seemed she had come here to escape something. Why else would she take a six month temporary job when she held such a position elsewhere?

But damn, he wouldn't have guessed that. "What happened? Did you hear through the church door that he cheated on you?"

She sucked in a breath, her ribcage expanding, the gorgeous, lush breasts lifting with her shock at his words. "Well, it's always good to be a cliche."

"I'm sorry! I thought I—"

She pressed her lips together as she nodded, the corners of her eyes pulled tight, and he watched as the tears started to fall. "I'm okay."

Obviously, she wasn't. He apologized again. "I'm so sorry. I didn't mean—"

"It's not your fault at all. Like I said, it's a cliche, right?"

"It's horrible is what it is."

She laughed a little through the tears. "It is what it is. Can you guess the next piece?"

"There's more?" Ash was stunned. *Who would do that to Brandy?* She was smart, bold, gorgeous, and funny. The asshole must have been an idiot, too. "It's bad enough that he cheated on you, and you found out on your wedding day. I don't want there to be more."

He watched as she sniffled, her palms raising upward as if to ask *what can you do?* She managed to grin through the tears she was trying to hold back. "Hey, maybe I'm not a full blown cliche. Or maybe I am. It was my sister."

His mouth fell open again and this time he couldn't close it.

How had he even been thinking about asking her out? She certainly didn't need a relationship.

Though, again, neither did he. His bullshit was thirty-seven years in the making. Hers had just been recent.

Brandy laughed a little and wiped at her eyes as her cheeks had grown wet. She tried to put on a brave face as she whispered, "I'll be fine."

But it was a lie. He could see it.

How much distance had he closed between them when she'd told him her secret? He was close enough to see her break as she laughed one more time before completely losing it. Her sobs hurt his heart and he got the impression that it might be the first time she'd actually let go.

Walking the last few steps between them, he wrapped his arms around her, pulling her close. She was tall, but it felt good to have his cheek rest on the top of her head. He couldn't help but close his eyes at the feel of her pressed up against him.

It wasn't the way he'd imagined it would be. He'd thought it would be steam and heat and tearing each other's clothes off. This was just comfort. But she felt right, and it felt amazing when her arms wrapped around him, too, as if maybe he wasn't broken.

How long did he stand there like that, holding her close? He didn't know.

Her sniffles subsided, the tiny jolts of her sobs wound down, until she was just breathing. Until she buried her face into his neck. Until her arms came upward, winding over his shoulders and pulling him close.

Ash told himself he shouldn't do it. He shouldn't take advantage of a vulnerable moment. She might not know it, but he was having one, too.

"Thank you," she sighed out the words, her breath warm across his jaw. Had she moved?

When he looked down at her, she was right there, so close, arms already around him. And he couldn't help himself. He leaned in for a taste.

CHAPTER TWENTY-ONE

H is mouth lingered on hers and Brandy felt the heady drunkeness of a great kiss fusing itself into her bones.

Pushing up on her toes, she kissed him back, her mouth opening slightly as if she could drink in this feeling. Her arms wound tighter around his neck, holding him closer than she would have if she'd been thinking. But she wasn't thinking, she was exploring.

The rest of the world had disappeared, and she hadn't known anyone other than Theo who could make that happen. Leaning into Ash, she let her breasts press against him, not surprised at the warmth that bloomed through her at the feeling of his chest against hers.

He crushed her tighter, the sensation comforting and mind-blowing at the same time.

He wanted her.

Almost as much as she wanted him.

His tongue swept against hers, his hands cupping the back of her head as if he had to hold her here with him. She was all in, everything else fell away now that he was touching her.

Her back arched and Brandy enjoyed the delicious feeling of

friction as she moved against him. It shot through her, sparking at the tips of her fingers and tightening her core. His mouth on hers shouldn't have that kind of power.

But it did.

Her fingers clawed at his back, the way they would if she were doing more than standing here on top of the mountain in the sun. She pressed herself to him as if she were horizontal and much less clothed, as if she'd already decided to give in to the sensation of being with this man.

Brandy was rewarded with the pressure of him against her, the subtle movement of his hips that said he'd be good on the dance floor and good naked in bed, too. His lips moved softly as he nibbled sweetly along her mouth. He pressed soft kisses at the corner, then down her jaw.

Did she moan? Gasp? She'd made some kind of noise because she could feel the shift in him. How had he gotten hotter?

His mouth was on hers again and he was bending her backwards even as she fought to push against him. Her fingers wound through his hair, holding on for all she was worth.

She was about to climb him like a tree. She was about to peel her shirt and make sure he touched her. She was about to lay down in the dog run and let him make her scream. But she needed oxygen, and she needed even the slightest shred of sanity, so she pulled back.

Brandy took one step away from him, her arms loosening. But she was still touching him, not quite ready to let go.

She sucked in a deep breath, the mountain air suddenly feeling muggy, the heat between them steaming. Her mouth was still open, lips still wet, she could feel him lingering on her skin as her eyes darted to his mouth.

Unable to completely disentangle herself, she let her fingers trail down his biceps, the softness of the T shirt followed by the sizzle of his skin. None of it was in her control. Certainly not the way she looked up into his eyes and caught the heat that flashed there.

Was it possible to burn up more than that kiss had just done?

"I can't," she said, not fully in control of her own words, but knowing it was the right thing to say.

Ash nodded in agreement, but still her fingertips lingered against his skin. His hands still held the backs of her arms as she forced herself to take one more deep breath. One more step backward.

Until at last, they weren't touching at all.

"We shouldn't do that again," she said, knowing even as she said it that she shouldn't, but she *wanted* to.

Finally, she made herself turn away in an attempt to break the spell that he held over her. It wasn't quite enough, but it did something.

"It sucked that bad?" he asked, making her laugh, the tension somewhat broken.

For that she was grateful. When Brandy looked back at him, she knew she had a smile on her face. Before she answered, she saw the grin on his. "No, it didn't. And you know it."

"Then why shouldn't we do it again?" Ash somehow managed to seem his usual jovial self. She was still burning up.

There were three Ashes that she knew. The first one wanted to do things his way—the man frustrated by having expected something different and thinking someone with no skill was trying to tell him how to do what he already knew.

Then there was the second Ash—the awkward gentleman. The one who opened doors for her and seemed to ask her on a date without quite making it clear that she was on a date.

The third was her favorite Ash—this man. The one who smiled at her with his eyes lit up. He was the one who had a good time teasing her. The one who made her grin back at him no matter what.

But she was forced to say, "I think it's pretty clear I'm not ready for any kind of relationship."

It didn't faze him. The smile didn't budge, and he didn't agree. "Who says there has to be any kind of relationship? Honestly, I'm probably not fit for one either."

There was a pause. He tilted his head looking her up and down as the smile became more sincere. His eyes zeroed in on her lips as the heat began to flare again in his eyes. "There's no reason we can't do what feels good."

CHAPTER TWENTY-TWO

Roz sat down in her office, grateful she had splurged for the comfortable chair. Though she hadn't expected to be in here that much, she'd thought she might need it at the end of a long day.

She'd been right. And it hadn't even been a long day today . . . yet.

She had intended to serve as one of the dog trainers as well as running the place. That would save her one salary, and cost her every minute of her day, she knew. But she also thought that having all of her time tied up might be good for her, might keep her from looking backward.

She'd chosen a beautiful, dark wood desk, thinking to make this office a little haven for herself. It had arrived with a beautiful, but wooden, hard-seated chair. She'd quickly traded it for this less attractive but padded and ergonomic thing.

Now she sank in, leaning back and letting the chair tip with her, her head resting against the cushion top.

It was always hard for her to tell if she was making good choices or reactionary ones. It was hard to trust her gut.

She hadn't had a lot of experience making her own decisions

and living with the consequences. But she'd certainly lived with the consequences of everyone else's. At least now, it would be her own fault. At least now, if it was possible to clean it up, she could do so. When she apologized, it would be for her own actions.

She'd just never trusted the choices she made because she had no experience with them. The few she'd made on her own always seemed to be the wrong ones. So now she had this chair. It had been more money than was budgeted, but she was grateful for the comfort.

Closing her eyes, she let herself sink away, her breath coming more deeply, more evenly. Had she closed the door or left it shut but not clicked? Could someone push it open and see her here basically asleep? Would that be bad?

She didn't know the answer to any of those questions.

But her bones finally were feeling like they melted. She was *resting*. How long had it been since she had *rested*?

Trying to clear her thoughts was harder than it ought to be, but easier now that she believed she was in a safe place. The office was her own. She was proud of herself for hiring Ash first. That had been a bold and very trusting move on her part. And she'd done it somewhat to prove to herself that she could trust someone.

Maybe part of the reason she'd scrambled to bring in Brandy as fast as she had was so that she wouldn't be alone here on the top of a mountain so far from anything with two men—two men she had never met other than through video interviews.

Her thoughts drifted, ideas twisting and changing, her wayward thoughts taking over.

She drifted off, half asleep until her phone chimed and reminded her to pay attention. Her workday wasn't done. Nowhere near it.

Roz opened her eyes and saw her monitor in front of her. She was old school, she knew. Desktop not laptop or tablet.

But that had been another conscious decision. She had her phone on her, had communication everywhere she went. She'd checked the cell phone coverage map before buying this place. Then she'd installed the most serious Wi Fi she could find, including individual boosters at each of the occupied cabins.

She would *not* be stuck, unable to get to the outside world. But she also didn't want the ability to pick up her work and carry it upstairs to her room with her. It might be too tempting.

Still, that meant before she headed upstairs, she had to finish.

She made notes on each of the dogs, double-checking her initial assessments of which dog would fit best with which kind of training. Her fingers flew over the keys, making her notes and hoping they were clear enough that anyone could follow them.

Beck had reminded her to prepare for up to twenty percent of the dogs to wash out of training. Statistically, that meant anywhere from zero to even three of them in this first round. Three would be too many. Zero would be great, but it didn't look like that would be the case.

She hated to do it, but in her notes, she added that it looked like Buzz might be their first to fail out.

When she'd mentioned it to Brandy, the engineer had become concerned. "Will he have to go back to the shelter?"

"No. We'll adopt him out ourselves to a forever home," Roz had explained. "Even if he's not suitable as a support animal, he is still a very highly trained dog. We'll find him the right place."

Ash and Beck seemed to have already known this. Which was good. Roz hadn't been up for calming all of them. But her explanation was fine and Brandy nodded along. She'd even added, "If it comes to that, you might tap Lynzee to find him a home. She's a bit of a social media guru. And that's in part because she is fantastic with wording and hype."

Interesting, Roz had thought, making herself a mental note to maybe test out any special skills Lynzee might have.

They were already employing Casey above just 'dog trainer.' He was working alongside Ash as his assistant for any and all veterinary needs. Casey could not have been happier, but he'd be gone soon. Off to veterinary school in the fall and she would have to replace him.

Lynzee was more of a wait-and-see hire. Ash was on a two-year contract. And Beck ...

Roz leaned back, her head falling against the cushion again. Beck was a 'wait and see' kind of scenario. The kind of thing she didn't know what to do about because she liked the guy. Maybe too much.

She thought he was doing a good job, but so many of her choices about what she 'liked' in the past had come back to bite her.

CHAPTER TWENTY-THREE

*I*t had been five days since he'd kissed Brandy.

Ash knew the number, even though he told himself he wasn't counting. It had been impossible not to count. He tried to keep his thoughts on Sidney and the routine checkup he needed.

He'd managed to steal one other small peck, to which Brandy had returned the motion. But then she'd smiled slightly and ducked away, claiming that someone might see them. She wasn't wrong, but what did it mean?

He couldn't tell if she had been avoiding him or if she was just actually busy around the sanctuary.

When he was melancholy, he decided he was doomed to always be uncertain about how she felt. He'd asked her out and managed to screw that up to such an extent that she hadn't even known. Then he'd kissed her, and when she'd said she couldn't get into a relationship, he proposed they not get involved.

She still hadn't quite replied to that. Not *no*. But not *yes* either.

Now, he'd heard nothing.

Maybe he was just bad at this.

"Is he done?" Lynzee asked.

"Yes. He checks out. Want to trade him for Curie? She's next."

Ash decided yesterday to throw it on the wall and see what stuck. Hell, if he was going to be awkward and confused, maybe he could get himself to where it was just awkward. Then he would know where she stood.

Right now, Brandy was just busy and so was he. They were all working extra hours with Buzz, trying to keep him from being the program's first washout. Though no matter what they did, the small dog's situation seemed precarious. He would improve, then do something bonkers like run off, or just decide not to listen.

It wasn't a good look on a service animal.

Beck was the only one who could get Buzz to listen. The problem with that was that service dogs had to be *on* all the time and for anyone. Their humans would certainly learn all the proper commands, but many dogs were trained to take over when their humans couldn't function.

Working with Beck was great, but it wasn't as if their best trainer could get adopted out too when Buzz went to his forever home.

Surely though, Ash could find a damn moment and get a decision from Brandy.

Still, it wasn't as if he could ask over dinner, not with Roz and Beck and usually even Casey at the table with them. They were still rotating who cooked. Adding Casey into the mix, meant all five weekdays were covered, meaning they each only had to cook one day per week. Lynzee was perpetually invited to dinner and continually declining. She was usually off the property as soon as her shift was over.

So tonight, of course, was his night. And Ash was ready. The Instant Pot would be full of brisket. He had potatoes already baking, and he would need to prep all the toppings as well as a side of green beans with bell peppers.

He always liked to think he'd done pretty well, but it was Beck who constantly swooped in with creative meals and a deft hand at cooking all kinds of things. He'd surprised them all with tofu, homemade spaghetti sauce, and salads with field greens. Certainly not what Ash would have expected from a man recently released from prison.

It seemed as if the tattoos across Beck's knuckles were fading, and maybe the influence of prison life was too. At least they all enjoyed the food.

With a moment alone before Lynzee delivered Curie to him, Ash scrolled through his email. Immediately, his heart sunk as he spotted a reply from his aunt.

His mother had sent out an update to a handful of family members. Though Ash had done what he did every time he saw an email from her since he'd walked out six months ago. He'd deleted it without opening.

But now, he was seeing every reply from every relative. Though he would gladly talk to his aunts and cousins, he wasn't answering these emails either. The first line was popping up in the list, "Congratulations." "I'm so proud of you." And "That's amazing."

He couldn't deny the mild curiosity to wonder what bait his mother had put into the world to catch these praises, but he wasn't curious enough to look. He dumped the replies into email trash, immediately feeling better that it was gone.

But how long until his leaving meant she was *gone*?

There was no good answer for it. Though he'd made his decision some time ago, the outcome didn't seem to be entirely in his hands.

He had walked out the door last time for the last time. He'd promised himself. No more second and third and thirtieth chances. Yet, just seeing the email knotted his chest, crunched the eggshells under his feet again.

Luckily, throwing it away got faster and easier each time.

Lynzee showed up with Curie and Ash shoved the phone back into his pocket. "Alright, let's get the patient up on the table."

He spent the next fifteen minutes walking Lynzee through the checkup routine again. She got it, she wasn't stupid, she just didn't seem to care to absorb it. Some of the job she took to like a fish to water, some of it she seemed to seek out, and some of it she just let bounce off her as if she would never have to do it again.

Ash was beginning to see the pattern . . .

He finished with Lynzee and Curie, then worked in the clinic until his alarm went off. He made his way to the kitchen, passing the dog run where Brandy and Lynzee were putting Tensing through his paces. Beck was out on the trails with Buzz. And Ash had it on his calendar that they would start training the dogs for everyday activities tomorrow.

By himself in the kitchen, he enjoyed the alone time even if grating cheese and chopping vegetables wasn't his favorite thing in the world. One by one the others showed up and built a plate until they were all sitting around the table.

The praise over dinner soaked in, far better than it should have, but he liked when things were rewarded or dismissed based on their merits and not whims. So, he merely said, "Thank you."

Beck, for all his tofu and vegetarian meals, dug into the brisket like a starving man. Luckily, no one at the sanctuary seemed to have any food issues, so Ash had been allowed to apply his limited cooking skills pretty liberally.

He sat to Brandy's right as usual, but nothing she said or did gave away anything. Then she finished and was gone, while he was stuck on dish duty.

It was dark by the time the pans were cleaned and dried and hung on their rack. He started the dishwasher on its industrial cycle and turned out the light in the kitchen as he left. Roz was already upstairs in her room, so he texted her to remember to come bolt the back door, then he headed across the wide back porch and across the open yard.

The moon was out, and his mind was made up.

Shoving his hands in his pockets, Ash tried to screw up his courage. It was the only way to get out of being stuck in the middle—not knowing if Brandy was brushing him off or waiting for him to make a move.

Still, he almost walked right by her cabin, telling himself it could wait until tomorrow. Then he called himself a string of stupid names and climbed the three steps to her small front porch, raising his hand and knocking before he chickened out.

He had to stay. What if she'd seen him?

Still, he was taking a step back so as not to crowd her, the porch was so small.

But as he was looking over his shoulder to not trip like a dumbass, he heard the door open.

"Ash?"

"Hi," he started to stumble over the words, but he'd gone over them so many times, he reverted to what he'd prepped. "I was wondering if you had a minute?"

He sounded like he was going to offer her a religious tract. She didn't answer. Instead, Brandy grabbed the front of his shirt and hauled him inside.

CHAPTER TWENTY-FOUR

Her fist was in his T shirt, her knuckles feeling the hard planes of his chest, as she dragged him into the tiny cabin.

Brandy had the door shut behind him before she even realized it was dark outside but still, she should have looked around to see who could see her . . . see *them*. It was too late now.

She'd been lying here, in her warm bed, reading her book and thinking about the offer he'd made. No relationship. No strings. Just . . . what?

Comfort?

Heat?

Someone who wanted her who couldn't cheat on her because he wasn't even hers in the first place.

D - all of the above.

"What is—"

She didn't let him finish. It should be damn obvious what this was, she thought as she pressed him against the door and pushed up on her toes. Her mouth was on his, tasting the sweetness that was there before he even got close to finishing the sentence.

Ash Cooper was kissing her back, leaning into it. His hands reached down to her hips, grabbing and pulling her close.

Yeah, he was into it.

Her breasts pressed into his chest. She felt his breath catch and wondered if she could do it again. Grabbing at his hair, she tugged his head down—just a little—closer to hers and kissed him again.

When she had devoured his mouth enough, she moved to his jaw, feeling the rough texture of the five o'clock shadow there. She pressed closer as he tilted his head to give her access. When her teeth closed over his earlobe, he actually growled. Maybe she still had it.

Maybe it didn't matter. Right now, nothing beyond these four walls did. She wanted to sink into this feeling, the buzz and the glow of this man wanting her, and just disappear.

Licking lightly at the spot she'd just bitten she aimed for the cords of his neck, surprised when his hands pushed her back.

"You've had your fun."

She frowned. *He'd said . . .*

But he was pushing at the sheer cardigan she'd thrown on, yanking it down her arms with no concern for finesse. He was just trying to get it off her. It was still hanging from one wrist, and she was laughing at his inability to finish the job when his fingers softly raked at the sides of her waist, tugging at the T shirt.

Her brain flashed away for a moment. It had been a long day. *Should she have showered?*

Ash was tugging at the shirt, up and over the mounds of her breasts, growling with appreciation.

What bra had she even worn?

She'd been wearing the better ones since his suggestion . . . Thank God.

A high-end sports bra, for working outdoors, but half sheer material. Another growl told her he approved as he went after the row of hooks and eyes down the front. Or maybe he just approved of large breasts.

She wasn't going to complain. Instead, Brandy reached down for the front of his jeans, sliding her palm along the zipper and the hard ridge behind it.

There were two hooks left on her bra, his fingers working quickly but maybe shaking a little and missing. So many hooks was the downside of having large boobs.

He gave up for a moment, running one finger across the exposed skin and the freckles there. They were everywhere. She looked up at him. A deal breaker?

But the heat flared in his eyes. Maybe he just wanted to get laid. Well, so did she. But his mouth was on the top of her breast and his fingers were back at the hooks he now couldn't even see, but she felt the pop as another one gave way. Two points for Ash Cooper.

Her fingers curled a little and she felt his hips move forward, pressing the length of him into her hand. Had it been a voluntary move on his part? She found she didn't care. But her bra was falling away, her breasts spilling into his hands, and she sucked in a breath at the touch of him.

She had to level the playing field.

Her fingers found the edge of the soft T shirt and she yanked upward. So much for thinking he was fumbling. She was, too.

He let her breasts fall to raise his arms, as anxious to be rid of his clothing as she was of hers. She watched as the rising cloth gave way to the hard planes of his bare chest, the rough cords of muscle on his arms. Her gaze wandered down to the dark trail that disappeared behind the snap and zipper of his jeans.

She could do something about that.

Yes, her fingers shook a little, too.

Was she actually doing this? How long had it been since she'd been with anyone other than . . . No. She wouldn't even think about it. She'd made up her mind and she wanted this, and she deserved to be touched like she mattered.

She pushed her finger behind the snap and popped it open just as he pulled the T shirt clear. He held it momentarily over his head as his eyes caught hers. He stared at her, almost daring her to go further. *Challenge accepted.* She felt for his zipper and tugged it down.

He tossed the T shirt to the side, not even watching where it was going. His now free hand dug into his back pocket, fumbling for a thin wallet, pulling out a condom and dropping the wallet onto the floor. From the corner of her eye, she watched a card go spiraling across the floor. Ash never looked.

He simply held up the condom and asked, "Yes?"

"Hell, yes."

CHAPTER TWENTY-FIVE

There was no air between them as he pushed forward, moving her backward until Brandy felt the bed at the back of her thighs.

It was a queen bed, high on the box springs, and luckily with only a headboard. Brandy was glad right then that she was tall, and she didn't have to climb awkwardly up onto the mattress. Instead, she tipped backward, Ash helping the process as he lifted her feet and pulled at her socks, then went for the shorts.

He tugged them down her legs, nibbling upward as he tossed them aside. She heard them hit a chair or the wall, but her head was falling back at the feel of his mouth on her calf, the inside of her knee, her thigh.

Ash didn't notice, or at least didn't care, that her underwear didn't match the bra. In fact, he might not have had time to notice as he tucked his thumbs under the sides and slid them down her legs. Again, he looked her in the eyes as he tossed them somewhere into the room.

She was fully naked, laid back on the bed now. While he was unzipped, he still had his jeans on, and presumably his shoes. She pointed up and down at him, "Your turn."

He leaned forward, grabbing her hand and pressing the condom into her palm before stripping the fastest she'd ever seen a man get naked.

"Good enough?" he asked, standing before her in all his glory. Long, lean arms and legs, muscular torso, blue eyes blazing.

She was here in only her freckles and her size fourteen ass and the heat in his eyes said he liked what he saw. One day she could tell someone about the wild affair she'd had with the hot veterinarian on the mountain top. But right now, he was waiting for something.

She crooked one finger at him, and he didn't hesitate, crawling up onto the bed, and laying beside her. He ran a finger reverently along her collar bone then down her chest, along one breast and to the peak of her nipple, holding her spellbound the whole time. His eyes followed his finger as her breath shortened with each inch he traced.

He lifted his finger and traced the back of her hand that still clenched the condom he'd given her. "You going to do something with that?"

She didn't need any more hints.

She ran her free hand flat down the front of him, until he was wrapped in her grip, his back arching and his breath sucking in. Brandy stroked him until he protested.

"Unless you want me in your hand, you'd better get that on."

She did not want him in her hand, not now. Maybe later. Right now, she wanted him on her, in her, riding her. Her fingers moved accordingly, ripping at the gold foil, rolling it onto the hard shaft that aimed right at her.

His fingers traced a new path, down between her legs. He touched and stroked until she couldn't breathe, until he ground out, "You're so wet."

"Please." She should have said something more, something sexier, but it was enough.

He moved, gentle pressure on her shoulder until she was flat on her back again. He was over her, his legs between hers, her own falling wide as if begging for him. She couldn't help it.

Holding himself on one arm over her, he reached down and touched her again, and again until she finally felt him start the slow, sweet slide into her. Her hips bucked, wanting more, but Ash was in charge now.

He held back, keeping it slow, sliding just a little farther each time, until her breath was coming in tiny gasps, until she was clutching at his arms, until she whispered again, "Please."

This time, he was hard and fast, the thrust enough to make her cry out, to make her head snap back, her back arch, her hips rise up to meet him. Enough to make him growl. Her knees pulled up, hoping to take him deeper, no conscious thought controlling her as she writhed in a symphony of pleasure beneath the feel of him.

"*Brandy.*"

Her name on his lips almost made her come. The guttural need behind it was heady. She begged, "Now!"

"Not yet."

Well, it was going to be now for her. And she felt the clench and the rush of her orgasm sweep through her.

Did she cry out? Scream? Call his name?

She didn't know. She just felt him, still pushing into her as she came. Harder and harder until he called her name again.

CHAPTER TWENTY-SIX

"Now what?" he asked.

Brandy stayed exactly as she was, breathing heavily, naked, and sweating on top of the covers. She was staring blindly at the fresh white coat of paint on her ceiling, wondering if the man beside her had done the work.

"Give me a minute," she told him without moving anything but her mouth. Like she could make any decisions at all let alone what the hell they were going to do next.

They'd already used two condoms tonight. The second round he'd insisted had been necessary, as he'd simply lost his mind the first time and he needed to show her a slow, languid kind of fun. He'd done that.

Now he laughed at her, a rich, deep chuckle that reached further inside her and tangled in places it shouldn't have.

If she took slow, deep, even breaths, she might get herself back to being anchored in the real world. Brandy was both trying to contemplate what she'd just done and maybe not think about it at all.

"So?" Ash rolled up on one elbow, looking down at her as

one fingertip traced along her arm. He grinned at her. "That worked for you?"

Finally finding some energy, she rolled over and slapped softly at him, her own smile returning. "I think you know what you did."

"Yeah. I did it a couple times, too,"

"Well, now you're just getting big-headed."

"I think I was already big-headed." He grinned. How was his brain so sharp after all that?

"Egotistical then."

"I think we're both allowed some ego after that."

"Okay." She shoved a little at him. "Maybe it's time for you to pack up and head home so I can get some sleep."

Roz said she'd put a queen bed in each cabin, so Brandy couldn't claim the bed wasn't big enough, but the cabin wasn't. She sensed him and what they'd just done as if it had permeated the furniture and snuck into the corners.

The bed was comfortable, but the cabins were each only a singular room. Though there was just enough room for a small table and two chairs, it wasn't what Brandy would call spacious. Certainly not intended for two people. Certainly not for the way Ash Cooper was taking up space.

"Are you okay with people seeing me traipse out of here in the clothing I was wearing earlier?"

It was the middle of the night. He was right. There would be no conclusion they could likely draw other than the correct one.

"Better than seeing you traipse out of here at six a.m." she said. Though who would see him except for Roz and Beck?

Honestly, the way she'd been acting this week, the two of them must have figured out that something was going on. Neither of them was stupid. While Brandy wasn't in the mood to parade this new whatever-it-was around the small campus, she also wasn't going to any great pains to hide it. That would simply be a waste of her effort.

"I don't get to stay for, say, five more minutes?" he asked.

"So now *you're* the one who needs to catch your breath?"

"Touche," he conceded. But instead of rolling over onto his back, staring at the ceiling like she was doing once again, he leaned over her. The mouth that had just done wicked things to every inch of her was now brushing softly across her own.

Her chest tightened at the gentle sweetness that he offered. It had been so long since a man had tugged at her emotions in a good way.

She and Theo had both been short fused for the last six months. At the time, she'd written it off to the pressure of family and a wedding. Of buying their first house together and making plans for a baby. All the big things they'd lumped into a short period of time.

Now she knew better. It had either been the stress of her subconsciously knowing he was cheating on her or him simply tapping out of the stress by putting his dick into her sister, Sammy.

What had Sammy been thinking? Brandy didn't even know, because the thought of one of her sisters' boyfriends approaching her for anything resembling a relationship or an affair would never have been something she would have said yes to.

Ash's finger traced along her jaw and Brandy's eyes flicked up. His were a bright shade of blue, so deep it was almost unreal. The faint glow of the little light that was always on under the cabinets outlined his silhouette. "Where did you go? You disappeared for a moment there."

She shook her head. "Nowhere good."

With another small soft kiss, he said, "Then come back to me."

She thought about it for exactly four or five seconds before realizing it was time to step away. "If we do this again, we won't get any work done tomorrow. And while I figure everybody's already figured this out—" she pointed back and forth between him and her. "—I'm not ready to advertise it. I don't want to be a bad employee."

His slight frown tugged at her. Had she hurt his feelings? But he only said, "Fair enough."

He might have already been an overly-good employee, cleaning out cabins, scraping away cobwebs, and clearing the trails, but she wasn't. Brandy had tried to do her part, but she did exactly what she'd been hired for. No superhero status there.

"I think you and I need to take a moment and think about what we've done." Her tone was slightly joking, but she certainly needed it. She'd thought about it for five days. Telling herself it was fine. She could do this, no relationship, no strings. Now she had to prove it to herself and to him.

Nodding at her, Ash rolled out of bed, this time swinging his bare legs over the side, his back with the straight spine and that ass now in perfect view as he stood up. He looked around for wherever they had flung his pants. At least the room wasn't big enough for them to get very far.

He had found them and was stepping into his clothing before she even had a chance to change her mind.

"Oh, I'll be thinking about what we've done," he promised her.

She grinned and wondered if it would be impolite if she didn't get dressed. They were, after all, in her bed.

Then he was leaning over to give her one more kiss. She slid fully under the covers. God forbid anyone be standing out on the trail as he opened the door.

The front door—the only door—offered a straight shot view of the bed. Something she'd not considered when she was the only person who was in and out of here.

"See you tomorrow," he said, something about the tone holding a promise she wasn't quite ready to cash in.

Then he was gone. Brandy snuggled down into the comforter, only then realizing it smelled like sex and Ash Cooper.

CHAPTER TWENTY-SEVEN

A sh stood at his own cabin door contemplating his choices four days later. Everything was measured in "time since Brandy."

The number of days since he'd kissed her the first time.

The hours since he'd kissed her the last time.

Every second since he'd left her bed and not returned.

When he faced his own unit, Brandy's was on the left and Beck's was on the right. Though the cabins were out of sight of each other, they were just barely so. When he had been staying in Charlottesville because the place was uninhabitable, Roz had had him start on the first cabin in line. Now Brandy's.

He looked to his left, again trying to see if he could spot the edge of the frame or the peak of the roof through the thick trees. It wasn't that far.

They'd next cleaned and painted and set up the second one, and the third, the fourth. Now they had six of the eight ready for inhabitants. Ash had taken the second one, liking the view out the back window. He hadn't met any of the other employees at the time, so he hadn't been stealing it from anyone he knew.

Beck had looked at all of them and said he wanted a cabin

far away from the others. But Roz wanted him in the third. She'd lined them up like little soldiers saying, "Somebody's going to come and go alone. At night, or when the place is otherwise quiet. It is, after all, your home and you should come and go as you please. But you'll do it in the middle of the night sooner or later. There are bears and wild cats out here."

Roz's reasoning was solid. Someone should hear them if they screamed. Now he looked both left and right, wondering if Beck had heard Brandy scream the other night. Or him?

The trainer hadn't come to check up on them. So, he hadn't been afraid Roz's concern had come true. Gratefully, he also hadn't given Ash any of that macho, fist-bump, way-to-get-laid-bro kind of bullshit that Ash hated. There was no telling if Beck knew anything or not. If he did, he'd politely kept it to himself.

Ash still stood there, wondering what to do. He'd thought about what they'd done, just like Brandy had told him to do. Just like he'd promised he would. He'd thought about it in his own bed alone and in the shower once. And he wanted more of it.

Did she?

The work was done for the day. The dogs were in their roomy kennels for the night. Beck was cleaning up after the dinner that he'd made. Ash and Brandy should be the only ones out here since Roz had picked up after dinner and run into town for supplies. Casey and Lynzee had both disappeared for the night.

Ash made up his mind and turned left.

The short walk happened faster than maybe he was ready for, leaving him at her doorstep before he was fully prepared with what he wanted to say. Still, he was here. It was too late to turn around. What if someone saw him here? He had to knock on her door.

She called out immediately, "Coming."

He groaned. Yeah, that's what he *wanted*.

But he wondered why she had to call out. It wasn't like she

could possibly be far from the door. Still, it took her a minute to turn the knob.

Peeking through the slim space where she cracked the heavy wooden door open, she looked out and spotted him. A small smile edged her lips before she peeked behind him and opened the door all the way, letting him in.

Her hair was wet. She wore pajama shorts and a white tank top with no bra, her heavy breasts beckoning to him in a way that he had told himself he wouldn't succumb to.

Not seeming to notice that he was about to salivate, she motioned him inside.

"Hi, I . . ." he couldn't talk. Was she going to slam him up against the door again? *Please?*

Instead, she tipped her head and raised her eyebrows, as if to ask him if the cat had got his tongue. But it wasn't the cat, and it wasn't that he didn't know what to do with his tongue. It was that he *did* know what to do with it and he *didn't* know if she wanted him to do it to her again.

"I was wondering . . ." He paused.

Brandy grinned, filling in, "If there is going to be a repeat performance?"

"That. Exactly."

"We said no relationship, no strings, but that doesn't mean that we can't occasionally make each other scream our brains out. Right?" She gestured with her hands as she spoke. But the top was nearly see-through and her motions made her whole body move with each gesture.

Ash bit his lip as if to stop himself. But could he?

He moved forward, reaching out, his finger tracing the soft skin of her jaw and then moving upward tracking the freckles that bridged her nose. "These are cute."

"They're obnoxious. The amount of money I've spent on makeup to cover them up is ridiculous."

He almost pulled back, shocked. "Why would you cover them up? I mean, obviously sunscreen, but they're so . . . sexy."

Brandy rolled her eyes at him. "You don't have to try so hard. You've already had me," she pointed out, turning away, heading toward the tiny kitchen where he only now realized she'd set out some food.

"I'm not trying that hard. Though don't get me wrong. I gladly would, if you told me it would work."

"Aren't you just the charmer?" She threw him a wry grin over her shoulder as she put the food away.

He stopped cold. "No. Usually I suck at it. Here I am telling you that I think your freckles are sexy and you think I'm *lying?*"

"You like freckles?" She asked it as though he couldn't possibly say yes.

"I like freckles," he said, a grin on his face that he could feel all the way through.

He liked this, he thought. A new life he was building for himself. Old ties cut. The anchors that weighed him down set free. If they wanted to drag the bottom of the ocean, they would have to do it without tugging him along or holding him back.

While it was scary to have no safety net, no family, it was wild to feel free enough to pursue this gorgeous woman and not have to worry about what anyone thought. Not worry about anyone checking in and needing to know the status of their relationship or telling him that he was making shitty decisions. That she'd never love him and that he'd never be good enough for her.

"I like freckles," he repeated. "But I am completely turned on by *your* freckles."

She turned back, hazel eyes burning.

"You're going to think I'm crazy," he told her, "but . . ."

CHAPTER TWENTY-EIGHT

Her phone had rung three separate times that day. Each time she'd seen her mother's name and tried to think what she should do.

The first time she'd simply been busy, and she heard the phone ring but hadn't looked. Buzz needed her attention. He'd gotten closer to washing out of the program. Despite being impressed with how much he had learned, Brandy could tell he wasn't as attentive as the other dogs were learning to be.

She hadn't even pulled the phone out of her pocket until she found a free minute. Then, seeing her mother's name, she checked the voicemail, concerned.

But the voicemail wasn't bad, only, "Honey, I have great news!"

It was nothing bad, but it still made her stomach drop. She wouldn't even bet herself what the news was. She was certain she already knew.

It wasn't anything that needed her to drop everything and run home. But even as she was tucking the phone back into her pocket and turning her attention back to Buzz, her mother called again.

Rather than hitting the button to send it directly to voicemail—because she wasn't sure if her mother was savvy enough to notice that it only rang twice—she'd let it ring through.

At her lunch break, Brandy still wasn't quite ready to call back and hear her mother share the dreaded news. Given the tone in the two voicemails her mom had left, her mother knew something that was *fantastic!* And Brandy did not want to fucking hear it.

Mom had called twice more that afternoon. She hadn't left a message either time, but it was clear that she wanted to share whatever the glory was. The more Brandy thought about it, the angrier she got.

It *had* to be about Sammy. It had to mean that her mother didn't know the whole story. She didn't know that Theo was involved. Which meant that Sammy hadn't told the whole truth . . . in fact, at this point, she'd probably only announced that she was pregnant at all because she was losing the ability to hide it.

When they closed up for the evening, Ash had asked Brandy if she was coming for dinner, noticing she was heading back toward the cabins. He'd grown concerned when she brushed him off, telling him she wanted to eat alone. But she didn't say why. Because she didn't know for sure. She was just heading home with her suspicions in her back pocket.

Avoiding the return call as long as she could, Brandy huffed and stomped around her tiny cabin. She'd brushed off dinner with the crew because she just couldn't deal with people. So here she was with a sandwich and microwave soup. She would have been shitty company. They would have asked, and she didn't need to tell.

It was bad enough that she'd told Ash the story before. The whole thing made her look like a fool and an idiot. She'd eaten the sandwich faster than possible and eventually clinked her spoon at the bottom of the bowl.

With the food gone and having put the detestable task off as long as she could, Brandy picked up the phone. For one last minute, she looked out the wide back window, across the peaceful mountains and watched the night fall.

Her mother was in Northern California, hours behind them, but there was no excuse to put it off any longer. Hitting a couple of buttons, Brandy felt her stomach knot tighter and tighter with each ring. The irony of her mother not answering the phone now wasn't lost on her.

Four rings later, Brandy had thought she just might get a stay of execution. But then there was the telltale click, and her mother answered.

"Brandy, Honey! You didn't answer today, I was worried."

"Mom, I have a job. I'm busy."

"It's just dogs."

The sentiment irritated her for a moment, but she held it in check. Her mother was generally good if Brandy explained. So, she did. She talked again about what they did, the important jobs the dogs would serve. Even though she'd told her mother all of this before, this time she said it with extra emphasis on the timing. "Later in their training, we'll train them to deal with impartial commands and interruptions, but not right now."

"Okay, okay." Her mother gave in, immediately adding. "I have the most amazing news."

There it was. "Do you?"

Brandy knew she wasn't completely able to contain the irritation in her voice. But still she hoped she was wrong, that maybe this wasn't about Sammy at all.

Was she horrible if she'd thought it would just be easier if the pregnancy didn't last? Because she'd thought it. More than once.

"I'm going to be a grandma!"

No, she wasn't wrong.

But mother was exuberant, so Brandy played along.

"You are?"

She wouldn't say anything to even hint that she already knew Sammy was making her mom a grandmother. If she did, she'd be giving it all away. Or at least most of it. Her mother didn't like secrets and she certainly wouldn't like being the last to know about this by several months.

"Sammy is going to have a baby! My *first grandchild!*"

It wasn't meant to be a slap, but it felt like one.

Brandy was supposed to be the one to give her mother her first grandchild. That had been the plan. "That's wonderful mom. I'm so excited for you."

She tried to sound like she meant it. She added the "for you" part because she simply couldn't drum up any excitement herself. Hell, she was so far from excitement, that she was still twelve feet deep into anger and rage. "Who's the father?"

Maybe she could get some straight answers with a seemingly innocuous question.

Even as the words came out of her mouth, she thought *this is going to be rich.*

"Some boy Sammy was seeing. She doesn't think he's going to be in the picture. Your dad and I are going to help however we can."

"Okay." Brandy let the conversation fall flat to the ground with a thunk between them.

Sammy hadn't told the whole truth. *Not a surprise.*

Sammy was not the sister Brandy thought she had known. Before any of this had happened—before she had heard Sammy accusing Theo of leaving her in the lurch and telling him how he needed to do the right thing by her—Brandy would *never* have guessed that Sammy could betray her so.

Sammy, three years younger, had always seemed to worship the ground Brandy walked on. She'd taken the same classes in high school, even considered going into engineering. At least, after the first year of college, Sammy had realized she was much better suited for design. And she was much better doing what she was suited for than what Brandy was suited for.

But this? This betrayal?

It was worse that Brandy had to carry it. Had it been anyone else, even one of her best friends, she could have cried on her mother's shoulder. Complained about Theo and what a lying piece of shit he was, and her mother would have sympathized.

But no. Sammy had stitched that shit right into the family, even if her mother didn't know it yet. Theo was still the father of her first grandchild, even if no one had intended it this way. If Brandy complained about him, she was complaining about someone who would be associated with the family for the next several decades.

And complaining about Sammy? Her mother would always make excuses for her children. Her mother would love her betrayer and Brandy couldn't stand to break her mother's heart by being the one to break the news. She didn't think she could bear to have her mother not be fully on her side.

So, she bit her tongue.

Again.

After a handful of seconds of silence, her mother said, "Well, I just wanted to let you know. And your sister's going to be a single mom. She's going to need your support."

"Of course," Brandy said, thinking even as the words came out that she meant it as *Of course, Sammy thinks she's going to get that.*

Let her mother interpret it any way she wanted. But later, when things came to a head, when that child looked a lot like Brandy's fiancé, there would be hell to pay. Just not right now. Not until she was stronger.

Not until she was ready for the conversation that Theo apparently hadn't even stuck around enough to take care of the younger sister he had gotten pregnant.

Then, when it was all out, Brandy would let them know how

she felt about the whole thing. She just couldn't stand to be the one to break the news. It would tear her mother apart. It would put an irredeemable wedge in the family.

"When are you coming home?" her mother asked.

"Probably not before Thanksgiving." And even then, she didn't know. She didn't know what would happen here. Didn't know if she'd be ready to see the effects of a very pregnant Sammy and all that meant. "It depends on the dog's schedules."

"I know you had your heart broken, baby, but you still need to come home."

"I'll see," was all Brandy could promise. Because it was hard to go home when that was where the knives were.

When the knock came at the door later and Ash said he was just checking on her, he saw the tears streaked down her face and came right through the open door.

CHAPTER TWENTY-NINE

"So how did Buzz do when you took him shopping?" Roz figured she wasn't going to like the answer but told herself she was prepared for it.

Across from her, Brandy fidgeted, tapping her fingernails sharply on the arm of the chair.

Roz liked having these weekly check-ins and she'd hoped that by making it a weekly thing her employees would come to realize they weren't getting fired, that it wasn't anything bad. She wanted it to be their opportunity to tell her what they needed too. What they wanted to do. Ideas they had for the sanctuary.

By now, Ash basically came in and sprawled in the chair and started rattling off lists for her. Beck was more formal, but never appeared nervous. Lynzee crossed her arms, but Roz realized that was her regular stance. Casey was nervous but eager.

Brandy had never quite warmed up to these meetings. If the engineer stayed the whole six months, there would be more than twenty of them. They weren't through half yet. She had to relax at some point, didn't she?

Though Roz told her there was nothing to worry about, the other woman still sat toward the front of the seat, her muscles tense.

"Are you concerned about Buzz?" Roz prompted when she didn't do more than tip her head for the first answer.

"I have to be," Brandy said finally. "It makes me sad. I wanted all the dogs to finish the program."

"So did I. But we knew . . ." Roz shrugged and hoped Brandy's discomfort was because of the dog and not her.

"I know." Brandy leaned back a little bit in the chair, both hands gripping at the arm, "but it feels like a personal failure."

"It's not. Please don't think it is."

"I mean, I picked these dogs out."

Roz didn't quite like her workers taking on that level of responsibility. "Well, yes and no. You pointed out dogs for the first round, but none of them came here without passing by all of us."

Brandy nodded softly.

Was she carrying too much guilt? Thinking that it was entirely her fault?

Sure enough. The next words out of her mouth were, "I just kept hoping if I worked with him a little more and a little more . . . that he would make it."

"It's okay," Roz tried to console her when Roz herself could use some. Wasn't that the way it always worked?

"Is it though? This is the inaugural class!" Brandy waved her hand toward the open window as if to gesture to the actual dogs outside. "Doesn't this first class of graduates *have to* succeed?"

"Yeah, they kind of do." She wasn't willing to admit just how much was riding on it. "But there's room for a washout. And the whole Sanctuary fails if we give someone a dog that doesn't work out."

That, at least, seemed to make Brandy sit up and agree. Roz pushed a little harder. "Imagine for just a minute, giving Buzz to a person with a severe medical condition—severe enough that they got a grant from the government for this service dog. Then they have a seizure or such and Buzz isn't paying one-hundred percent attention."

Brandy blinked, sad at coming to the decision herself now.

Roz wasn't sure if that was better or worse. Maybe it would be best if she simply told Brandy that Buzz's training was over, but Brandy was already nodding along. "You're absolutely right. We need to start looking for his forever home now."

Roz hated to agree. They'd put so much time and effort into him—into each of the dogs. Still, it was time to cut losses. Maybe the other dogs would train up a little faster with more direct attention and time.

"Okay. All right." Brandy was clearly talking herself into it. "Do you want me to help Lynzee with it?"

"I think that would be great. Just don't let it take up too much of your time."

"Okay." Brandy pushed down on the arms starting to stand, but Roz held up a hand to stop her.

This was the part she had not looked forward to. This was the part that would make Brandy just as nervous coming in for the next meeting. But it had to be done.

"I wanted to ask a question," Roz started, the tentative tone in her voice giving her away. She watched as Brandy's gaze grew wary. "I'm just going to get right to it. You and Ash?"

Brandy looked up toward the ceiling and shook her head slightly. "Is it a problem?"

"No," Roz assured her trying to use her gentlest, most sincere tone. "Not unless it becomes a problem. You're adults. So far as I've seen, the work is still getting done. Everything's on time. Honestly, the two of you are getting along better."

Brandy at least laughed a little at that.

Roz tapped the pencil she was fidgeting with on the desk. "I don't know if that's better for the sanctuary or not."

That caught Brandy's attention. "What do you mean?"

"When you and Ash were constantly trying to one up each other and always arguing, I really felt like whatever we eventually decided on was going to be the best option. Now, you seem to agree a lot more and I'm not getting as many options." She laughed a little though it was true.

Brandy grinned. "I will see what I can do about arguing with him more, and I will let him know that it was a directive from you."

"That would be wonderful," Roz said, hoping Brandy didn't feel so nervous. The worst was over. "I am finished now and you're free to go if you want."

Brandy stood up and headed to the door but as she put her hand on the knob, she paused. Before she opened it, she turned back over her shoulder. "Did you ask the same thing to Ash?"

"I did," Roz assured her again and watched as Brandy nodded and headed out the door. Too much of an adult to ask what Ash had said. Or at least knowing by now that Roz wouldn't tell her anyway. She hoped the woman knew she wouldn't tell him anything she said either.

She leaned back as she heard the door click shut. Her head rested on the cushion, but she wasn't relaxing. Buzz washing out was going to hurt.

The sanctuary would operate at a loss for the first class. Probably the second and maybe even the third, too. They had grant money to start, but the second payment depended on how many working dogs they could put into homes.

She reminded herself it depended on the number of *successful* dogs. The first class of graduates would be watched more closely, Roz knew. More evaluations. Maybe more home visits, deemed acceptable for animals that government or charitable funding was covering. The average family could not afford one of these highly trained, very skilled wonders.

But she saw no way to make Buzz into a successful medical

dog. Roz had been racking her brain, asking Ash and Beck what other type of support animal he might be suitable for. But a standard low end emotional support animal was the best they could come up with. ESAs were often granted legal status from therapists and even online certification farms. Their training and adoption wasn't covered by the grant money.

Still, this was the lesser of the two hits, and Roz reminded herself that she had planned for this. Still, she felt the loss in her core.

Each time some small part of the sanctuary needed more than she had budgeted or didn't work according to plan, she heard *his* voice in the back of her head, telling her she would fail.

CHAPTER THIRTY

Ash rolled over, his eyes open. He wasn't going back to sleep no matter how much he wanted to.

Pulling his phone out of the pocket of the jacket he'd hung from the headboard, he clutched at it, not quite ready to check the time.

He'd left the jacket on Brandy's headboard on purpose. There was only a nightstand on her side of the bed—the same as in his cabin. These little places had never been intended for dual occupancy. At least not for more than a brief vacation, if that.

There wasn't room for him to put anything here. In fact, if he stood up, he had only about three paces to go before he stubbed his toe on one of the two chairs at the small table. So, he'd hung the jacket, using the pockets for his keys and phone and whatever else he needed handy. Brandy hadn't complained.

Though she'd stayed over at his cabin twice, they'd most often simply ended up here. Ironic, he thought, that they seemed to have chosen her place when it wasn't any nicer or bigger . . . they were living in basically the exact same little house though he hadn't said anything about it.

His real concern was that his place was closer to Beck's and that he'd succeeded in making Brandy scream often enough that they would either bother or concern his neighbor.

He rolled back, staring at the ceiling. Brandy wasn't an early riser.

Ash missed his view. At his place he would have his coffee in the morning looking out at the mountains dropping into the valley before him. Her view was fine but didn't have quite the majestic scenery as her cabin faced a different direction. Also, there were trees directly between her and the open sky.

He swiped at the phone, the light of the screen jarring his brain. Ash quickly swiped again, turning the brightness down, hoping he didn't wake her.

Five a.m. and not the first time he was tempted to get up and get dressed and walk back to his own place. To make a breakfast omelet with eggs and onions and peppers instead of having the high-end cereal or oatmeal and berries that Brandy kept her cabin stocked with.

He sighed, but she didn't stir. Brandy had certainly seemed to have learned to sleep through his getting up and puttering around in the middle of the night. It sucked, because aside from stepping out onto the front porch, there was nowhere that he could go.

If he made any noise, he might wake her. Turning on the bathroom light would let it shine brightly from under the door —he knew that from experience. Even reading on his phone would make light and . . .

The tiny space was fine when it was only him. He imagined the same was true for her. But it wasn't really enough for two people.

Pushing the phone back into the jacket pocket, he thought he could roll over. Next to him Brandy was warm and naked. He breathed in her scent, thinking that pressing his bare skin to hers was better than any omelet, but it didn't take long to realize that she was out cold.

Warm and naked or not, she was not going to wake up and put that to good use. He didn't want to be stuck lying here looking at the ceiling, so Ash rolled softly out of the bed, his feet quiet on the plush carpet that had appeared on his side after he'd stayed over the first couple times.

Unlike before, when his clothing had been strewn around—pants caught haphazardly on the headboard, his underwear under the kitchen table, shoes in two opposite corners—now it was hung nicely over the back of the chair. He managed to quietly step into all of it without waking her.

Tying his shoes, he stood up and leaned over the bed, thinking to kiss her goodbye. But she was so sound asleep, he didn't want to disturb that. So, he crept out the door into the chill of the night air.

They were high enough in the mountains that, while the days were warm in the open sun, the nights were starting to bite. Fall would be fully underway soon. Brandy was getting close to halfway through her six months.

Checking his pockets, Ash made sure he'd loaded his keys and phone. His wallet was locked safely back in his own cabin. He rarely carried it around the sanctuary, there was no need unless he was leaving. Quickly, he tapped out a message, knowing that her phone was on Do Not Disturb and that she would see it when she woke up.

— Sorry. Woke up restless, didn't want to disturb you. I headed back to my own cabin.

As he pushed through the door he still felt restless. He didn't last long there either. The upside of being on top of a mountain was that nothing blocked the sun. The sunrise came very early.

And the upside of Roz was that she was a firm believer that the early people should show up early and leave work early. And the people who liked to sleep in should show up late and stay later. He could take a morning as it struck him to do so.

His own cabin didn't offer much more to do than Brandy's

did. It simply had one less person to disturb. Changing quickly into his running gear, he pulled out his music. As per his own instructions to Brandy, when he'd scared her on her run, he put in only one earbud.

It was just bright enough to hit the trail and Ash felt his body and his mood shift as his feet hit the dirt. The mountain top opened before him and he kept his eyes out for any early creatures. But the fresh air and movement did him a world of good.

He arrived back almost an hour later. The sun was fully up, the day starting to hit its stride. Still no return message from Brandy.

Hoping she wasn't mad, he let himself into his cabin. Stepping into the tiny bathroom, he peeled his clothes and turned on the shower. Ash lingered there, the water hot and absorbing all the strange emotions coming off him. He'd been clean for a while, but he didn't know what to do.

Was it good or bad that his time with Brandy seemed to have an end date?

They'd said they were just sleeping together, but it was certainly starting to feel like more. And when Roz had asked him what was going on between the two of them? He hadn't had a good answer.

"We're just fucking," had seemed beyond crude and certainly didn't cover when he'd walked in the door and found her in tears. When she'd clung to him. It didn't cover the slow languid lovemaking afterwards.

But neither of them had declared that they wanted anything more. They both knew their time together was terminal.

Thinking he heard something in the cabin, his immediate thought was that a bear had come in through a window, even though he knew it was unlikely. Turning the handle, he shut off the shower. It was time to get out anyway. He breathed in the steam only to hear Brandy's voice.

"Hey, Ash. I let myself in!"

He smiled at the thought. She showed up completely unannounced, let herself into his home, as small as it was, and that made him happy. He was glad she was here, glad to see her before he started work.

They weren't just fucking. There was definitely something more here, even if neither of them had said so.

He was still smiling, a few moments later when she knocked on the bathroom door. "Hey, your phone rang. It's your brother."

"I'll call him back!" Ash called out, running the towel over his head before slinging it around his waist and tucking in the corner. With his grin still in place, he pushed open the door, only to find Brandy standing there, holding the phone out to him. The light on the screen told him it was on.

"I answered it," she said out loud, then pointed to the phone and mouthed, "He's on the line."

With a slight frown, Ash took the phone from her. "Hey Marcus, what's up?"

"Mom was in a car accident."

"Okay." He didn't know what else to say to that. Whatever air and moisture was in his lungs froze, and he wondered what he'd be asked to do now. How he'd be asked to participate in this.

It occurred to Ash that he should have felt fear that something might have happened to his mother, but he didn't. It didn't even register with him.

Brandy was looking at him, obviously concerned at the impact of his brother's statement.

"She's going to be okay," Marcus added. "But she's going to be in the hospital for a few days and need care at home after. We're all going out to help."

"Okay," Ash said again.

There was a pause and then Marcus asked, "When can you get here?"

No, Ash thought, *not again.*

Every single time he had to go through the work of explaining it all again.

"I'm not coming," he told Marcus.

"What do you mean you're not coming? It's a car accident. She's in the hospital."

As if he hadn't heard the first time. *What was Ash supposed to say?* He wasn't even going to say *"Tell her I said hello,"* or *"I hope she gets better."* He had worked so hard not to have to say anything.

Yet when it was about his mother, there was nothing he could do. It just kept crashing into his life.

"I'm not coming," he said as calmly as he could. "I told you I'm done."

The force of getting those words out again made his knees wobble. If Brandy hadn't been standing there looking at him, he would have sat down on the nearest thing—the toilet.

"You can't do that," Marcus said.

But he'd spent so long—too long—learning that he could. That he had to.

"You shouldn't have called," Ash told him, "But good luck."

With that he pushed the button, hanging up the phone on his brother. Squeezing his eyes shut, he pinched the bridge of his nose. When he could breathe again, he tried to take a deep inhale, but it didn't work, and he ran his hand through his hair.

When he finally looked up, he saw Brandy, an incredulous look on her face.

"What the hell was that?"

CHAPTER THIRTY-ONE

W*hat had she just seen?* The tension in every muscle made Brandy think her bones would snap.

How was this possibly the man who scratched behind the ears of every dog he ran into? They all loved him. He administered vaccinations with such a gentle touch that they didn't even flinch.

"Your mother's in the hospital." Brandy enunciated each word because she did not understand how he could be so callous. The adrenaline coursed through her system at the thought of what it would be like if *she* had gotten that call.

He let the phone swing down in his hand, hanging at his side, as he pushed his way past her. His wet torso left swipes of water marks on her shirt, the little cabin suddenly far too small.

"I told you. I don't speak to my mother."

He had said that, but . . . "Look, I get it. You're mad at her, but she's in the hospital. You will regret it if you don't go do this."

An Ash she had never seen before turned on her. His eyes flared. She could almost imagine his teeth bared, showing fangs like the dogs he worked on, growling at her.

"I'm *not* going to regret it!" He almost yelled it, his tone controlled tightly enough to worry her. "I'm so fucking tired of people telling me that."

Brandy pulled back. It felt like he had reached out and slapped her, but she sucked in a breath and tried to be reasonable. "Look, I'm sorry, but I get it. I've never been so mad at Sammy in my entire life. But if she was in the hospital, *I would go*. Even like this, even if they thought she was going to pull through fine, even if there was enough other family around her to take care of her. I would *still go*."

There were six of them, between her and her brothers and younger sisters. Ash was the middle of three. He'd told her about Marcus, who was older, and Delia who was younger, which was why she'd answered the phone when she saw Marcus's name on it.

"This is not like what's going on with Sammy," he told her. The towel somehow still on despite the tension that turned his whole body to wire. "I get it, Sammy lied to you and Sammy betrayed you. But you and Sammy used to get along. This is a *bad thing* that Sammy did. That is not what the case is in my family."

Turning around, he faced away from her. His hands reached out but didn't grab anything. He looked as if he was going to get dressed but didn't. Instead, he reached into the tiny closet, pulled out a few items and stomped into the bathroom, closing the door behind him.

He emerged a few moments later, the T shirt clinging, the water not entirely gone from the shower, his hair still wet. He rubbed the towel over it, but the movements were jerky. He wasn't calm.

She tried to help. She'd been taking deep breaths the whole time and she wanted to be understanding. But this decision wasn't good. This was the kind of thing he would regret. She hated that he would suffer later even if she wasn't here to see it.

She waited for him to calm down. Let him putter around, pulling out socks, sitting in the chair, putting on his shoes. She sank onto the bed, not wanting to hover over him and laced her fingers together.

"Look, you should go. I'll let the guys here know. I'll take over all of your work—"

But he didn't agree. Instead, he looked up at her, eyes glaring.

"*No*," he interrupted. "I'm not going. I don't know what part of that you don't understand."

"She's your mother," Brandy tried again. "No matter what. She loves you—"

He was on his feet in an instant, leaning over her, jaw clenched tight enough that she wouldn't have been surprised if she could hear his molars crack.

"You haven't been listening." He ground out each word and she could tell he was fighting to rein in whatever he was feeling.

Brandy was both curious and afraid. "I have been listening." She put her hands flat on the edge of the bed, clenching the comforter in her fists, so that she didn't grab anything else. "I know you're mad at her. And I know you, you probably have every right to be! Just like I have every right to be furious at Sammy. I have every right not to answer the phone or talk to her. But this isn't *that*."

"No," he told her. "This—" He pointed at his own feet. "— isn't *that*." He pointed at her. "What is between me and my mother is not the same as what's between you and Sammy."

"You'll regret it if you don't go!" She tried again, pleading up at him. Just imagining the pain of standing by her own mother's coffin—or even Sammy's—almost brought her to tears. Car accidents were bad, and lots of times the doctors thought people would pull through, but they missed something. "What if she dies?"

"I won't regret it!" he roared. His hands out at his sides, almost in claws, his anger radiating off him.

She couldn't tell if he meant that he wouldn't regret not going or if he meant that he wouldn't regret if his own mother died. Brandy struggled to process that, but Ash was still furious, still ranting.

"What I have regretted is every single time I have gone back. I regret every single time that I have tried."

"Your mother loves you."

This time he wheeled around fast enough to startle her. His glare would be deadly if she was picking a fight with him. She felt it as if it were a physical touch, as if *she* were the one he hated.

"No, she doesn't. I'm confident she's mentally ill and she's not capable of it."

That struck Brandy as odd. Ash didn't seem like the kind who would be cold and unfeeling. "But if she is mentally ill, then it's not her fault. Doesn't she deserve your love?"

"No!" he said. "Look, you're right, mental illness might not be her fault, but her inability to acknowledge it, her inability to want to be better? That is. And I'm not going back. I'm done being her punching bag."

"I get that you're at odds with her," Brandy tried one more time. She was in a rough spot with her own mother right now. But again, the thought of losing her, of not having made up? In fact, she was changing her own mind right now. Even as she sat here trying to convince Ash, she wound up convincing herself.

"I am not *at odds* with her," Ash said, this time calm. "Marcus and Delia are more than welcome to go and take care of her. But I'm not going."

Brandy stood up, looking him up and down and trying to reconcile this man with the warm and caring creature that she'd known. His walls were up. He was closed—an ice fortress that even she couldn't penetrate. She hated to see him like this. She tried again.

"Marcus and Delia have obviously put their issues with her aside. And it doesn't have to mean that you forgive her for everything. It just means—"

"*Get out!*" He growled it at her, hands clenching at his sides, eyes staring blankly out the window at the view she knew he loved, but couldn't see right now.

"Ash—"

"*Get . . . Out.*"

CHAPTER THIRTY-TWO

He sat in the little hard chair at the little table with his head in his hands. If Ash was feeling any particular emotion, he couldn't identify it from the hurricane that roared inside him.

He was mad at his mother for still existing. Mad at her for getting into a situation that would cause his brother and sister to come to suggest that he "come home." It wasn't home—it never had been.

Neither Marcus nor Delia had ever understood that.

Ash was furious at Brandy, too. *How many times had he told her?* She either hadn't listened or had simply decided that he was a fool who didn't know what he was talking about. Neither was acceptable.

Or maybe it was okay, he thought, after all. Maybe she was just somebody that he was fucking.

Still, it broke his heart. And he didn't have time to have a broken heart, not when he was stuck in the middle of the same struggle that somehow always hurt the same way. He was dealing with this same bullshit all over again.

He had left. He'd said *No.* He'd put his foot down and he'd stayed away. Why was it never enough? Why did they always come back and find him? Did they think this time would be different? And could he fault them? He'd gone back too many times thinking exactly that.

But it never was.

His phone rang and he wondered what shit show was finding him now.

Heading toward the sound, he found the device on the tiny counter in the bathroom. Flipping it face up he saw that it was Delia. Marcus had probably called her and told her Ash was causing problems. Perpetual middle child that needed attention.

How long had he believed that about himself because they always said it?

Decades.

But he'd also learned that he should deal with shit now.

As soon as he hit the button, he thought maybe he shouldn't have answered at all. Not put it off, but just never answer. His intent had never been to cut off his entire family. He didn't want Delia and Marcus out of his life.

Ash still suspected he knew what Delia would say. But he answered anyway, his anger getting the best of him. "Hey, Dee."

"Marcus said you're not coming back."

Well, at least *someone* had heard him. "Marcus is correct."

"Ash," she chided. Not a good look when she was younger than him. "I know you and mom don't get along—"

"Then you *don't* know."

Delia had been there for all of it, but she was younger. She'd seen it all through the eyes of her mother's favorite child. Though she understood some of what had happened because she'd seen some of it, she hadn't seen anywhere near all of it. And it still hadn't quite processed for her and maybe never would.

Ash and his brother and sister had grown up in the same house but in separate worlds.

149

Delia, the favorite, the baby, got dance classes. When she tired of ballet mid-season, their mother had talked the teacher into taking Delia into the jazz class instead.

When Delia didn't like the piano, their mother had immediately bought her a tiny violin and hired her a tutor. When she hated the violin, her mother talked the band teacher into taking a fourth grade Delia for flute. Delia didn't have to wait until fifth like all elementary school students are requested to do.

When Ash had wanted to play the tuba, he had been told that he didn't have the ability to stick with anything and it simply wasn't worth their investment. When he'd wanted to join the high school baseball team, his mother had reminded him how he hadn't liked T ball in elementary school, and therefore he wouldn't like this either. As if his seven-year-old tastes and ability to persevere with something would be what he was stuck with for his lifetime. His baseball just "wasn't something that the family was interested in putting their time on."

Delia didn't know how many times his mother had simply forgotten to pick him up after high school theater practice. How many times he'd had to call his father at work and then Ash had waited and waited. Everyone else had already gone home, even the teachers had left, because this wasn't the first time, and they knew that eventually someone would get Ash.

She didn't know the number of times he'd wound up walking, because his father had been busy and no one had remembered that he'd had theater practice. His mother had showed up for the play, highlighted his name in the program, and at the end of the night, she had given him corrections. Despite the fact that she was no actress, and had no real theater experience herself, she'd spent an hour making him listen to exactly when and how she thought he'd failed to show the appropriate emotion for the scene.

The following year, when he said he wanted to be in the

school production again, she complained about the amount of time that it had taken and told him he would need to find his own rides.

Delia didn't see those things. She didn't remember them. And they hadn't happened to her, so she couldn't relate. They weren't even the whole story.

Marcus on the other hand was the smart one—always excelling in his classes. Always praised for his A's and B's while Ash's 3.95 GPA had been brushed off repeatedly. His cords and honors at graduation given no notice.

His parents had laid a payment system to help him out with college. They'd even all written it down, and he'd had stupid, stupid faith in that piece of paper. But that, too, had simply dried up halfway through his undergrad. His father made rough excuses for his mother, letting him know that Delia had picked a more expensive school, so they needed to cover that for her.

So no, Delia and Marcus did not understand. And they probably never would.

Ash had done far more reading about what it was to grow up as a scapegoat than either of them would ever know. They knew —acknowledged that something was wrong with Mom. When their father passed away a few years ago, the three siblings had some serious conversations. But being the ones she favored had made their opinions very different than his.

They acknowledged when he showed them what he'd read, detailing how she had divided them and turned them against each other as kids. But as adults, they'd done nothing about it. So, no, they didn't understand that his mother's treatment of him—even of them—had been a classic case that no one had diagnosed. He'd learned lately that no one was ever going to fix it.

"I think you should come," Delia told him softly. "Just for a few days."

"No," he said again, still biting his tongue at the common

pleasantry that was ingrained to roll out of his lips. *"Tell her I said hello."* He wasn't going to say that.

This time, he repeated what the therapist he had visited a few times had told him to tell himself. "Delia, *no contact* means *no contact.*"

"Jesus Ash! When is this going to be over?"

"When mom straightens herself out." He laughed a sharp, harsh bark that yanked straight through him. "So probably never."

"You're just going to live the rest of your life without mom?"

Wow, it hit him hard just how *good* that statement sounded.

"Yes."

"Don't be that way." The words were snide and too young for the adult woman his sister had become.

"Travel safe," he told her, the best he could do before he hung up.

He needed at least three deep breaths and paced the small space four or five times before he messaged Roz.

—Need a mental health day.

She messaged back immediately.

— No worries. Plz take it.

Then another ping from her.

— need more than one?

He smiled. Why was this woman who was barely ten years older than him so much better to him than anyone in his own family?

— I hope not. I'll try to make good use of today.

But he was already grabbing his wallet and keys, shoving them in his pocket. He closed the cabin door behind him. Though it had a latch and a bolt, he didn't lock it.

For a moment, he wondered if he'd find Brandy in here when he came back. And what would that mean? How would he handle it? Would she understand? Apologize?

Ash had no answers. His insides churned but it didn't stop

him. Climbing into his car, he snapped at the key and started the engine for the first time in several days. It struck him then how infrequently they left this space.

But he hit the gas a little too hard, churning gravel as he backed up, spun the car around and headed down the long drive.

As the compound disappeared in his rearview mirror, he thought he caught a glimpse of red hair.

CHAPTER THIRTY-THREE

Ash headed toward Charlottesville but, on a whim, took a turn on a road he hadn't driven yet.

He wound up on winding drives tracing his way through the mountains. Something about it pulled him into the past, to a childhood he wasn't sure he ever wanted to revisit.

He'd grown up in a small town in the mountains in North Carolina. Just beyond the neighborhoods, there had been roads like this. Places, that once he'd learned to drive, he'd explored in depth, just to get out and be away.

He hadn't loved those times. The reason he needed to escape wasn't lost on him. But the mountains were calming then . . . and now.

Putting the windows down, Ash let the heat of the day start to seep in. He let some of his anger seep out, too. He was mad at his mother, again. He even entertained thoughts that her car accident wasn't so much an accident as just another thing that would get her attention.

He'd learned terms in therapy for what it all was. One of them was a phrase his therapist used for his mother, a casual narcissist. Maybe the worst kind because that made it harder for everyone else to see it.

Ash was mad at Delia and Marcus, too. Mad at them for being their same old selves and never getting any better at seeing or acknowledging the bullshit. They were getting taken, too. They just still bought in. Ash tried to let that go, he couldn't change anyone but himself, and he'd lost enough time trying to educate people who didn't want to see.

He was mad at Brandy for being the same person he'd encountered so many times before. The 'family first' and 'family above all else' who couldn't see some families didn't look like their own.

He tried to let that go too. But that one was harder.

Ash put his hand out the window, letting the passing air drag at his fingers. No one else was on the road, just him and his broken wishes.

He held no real hopes for Delia or Marcus to come around. But he'd made the mistake of believing that Brandy understood him. Or that, even if she didn't, she would have his back. Instead, she sat there and told him repeatedly how wrong he was about a decision that had taken decades for him to come to. One that she knew nothing about.

Ash spotted his fingers gripping the steering wheel, his knuckles white, and he didn't even feel it. Forcibly, he relaxed, letting his shoulders sink down, his jaw unclench, and his fingers loosen.

Time to turn on the GPS. He had an idea how far off track he'd gone. Once the program found him, he realized he wasn't that far out of Charlottesville. He cut through a tiny town—if it could even be called that. It was mostly just a cluster of homes.

He was familiar with roads that held a variety of old houses. Some mansions with columns that held up dual front porches. Next to that were trailers. Then, older, sagging homes that had a junkyard in the front yard. The junkyard was never a random pile of trash. You could tell just driving by that someone who lived there collected something specific. Maybe old washing machines, VW bugs, or lawn mowers—usually machinery of some kind.

He passed by the neighborhoods that sprawled through Albemarle County, just outside the city limits of Charlottesville. Some of the houses were still being built.

Tiny bedroom communities beckoned him in. But he didn't heed, instead he headed toward the shopping area. He needed new running shoes. Today was as good a day as any to get them.

It startled him as he pulled up to realize the store wasn't even open yet. How had things gone so wrong before ten a.m.?

He considered hitting the coffee shop where he'd taken Brandy. Though he told himself he wasn't that immature to avoid it just because she had been there, it was still difficult to go back and relax there when he was specifically still mad at her from just an hour ago.

He found a new place where the coffee wasn't quite as good. Somehow, he'd lucked into the best one first. Next, he found the stores open and bought the running shoes. He grabbed a new phone charger and a few other items that he didn't really need but wanted.

Aside from the occasional grocery run, and a little bit for gas, he was mostly saving his salary from working at the sanctuary. He had no housing to pay, no utility bills. Though the actual salary itself was definitely on the low end, most of it was going into his pocket, which was a welcome change from the meager money when he worked with Dr. Dickens at the barn. It was also a change from making good money doing his stint in Redemption, Nebraska. Zadie had paid him well, but Ash had empty weeks on either side that he'd had to save to cover.

He ate lunch on the patio of an Italian place, stuffing his face with amazing pasta and enjoying the slightly too hot day. The patio was mostly empty, people preferring the air conditioning.

But Ash knew this was about to be the last of the warm days. The mountains got cold, fast.

After his late lunch he went to see a movie by himself. How long had it been since he'd done that? The sun was setting by the time he emerged, so there was no glaring brightness to shock him into squinting. As Ash headed toward his car, he realized he didn't know what to do next.

He wasn't ready to go back. There was still too much evening to cover, and he wasn't ready to talk. Wasn't ready to make nice. He was hoping to arrive late enough not to run into anyone.

There were *hours* between now and then. He sat in the car for a moment, before looking up the name of the nearest veterinary clinic. He wound up with three of them to check out. Not that he was intending to leave Jade River Sanctuary. He wasn't even sure he would leave when his contracted two years were up, but he also wasn't sure that Jade River Sanctuary would still be here in two years.

He didn't discredit Roz. She was doing her absolute best. It was a startup and startups sometimes failed. He told himself he needed to be ready if that happened. He would need a plan.

He headed toward the nearest one and pulled into the parking lot. He didn't go inside or introduce himself but sat for a moment and looked up the website. How many veterinarians did they employ? What did the pictures of the inside rooms look like? How up to date was the equipment?

He told himself he wasn't making plans, but then he looked up two more clinics. Not that he would necessarily stay in Charlottesville, he told himself, but he was discovering there was something about the mountains that felt like home.

Sitting at the fifth office with two more on his growing list, he got a ping on his phone and saw a new text.

— Heard you were out today in Charlottesville.

Ash frowned at the phone. He didn't recognize the number.

Not only was it someone who knew he was out today but knew that he might be in Charlottesville. Who would even ask that? Zadie was still in Redemption, on the other side of the country as far as he knew. Also her number was in his phone, it would have said her name. He had told her he'd moved to a place just outside of Charlottesville.

Brandy's number was listed with her name and a picture of her smiling. One that he'd snapped when she hadn't noticed. He rolled his eyes at himself as he pulled out of the lot, taking the next turn his GPS told him to.

Why had he not admitted to himself he was so far gone? *They* might be casual, but *he* clearly wasn't. He'd let it go too far without saying anything and now he was stuck.

A second text popped up.

— Let me know if you want company. Okay if you don't. There's a great bar off Huntington. The bartender's an old friend from my halfway house but the bar itself isn't crazy rough just kind of laid back

Ah! Ash thought. It was from Beck.

Then he pulled into the parking lot of the next vet clinic and tried to look with a critical eye. The small brick building held a green tin roof. The big sign out front was shaped like a bone and made from carefully curated, rusted-looking metal. A cutout of a dog and a cat held up a handcrafted sign with "Pen Park Veterinary Clinic" across the top.

The cars in the lot were higher end, and the neighborhood had been multi story houses that were cookie cutter, but with enough variation for the owners to think that maybe they weren't. This was not the place for him.

He grabbed the phone and added Beck's name in place of the number then messaged back.

— I am here. Where is it? I'll meet you there.

Because, *why the hell not?*

CHAPTER THIRTY-FOUR

"I have to quit after this one," Ash said as the tall glass was pushed across the bar toward him. The foam on top sloshed but expertly didn't spill, as if it were all just for effect.

Or maybe he was just a little drunk, and he should have quit before he ordered this one. But he was having a surprisingly good time, just sitting here talking to Beck and occasionally to the bartender Liam.

"You want me to ring you out now? To make sure you stop?" Liam asked.

Ash took his first sip. This was the fourth draft beer he tried that Liam had recommended. "It's good." He told Beck whose own glass of it was sliding across the bar to him.

Then Ash looked back at Liam and assumed a slightly affected voice. "I can detect a note of pear."

"You would be correct, sir," Liam smiled, but motioned again and this time Ash nodded.

"Yeah, ring me out. Your recommendations are good enough I might be tempted to get another." He reached for his back pocket, but Beck stayed him with an outward palm.

"I've got it."

"You don't have to," Ash countered. He hadn't come out of charity. Hell, Beck might be working *him* as a charity case.

"I know I don't." Beck handed over his card to Liam who was already ringing them out. "You can get it the next time."

Ash tipped the tall glass at him in a small salute. Hopefully, like him, Beck didn't have much to spend his money on and this wasn't stretching anything.

Though, honestly, Ash was learning more and more about his coworker. Maybe he was just finally feeling the buzz enough. They'd danced around all kinds of topics—discussing the dogs and the sanctuary. They'd already made the executive decision to swap the training for two of the dogs. Though Curie was a beagle, her scent training wasn't as strong as Norgay's was. He would make the better medical assistant. She would be better as a hearing ear dog.

Beck must have sensed a shift in the evening, too. He made a move. "So, you and Brandy?"

Ash began reading the labels of the bottles stacked behind the bar. "Yes, but then . . ."

He shrugged, turning to Beck and motioning that he didn't know what. Then words fell out that he hadn't expected. "I thought you were into her for a while."

What a stupid thing to say. How grade school. He should have quit before this beer, but his friend had paid for it, so he took another sip.

Beck shrugged. "Who wouldn't be? All those curves, that red hair. She's gorgeous. But . . ." he made a small motion of concession. "It's clear who she has eyes for. And my tastes run a little bit elsewhere."

Relief coursed through Ash, though it shouldn't have. But then his senses tuned, and he realized there was something in the way Beck said the last part that made Ash think it wasn't a generic statement. There was someone specific his tastes were running to. And it wasn't the obvious choice of Brandy.

He laughed. "You know, I think Lynzee has a crush on you."

Beck's eyes rolled and his head tipped back. "Roz thinks so. I've been telling myself that I was reading it wrong."

Ash clinked his glass against his new friend's. "I do not think you were wrong."

"Crap. She is way too young and way too . . ." Beck let the words trail off.

Ash frowned. Lynzee was so rebellious, so, so borderline goth. He'd had too much to drink. Had he said it out loud? Because Beck turned and laughed at him.

"What? She's just so ornery that she'd be perfect for the ex-con?"

"No. Not what I was thinking." Ash started to hold his hands up in surrender but realized at the last moment that he was still holding the glass.

Though maybe he had thought that. "You're not what I expected."

Beck was an insanely good listener and maybe it was time to say something. Tell him why they were here letting him hit a fourth beer in fewer hours. He'd have to stay and sober up before he drove home, but the wait wouldn't hurt him.

"I had a huge fight with Brandy this morning." That wasn't enough. He explained. "My mother had a car accident and Brandy is trying to convince me to go home to take care of her. But I haven't spoken to my mother in six months."

"You cut her off?" Beck asked. There was no judgment in the tone. Ash was shocked how quickly the other man had come to that conclusion.

"Not for the first time, either. I'm just the fucking idiot who keeps trying to make it work."

"Of course, you do. She's your mother." Beck made all the wasted time sound like something a reasonable person would fall prey to. "But being your mother doesn't automatically make her a good person."

The relief washed through his system again, a much bigger wave than when Beck said he wasn't into Brandy. Hell, how much was he still holding on to with this shit?

Reaching over, he clinked his glass against Beck's again. This time a little too hard. Liam hadn't made it spill even with all the foam on top, but Ash did.

Beck grabbed a napkin and wiped the side of his hand with a laugh but added, "Cheers!"

"Why do you understand this so much better than everybody else?" Ash asked, amazed.

Beck laughed again. He was on his fourth beer, too, but he seemed to have his shit together better.

"I've been in prison for eleven of the last twelve years."

Ash put his hands out, his shoulders ratcheted up, his head shaking back and forth. How in the hell did that math work? And why did that explain anything?

As usual, Beck understood the assignment. "I understand about mothers. How do you think I wound up in the clink?"

Did people actually say *the clink*?

But Liam was leaning over the bar smacking his hand flat on the shiny clean surface and saying, "Amen to that."

"Your mother got you in prison?" Ash was still dumbfounded, though Beck and Liam seemed to be bonding. Then again, they'd known each other for a while. Or so Ash had gathered.

"Yes. She had me selling weed by the time I was ten—"

"*Ten?*" Okay, he needed to stop sounding like a fucking idiot.

"I moved up to dealing coke by fifteen, and then at eighteen I barely managed to graduate high school. No college for me, not then. The only seemingly real job prospects were to continue doing what I was doing, because the money was fucking amazing—"

"Amen." Liam said again, though this time with tempered enthusiasm.

Who was he even at the bar with? Ash wondered. Then again, at least it wasn't murderers.

Beck's tone changed. "I got snagged. In the process of getting charged, I found out my mom's new boyfriend was running kids."

"Running *kids?*" Oh, good God, he had to sound so naive.

"Exactly as bad as you think. So not only do they have me on intent and distribution, I was associating with a ring doing much worse than anything I did. I was never charged for anything regarding trafficking, and I *honestly did not know.*" Beck took a deep breath. "I do know it made my sentence longer. I was unwittingly a part of it. And that I will never forgive myself for."

"Shit man," Ash said. The pall hung heavy between them for a few minutes.

Luckily, Beck was still sober enough to steer the conversation back on less disturbing ground. Still, what he said next surprised Ash in ways he had not been prepared for.

CHAPTER THIRTY-FIVE

The room was empty. Brandy sat still on the end of the bed.

Because it wasn't her own place, puttering around, fixing food, or touching anything didn't seem okay. She wasn't on good enough terms with Ash right now to mess anything up.

Still, she wanted to be here when he got back.

Her workday had ended. The sun had set while she had dinner with Roz and Casey. Then she'd come here, thinking Ash might already be home, that he might be ready to really talk.

But the night had grown longer, and he hadn't showed. She'd become worried that he wasn't coming back. *What had she done?*

She'd sat and waited long enough to grow bored and agitated. One thing she knew she had done though was convince *herself* to mend her own relationships.

With nothing else to do, and in need of something to occupy her time, Brandy decided to start with calling her sister. She hadn't spoken to Sammy since yelling at her to go away through the church door. She'd been sitting in the bathtub, in her dress with her beer in hand, crying and drinking away all her sorrows.

Even now, she still had the penny tucked away in a drawer in the cabin. It meant more than what Gamma had intended it for. It was a backup plan—a symbol of how much her Gamma loved her. Because the penny was valuable, and Gamma didn't have much.

A depression baby who'd had her own children older in life, the woman hoarded everything. Brandy thought to herself that despite the failed plans and the shit circumstances, Gamma would be excited to see Sammy's child. It would still be her very first great grandchild.

What Gamma wouldn't be excited about was Brandy and Sammy being at odds. Though Brandy had called Gamma a month ago and offered to give the penny back, the woman had bade her keep it. It was important to have something that could easily be hidden and carried and traded if an escape was ever needed.

It felt good that Gamma had her back truly no matter what. Even though she didn't know the whole situation. And maybe that's what she owed Ash.

She would tell him . . . if he ever came back.

She'd dicked around long enough, though. Pushing the button, she let the phone ring, her guts in knots as she waited for Sammy to answer.

Just when she thought she would get the voicemail and she could hang up, the telltale click came over the line.

The voice on the other end was tentative. "Hey."

For a moment, Brandy didn't know what to say. She'd prepped so many things to start with. She'd expected a hostile answer or maybe one that gloated. None of that was in the shallow voice that answered.

She sat there, startled, until her sister said, "Brandy, are you there?"

"I'm here. I'm sorry. I just wanted to reach out I guess." She paused, stuttered, stopped, and started over.

"I'm glad. I don't want to be so mad at each other."

That made Brandy's head snapped back. *Why was Sammy mad at* her?

Brandy felt she had every right to her anger. She had a right to carry it a long, long time. The cut was so deep and Sammy had to know it. But . . . maybe she should figure the rest out. "Why were you mad at me?"

"I shouldn't have been," Sammy confessed. But that meant she was. "It was stupid."

It might have been stupid. But that didn't change that Sammy and Theo had fucked everything up. It was almost worse that it was over something stupid. Maybe if they'd been magically in love and Brandy was just playing the part of the "wrong girl" she could have lived with it. Somehow this managed to make her feel even more awful.

She shouldn't have called. But she was already on the line, so she stayed silent, letting Sammy fill in the blanks.

"I graduated," Sammy said, "and no one noticed."

"That's not true."

"It *is*."

Shit. Brandy thought. It wasn't fully true. They'd gone to her graduation. There had been a family party, but that didn't excuse anything, because at least in part, Sammy was right.

She had finished her classes in December and finished her thesis in January. That left her hanging for several months until she could actually graduate in the spring with her class. Right around the time of Brandy's so-called wedding.

"Everyone came," Brandy reminded her, though she understood that it wasn't the same as when Gary Jr had been the first. And not the same as Brandy's college graduation.

With Sammy's spread-out schedule, everything hadn't happened at once. There had been little celebrations along the way. Daddy had taken her out to dinner when her thesis was approved and so on. They probably hadn't made quite as big of a deal out of it as they could have.

"I graduated from one of the most prestigious Art Institutes in the country, with honors. And do you know what everyone talked about at my graduation?"

Fuck. Brandy knew the answer. "My wedding."

"Yeah." The sound was short and righteously angry. "Because your decision to become Mrs. Theo Longmeyer was more important than my years long accomplishment."

"That's not true Sammy."

"Evidence says otherwise." Brandy was opening her mouth to point out that it wasn't entirely true. Everyone had still been mostly in one place for Gary Jr's graduation. It had been easy. By the time Sammy graduated, only Dakota and McKayla still lived at home. The others had had to travel from all over to see her walk.

Brandy was trying to point that out, when Sammy added in, "It's no excuse for what I did. I ruined your wedding. And I'm so sorry."

Interesting. She was sorry she ruined the wedding but not that she fucked the man Brandy loved? Maybe it was as much of an apology as Brandy was going to get.

It definitely left things still unsettled. Maybe it could be enough for Brandy to be able to sit at a Thanksgiving table. Maybe it would be enough for one night.

She thought she heard tires in the distance. "Well, I have to go."

Sammy paused, then said, "Thank you for calling. I do love you, big sis."

"I love you, too, Sammy."

Brandy hung up, thinking some days it was harder to love her family than others. But wasn't that the way that love worked?

Sammy might be sorry that she'd ruined the wedding but as time had passed, Brandy discovered that maybe *she* wasn't. She had a whole new life, and it was settling in okay. Losing Theo had been hard. But maybe that had been about losing her plans for her future, too.

Sitting again with the phone in her hands, she wondered how long it would take Ash to make it past the lodge and down the trail to the cabin. *If* she had heard tires at all.

Growing antsy, she stood up and paced, tried to think about what to say to Ash.

Should she apologize for what she'd said? She didn't want to, but she knew she was wrong in the way she'd done it. She didn't even know what she wanted, just not to leave things with Ash like this.

In her hands, her phone buzzed. Excited, she turned it upright, hoping it was him.

She froze when she saw that it was Theo.

He'd called her for weeks after the wedding-that-wasn't. She'd ignored him until he got the point. He hadn't emailed or texted or called since.

Until now.

Until five minutes after she hung up with Sammy.

That couldn't be a coincidence.

She watched the face of the phone, stunned and motionless until it stopped ringing. Then she waited, her breathing heavy, as she berated herself for letting him affect her so much. She watched for a voicemail that never pinged.

Brandy was still standing there, still staring at the screen as she heard footsteps and then Ash's hand on the knob.

She gingerly set the phone on the bed, face down, as if not seeing it would make it all go away. She didn't want any distractions between her and Ash.

But as he opened the door, he didn't see her because he was

looking over his shoulder. She was surprised when he called out to someone beyond where she could see.

"I'll see you tomorrow. And thanks!"

CHAPTER THIRTY-SIX

"I'm sorry." Brandy made sure they were the first words out of her mouth. Before she asked who he was talking to. Before she let any wild jealousy run away with her.

Ash closed the door behind him, his hand still on the knob, and he leaned against it. As he looked at her, she could read the accusation there. *She was sorry, but what for?*

She did her best. "I'm sorry that I reacted the way that I did. I obviously don't understand."

"You obviously don't." His tone was flat. Her heart already felt like she'd been steamrolled, and his tone flattened it a little more.

"Can you explain it to me?" She felt so lost.

Everything between them had been easy, so simple, no expectations. Every time she'd needed something, he was there, he listened. She listened to him. But, somehow, she had managed to fuck this all up, and she still wasn't quite sure how.

And she still didn't understand *him*. He was so smart. How could he not at least imagine the outcome to his choice? How could he not see that the decision was a bad one?

But somewhere during the day she'd realized it wasn't her

decision to make. Maybe she just needed to let him make his own bad decision. She might also need to admit that he wasn't her boyfriend, and that this was all casual in the first place.

Instead of saying yes, he would explain, he slumped a little more against the door and simply said, "I don't understand what you don't understand. I did explain it."

"She's your mother." Brandy offered up the obvious again, thinking of her own mom and how much the distance between them had hurt these last few months. "Do you think she simply doesn't love you?"

He sighed, that gorgeous chest rising and falling slowly, his now-too-blue eyes looking off to the side. Stepping away from the door, he didn't answer as he headed toward his tiny kitchen, grabbing ice, then filling a glass with water. He took a large drink and didn't offer her anything.

This time he leaned back on the counter, the glass still in his hand. "I do think she loves me."

"Then why don't you go?" Brandy asked. "Why do you think—"

"Shut up!" he said. The glass smacked down on the counter. "Stop second guessing me! You know nothing of my life."

It was all she could do not to actually recoil from his anger. She thought she *did* know about his life. She knew how he'd worshipped the one doctor, and that man had let him down. She knew how Ash had bounced from job to job, and that he'd almost run out of money several times. How he put himself through veterinary school.

"Look," he said, a little calmer, "I'm glad that your family was good. I'm glad that your mother loved you and that her love helped you. I'm sure you're a better person for having been raised by her."

Brandy nodded. It was a good way to put it. Her mother helped absorb the shock when she was hurt. Her mother was the one she turned to, then maybe one of her sisters. Together, they would brunt the blows that life inevitably brought.

It was what had been so hard about this last one. Dakota and McKayla were too young to have the the kind of conversation Brandy needed. Sammy was the problem. Her mother couldn't be told, or Brandy would be the one driving the wedge through the family since Sammy hadn't told the truth yet. And maybe never would.

Gary Jr. would tell her to walk it off, that sometimes things didn't work out. And Rick? Hell, Brandy didn't even know what Rick would say. Even so, it was difficult to imagine cutting any of them off.

"Your mother didn't make you a better person?" she asked. "She loved you but somehow she didn't help?"

She was just trying to put together the pieces he'd handed her. They didn't fit.

"Am a better person because of her? Yes."

Progress! She thought.

But he continued. "I'm better because of all the things I said I would never do because I watched her do them. I'm really good at school because I was petrified of getting even a B. And because school was the only place I was ever praised for what I did well."

"If your parents were really strict . . ." Brandy tried to lead into something that would work. Even so, people loved their strict parents. They didn't do this.

The Ash she saw now seemed so different from the man she'd gone to bed next to last night.

"Oh, no," he said, surprising her. "They weren't strict."

He was being even more confusing! How did he possibly expect her to understand when he didn't make any sense?

He drank more of the water, this time setting it down more gently, not frightening her that he might break the glass. He pulled out one of the two chairs at the small table—identical to hers—and sat down. "They were only strict with me. My brother did passably in school but was praised for being so smart. My sister was given everything she ever asked for. And I was told I didn't have the ability to stick to anything, so I shouldn't get classes or play an instrument. I was told that the two Bs I got in high school were horrifying. I was punished for them. Neither of my siblings was punished for a bad grade. Ever. Even the Ds Delia brought home a few times."

He paused, his fingers lacing together. He didn't look at her but continued. "It was later explained to me that they knew I was smart and that I could do better. But that's a shit system, Brandy, and it's a shit system to put on a *kid*."

"If they treated you that differently from your brother and sister . . ." That still didn't make any sense. Kids were supposed to be raised differently. They weren't all the same. She'd seen it with her own brothers and sisters. She knew kids often remembered things wrong. *Was he doing that?*

"I'm an adult." He looked at her now, that blue gaze piercing her soul. "I'm an adult who lived this life. And you didn't. I'm sorry I didn't download every shit thing from my childhood when we were talking because I don't want to deal with it anymore! I'm trying so hard to be done with all of it."

He paused, but she could see he had more to say.

"If I had started the day we met, I still wouldn't be finished."

"But you're not a child anymore," Brandy pointed out, still hoping this could be solved. "You can go back and be an adult. You can have a different relationship with your mother now."

Ash laughed, as though she'd said the funniest thing ever. Then he laughed again. Each time the sound got bigger, she felt smaller. *Shamed*, though she wasn't sure quite why.

"That's beautiful—that you think I haven't tried it. I've never done that to you. I've disagreed with your choice of materials to build dog kennels. But I never suggested that you'd made the wrong choices with *your own life*. With the one thing that you are the only one who one hundred percent knows about." He huffed out a harsh breath. "I have not had a single adult interaction with my mother that didn't eventually end with some of the same bullshit. And I refuse to spend the rest of my life walking on the eggshells I grew up on."

Maybe, *maybe*, it was as bad as he said. Maybe he was right. Though Brandy couldn't fathom it. He'd never once said he had been hit or sexually abused. None of the things she really understood would make a child not want to be near their parent.

She was trying to figure out what to say next. When Ash said it.

"I've had a long day and I'm tired and I'd like to go to bed." He looked at her, the gaze flat and tired and uncaring. "By myself."

She felt the tears welling at the sides of her eyes, but she managed to nod. She stood up from the end of his bed and walked out the door into the cold night air.

CHAPTER THIRTY-SEVEN

R oz stared at the spreadsheet on her screen. Her vision had gone fuzzy, and she'd reached the point where she was trying to break everything into smaller pieces because the "big picture" was simply too much to handle.

The good news was that Lynzee had gotten thirty-two adoption applications for Buzz. They were going to get him into the perfect home and very soon.

The good news was Beck and Ash seemed friendlier. They'd come back together from Ash's day off late at night, and the low grade oil-and-water feeling was now gone.

Roz had been up in her room, reading a romance novel, when the headlights had swept across the wall, followed quickly by a second set. She tried not to be a mother hen, but she always knew who was at her Sanctuary and who was out. Normally, she waited up for them to get back, even though she knew they were adults and not even her own family.

She told herself not to but hadn't been able to help heading to the window and peeking through the curtains. Ash had looked fine to her—he wasn't stumbling around or making jerky movements. Roz wouldn't have thought anything of it except that Beck was clearly watching over him. Beck seemed to have followed Ash in.

Beck had told her—maybe a little too casually—this morning that they'd met up for beers in Charlottesville. Which then made Roz wonder if Beck had been watching over Ash from even earlier in the evening. She didn't ask.

She just took a deep breath and tried to relax into her nice office chair now.

Unfortunately, the bad news was that she'd still somehow made her employee salaries too high. They weren't too high, not in reality.

She knew they were barely middling range and cut slightly lower for the fact that housing and a good portion of food was included. But according to her budget, they were way too high.

The good news was that with Buzz finding his forever home soon, she would have one less mouth to feed. Sadly, the irony was that Buzz was the smallest dog and ate the least. Aside from feeding the dogs, all the other expenses were mostly included with the day-to-day costs of running Jade River Sanctuary.

She wouldn't cut an employee because she had lost a dog. And Roz wouldn't get any more money back on the place. While she was using five kennels, they had built ten. Her high hopes and lower per-kennel cost had her planning ahead for when the training center was fully up and running. They would have larger and larger classes, more and more room for dogs to wash out. More and more history of providing well trained dogs, the Sanctuary's ratings would be high.

More importantly, to be sure, she would know that people who had dogs from Jade River recommended them and lived better lives for having them. But that was all still a ways off in the future and the crushing pressure of making all that happen right now with this first class was killing her.

She tipped her head into her hands, knowing that it should

help to just stop staring at the bright screen for a moment. She also knew it wouldn't help anything.

When she looked up again, the night had fallen around her. She should have been up in her room, already reading, but . . . she had to figure this out.

The van? It was valuable.

She'd bought the van because they needed it, and they'd proved that by using it so many times already. It had been an incredible deal. She had snapped it up thinking she couldn't afford *not* to get it. But maybe they could have just put the dogs into the SUVs.

Could she sell the van? Hopefully. Maybe for as much if not a little more than she'd paid for it.

But the dog training world was small. She'd learned that early on.

Another hard lesson she'd had was that when circles were small, someone could spread word and it could roar like wildfire through a tiny community. That burn could wipe out everything—true or not.

She'd bought the van from someone in the community who was selling because they were retiring. If word got out that she'd already sold it . . . well . . . It would reflect badly. If she sold it for more than she paid for it—which was what she needed to have happen—it would look like she was scamming people.

In the long term, Jade River would not survive that.

So that cash flow was off the table.

She told herself she would survive, even if she wasn't quite sure she believed it. But Roz reminded herself that she had survived worse days than this. She had survived all of her worst days, though some of them barely.

She'd been in the hospital more than once. In the ICU and on a ventilator more than once. She told herself, this wasn't that.

Now, the zeros in her bank account were at the front of the numbers and not marching after them.

She needed a loan. *Bad.*

The problem was, there wasn't any income until these dogs were trained. And she didn't have the kind of collateral to cover everything until then. She'd already mortgaged all of it to the hilt.

There was one person she could call and ask for money, but the thought of doing it was so repugnant. She hadn't spoken to him in forever and asking for money was not the first gesture she should make if she wanted to make a gesture at all.

He'd been so warped by forces beyond her control. Though she never fully gave up, she had certainly stopped trying to have a relationship. She would save it as a last-ditch effort. She had the awfully manipulative thought of reaching out now, for nothing in particular, so that if she had to decide that her sanctuary was worth more than her pride, it wasn't the first contact.

Roz swallowed the bile at the back of her throat and the slim wisp of hope that rose up, wishing for a different outcome this time. A different man on the other end of the line. But she shoved that back down and tapped out the email.

"Hello. I just wanted to say hi and see how things are going. Would love to hear what's up these days."

Her finger tapped the 'send' button before she could change her mind.

She was tapping her pencil on the desk and wondering what the hell she'd just done, when the door opened.

Beck leaned against the opening, large arms crossed over his chest. The black T shirt seemed to light up the tattoos that he wore like sleeves. "You're still here?"

"I am." She held her palms up as if she could be casual about still being in the office so damn late.

He saw right through her. "You shouldn't be. And that means something's wrong."

"No."

"You're a shitty liar, Roz." He shouldn't have grinned when he said it.

Really? She'd believed she was a pretty good liar. She hadn't repeated herself. She hadn't overly explained the situation or stumbled across her words. Yet, somehow, he had seen through her anyway.

He sauntered into the room, grin gone, replaced by worry.

He seemed to take up all the space and steal the air she'd been struggling to breathe even before he opened the door. Leaning over the other side of the desk, he stared at her and said, "Let me help."

CHAPTER THIRTY-EIGHT

Several mornings later, Brandy showed up for work with her eyes a little bleary.

Ash didn't say anything. They hadn't spoken much in the past two days, not since she'd walked out his door without so much as an "I understand." Or "I hope things work out."

It wasn't his place to mend their broken fences. She wasn't his girlfriend. Whatever they were, it wasn't solid. He wasn't even sure if they were anything anymore.

If he didn't have a solid definition of who she was to him, then he didn't have anything that he needed to protect. Neither did she. They'd just proved that the relationship—if it could be called that—was tenuous enough that they could crack it with the slightest provocation.

Better to call it a wash now, even if it twisted him up inside. That would pass.

Wouldn't it?

They worked together silently, speaking only what was necessary to get the job done. They passed each other on the Sanctuary grounds, and last night, they'd managed to have dinner with everyone. Though they'd both talked with everyone else, they'd hardly said a word to each other except to ask that something be passed.

This morning, however, Beck had needed them both out on the trails.

With dogs in hand, Brandy and Ash both remained remarkably quiet. For Beck's sake, Ash tried to make conversation. But he couldn't bring up anything from the bar. It wasn't his to tell and Brandy was here.

Beck had two dogs with him, a leash in each hand. Ash and Brandy each had only one. Ash considered turning around and offering to take the leash from her so she could turn back on the trail and go do something else.

It had to suck to be Beck dealing with the two of them, but Ash couldn't fix that. At least after drinks the other night, Beck had an idea what was going on and he wasn't walking down this trail wondering why his two once-so-chummy coworkers were now cold.

But Beck was in charge of this portion of the training, so Ash didn't offer to take Brandy's leash. Maybe Beck was just trying to fill the silence, but he started talking.

"The dogs have started their public training. Now we have to begin separating them and working on some of the specifics."

"Like what?" Ash asked, trying—as always—to be a good student. Though he'd wondered about Beck when he first arrived, he now realized the man had a lot to offer and he should listen.

"We need to get Sidney used to interacting with someone in a wheelchair. We need to get Norgay to learn to stand over a down person and alert passersby. Katherine needs to not just wear the guide dog harness but start making the decisions to cross the street."

Ash remembered Beck had wanted to switch Curie to assist the deaf and Norgay to be the medical dog.

Beck finished, "We're going to train Curie how to set off a

flashing light and how to alert her person that a concerning noise has happened."

"When do we start?" Ash asked, still finding it hard to put aside all his feelings for Brandy. As much as he told himself it didn't matter, that didn't change that he still felt like shit. That he missed her, but he'd learned long ago that he couldn't be with people who didn't trust him. He'd grown up without it and knew it would kill any relationship.

It was crappy enough that he was having to deal with his brother and sister. But this break-up with Brandy on top of it had simply been the cherry on the shit cake. He couldn't help but think that he'd managed to not even interact with his mother at all. Yet somehow, she'd still managed to ruin everything for him.

Beck wasn't following Ash's inner turmoil. Or if he was, he gave it no credit. Looking over his shoulder he made eye contact with each of them. "We'll be starting this afternoon."

"I thought we were starting sign language class this afternoon," Brandy piped up. Her voice even sounded just a little bit froggy, but maybe Ash was imagining that.

Had she sat up all night crying? He hoped not. It wasn't what he wanted. What he wanted was the kind of support that he should get from a partner. But nothing could have made it clearer that she wasn't what he needed. They were merely casual friends who fucked.

Though he'd thought it was moving towards something better, clearly it wouldn't, couldn't.

"Are you going to do that?" Beck asked Brandy.

Ash knew Roz had offered Brandy the chance to opt out of the sign classes. She wasn't going to be here past the first class graduation anyway.

She would still be here when the dogs were matched with their humans. But the people would stay here at the lodge for their own training for at least several weeks. They had to learn how to handle the dogs and the dogs could learn whatever personal training aspects they needed.

Maybe specific signs for Curie. Things to fetch for Sidney and so on.

They would need time to bond with their new people before they moved to their new home. Brandy would be here when the class arrived, but Ash hadn't counted the specific days. He didn't know if she'd actually be here for the pairs graduation before they all left and Jade River Sanctuary started to choose their second class.

"I want to do it," Brandy said. "I don't want to be the only one who can't talk to our deaf client. I do know how to fingerspell already."

She shrugged a little awkwardly, and Ash was pleased to see that Norgay stayed the path. He didn't move or turn because tugging oddly on his leash wasn't a signal.

Now that Buzz had been placed with a family who absolutely adored him, the four remaining dogs were doing wonderfully, benefiting from the extra attention. Ash didn't expect any more washouts and didn't think Beck did either. There's always the possibility for an accident or for something to go horribly wrong, but barring that, the first class would be enough.

They came up on the end of the loop, having made the full trek.

"We need to start hitting different trails, don't we? So, they aren't just in places they're familiar with?" Ash asked.

"Absolutely. We'll be in Charlottesville tomorrow. We're going to train out at Northeast Park."

"You don't think the people will be too much of a distraction?" Brandy asked, frowning.

Beck grinned. "That's the whole point."

Ash watched as she nodded, thinking once again that she looked a little out of sorts. She didn't have to be. She wouldn't be if she had simply trusted that he knew what he was doing with his own life. He just wouldn't take not being trusted from anyone. Even her.

When they made it back to the edge of the grounds, Beck gave them a silent signal. The three of them leaned down to unclick the leashes and told the dogs, "Go home."

Then they hung back, watching as each dog trotted along, entering the sanctuary, making the turn and returning to their own kennel.

"They do that one well." Ash said.

"True," Beck held his hand out for the leashes. "But they'll have to retrain when they get moved into the rooms here when they get matched with their people. Then again when they move to their new homes."

He wrapped the leashes together and headed in, leaving Brandy and Ash standing at the edge of the Sanctuary. It seemed like a little too much of a metaphor for him and Ash started to walk away.

"Wait," Brandy called out.

He stopped but didn't turn around, almost angry at himself for obeying her commands so readily. He put his hands in his pockets, not sure if he was protecting himself or making a gesture to let her know that he wasn't quite on board.

"You kept insisting that I didn't know what I was talking about."

Oh, dear God. This again. He sucked in a deep breath trying to stay stable when it was already hard enough.

Behind him, she was already talking. "I tried to look it up. I just started searching the things that you said." She paused, then asked, "Do you think your mother is a narcissist?"

Ash turned around. "No, I don't *think* she's a narcissist. I'm *confident* of it."

"A lot of narcissists have adult children who don't speak to them," she added.

"That's true," Ash said, a bit surprised she'd found that much.

"I didn't realize there was such a rabbit hole to go down looking things up. I had no idea, but you're clearly not the only one."

He knew that. They weren't usually vocal about having cut off a parent, but even just acknowledging that someone else like you existed out there, helped to say that maybe your decision wasn't horrifyingly wrong. It helped when there were people like Brandy who tried to tell him that he didn't know what he was doing, that he would regret it, and so on.

"You know, I quit speaking to her the first time when I was twenty-four. And I quit speaking to my father at the same time too, because he told me if I couldn't be a good son to my mother then he didn't need anything to do with me either."

Her eyes went wide at that. "Did your father have issues too?" Her tone was soft, and Ash was vulnerable enough to just answer her even if he couldn't face her.

"I think his issue was just that he felt he needed to support her because she'd been the primary one at home. I think he believed her too when she told him the things that I'd done."

"Things you had done?" Brandy clearly didn't understand again.

But was she at least asking the right things now? Was she listening? Ash told himself again not to care.

"I wasn't a bad kid. I hadn't done the things she told him. Never in the way she had said, and sometimes not at all." Interesting, he thought, turning around, looking at her now. "You looked it up last night?"

"I hate where we are, and I was the one who didn't understand. I put some of the things you said into the search bar. I was up until three a.m. There's a lot to read."

"There is a lot."

She fidgeted with her fingers, looking at her fingernails as though they might tell her what to say next. "I found a lot on

Borderline Personality, too. Although you've probably already looked at that."

He nodded. "My therapist suggested it was a possibility and when I found the list of how those kinds of personalities parent, it read like a checklist."

He was stepping closer before he realized what he had done.

"I still don't understand," she confessed, her voice soft. "Because everything I've read says that she does love you. She just doesn't really know how."

"Probably true," he admitted. That was the part he hated. That there was a path to a better place. "But she won't get diagnosed. She refuses to believe anything she says is possibly wrong. When things go wrong, the blame will fall to me. It's entirely possible that if I go back and take care of her after this car accident, that I will somehow become responsible for it."

"How could you possibly be responsible for her car accident?" Brandy waved her hands around, and Ash was opening his mouth to say, but he watched as the understanding caught in her eyes. "I read that—about irrational assignment of blame."

"Very good. You did your homework," he said, though he didn't really know what it meant.

"I tried and I'm really sorry."

They stood there for a moment, looking at each other and then Brandy held her hand out, palm up, waiting.

Ash didn't know if he could take it or not.

CHAPTER THIRTY-NINE

"Wait!" Brandy called out to Ash.

He not only didn't stop walking away, he actually laughed at her.

This was good. It had been a slow climb to here, but it was good, she hoped.

She rolled her eyes at him though.

She understood.

"I'm not waiting because I can't hear you. You didn't get my attention."

"Yeah, Yeah," she called out and watched him laugh again. It felt good to see this man laugh. To see him smile at her again.

"I did hear that," he called back but he was still walking away.

It had been several weeks since their big blow up. Bit by bit, they'd worked their way back. She'd stayed in his bed a couple of nights. He in hers a few, and they'd spent a few apart.

She told herself those nights were a chance to get a full night's sleep. A chance for him to miss her. Though she never knew if he missed having her next to him as much as she missed having him with her.

The days were getting shorter, but the time for working with the dogs was getting longer. Beck wasn't out of line, but Brandy noticed an extra hour or two on the schedule. That graduation had been pushed forward by almost a month.

To get in the minimum number of training hours, there were two or three more hours in the day than there had been previously. Beck had just casually started adding in extra tasks. Also, his car had disappeared, and he drove Roz's SUV much of the time. If anyone knew what had happened to his car, no one said.

They'd also been learning sign language and prepping Curie to be ready for her new owner. Hence Ash's refusal to "hear" her right now.

Brandy stomped on the ground and Ash stopped. Turning around, he looked at her, a grin on his face.

She watched as he signed. "Good work."

In reply, she flipped him off.

He laughed at her again.

The signs for "good work" had come easily for him, but she watched as he searched for words for the next thing. "What . . . you . . . want?"

Brandy started to answer him.

She'd thought she would blaze right past them all in the ASL class, but she hadn't. It was Lynzee who took to the language like a fish, adding each new word fluently into her repertoire.

Brandy was not the star of the class, and she was wondering if she'd be ready for real communication by the time the dogs' people arrived.

She signed back to Ash, "We need to get Curie . . . and go into . . . town . . . and use only sign for three hours."

She watched to see Ash process each sign and put it all together. Slowly he nodded then replied slowly and haltingly. "Which . . . one of us . . . doesn't speak?"

Whoever was determined to be the main handler for the day

could not speak to the dog in any form other than sign. Curie would have to take her commands from that person only, and in only sign. Also the main handler couldn't speak or react to anyone else unless it was in sign, which Curie needed to get used to—which was why the second person had to come along.

"You don't." She pointed at him and then she made a motion toward her mouth of locking the key and tossing it away as if to tell him *you get to shut up today.*

Ash grinned, the smile wide, his eyes lighting up. "O . . . K," he signed the two letters entirely separate and not one piece the way they should be. Then he added, "I need to go back to my room. Meet you back here in twenty minutes."

It took far too long for him to say all of that. Curie would certainly need to learn with someone who was actually fluent in the language. Hopefully that would be Lynzee soon, but she hadn't been available today. Given Beck's crazy schedule pertaining to all of the trainings, he wasn't either.

Brandy headed back to her own cabin and dressed in clothing for going into town. It wasn't fancy, but not the shorts and hiking boots that she tended to wear on the mountain top. She figured she was probably on her last days in shorts. She ran hot, but even she wasn't going to last much longer.

Making sure she had dog treats on hand, she was already at the kennel when Ash arrived. He had the yellow vest that he fitted on Curie.

If Brandy had ever had a doubt about all the training, this would have squashed it. She'd initially asked Roz if it was okay to work the dogs that much. Roz had explained enough for Brandy to feel comfortable with it. The dogs liked the attention and they'd chosen dogs who liked work and be needed. It seemed to be a two-way-street.

But Roz had told her about this amazing moment. Brandy saw it for herself now.

It wasn't the first time Curie had been in the vest, but now she seemed to understand what it was for. She took it seriously, as she should. The Beagle lit up at the sight of her outfit. She sat with her chest puffed out as Ash fastened it, and her head was held higher as if she was proud of the work she was doing.

Reaching down, Brandy passed her a small treat.

This wasn't the final vest either. It was a training version that let everyone know not only was she a working dog, but that she was a dog for the deaf and in training. Hopefully that would keep too many people from asking too many questions and making too many interruptions.

Needing to maintain the "no speaking out loud" rule, they stayed mostly quiet on the way to Charlottesville. They simply didn't have the skills yet to carry on a robust conversation. But as she looked out the window, Brandy realized the silence made her want to practice more.

Roz had begun training all of them—including herself— through videos. Brandy had expected a human teacher, though she couldn't remember if Roz had told her there would be a person or if she'd just thought that. Roz tried to sell them on the videos.

"You can each go back and rewatch whichever lesson or lessons you want and work on it on your own." Roz had demanded that they come back with a certain level of added vocabulary each time they returned for the next class.

Right now, they were sitting down to learn every other day. They had almost forty eight hours to do their homework. It was up to them to work on it, however long was necessary.

The trees passed by outside and Ash reached for the radio to fill the air. Brandy moved her hand in front of his, cutting him off and reminding him it wasn't allowed.

She turned back to the mountain roads, thinking about the number of times she'd seen his brother's or sister's name flash on his phone. Ash hadn't answered. She hadn't said anything, knowing now it wasn't her place. She couldn't help but notice that each time he saw the name, it made him tense.

One voicemail had simply said their mother was improving and hadn't asked anything of Ash. Marcus hadn't asked about Ash either. Ash had only responded with a text saying that that was good news. And thanks for letting him know.

That had been the extent of it and Brandy had wondered what it would be like if that was the relationship she had with her own brothers and sisters. The thought was horrifying.

With nothing else to occupy her thoughts, she made a decision. She would call Sammy again, confront her sister, and push her to tell their mother what had really happened. Because Brandy was tired of covering up for some pretty fucking epic bullshit.

By the time she reached Charlottesville, she'd picked a date. Three weeks from now—which would be three weeks before Thanksgiving—Sammy would have to tell, or Brandy would. And Brandy wouldn't hold back on what she knew, how long she had known, how long she had waited for Sammy to come forward.

Hopefully that would be enough time for her mother to calm down and figure out how to handle the situation. Maybe Brandy could go home for the usual Thanksgiving family gathering with all the drama finally put aside.

So, either Sammy could tell their mother by the deadline or Brandy would. It sucked. Even this decision left her with the tension of possibly having to be the one to do it. Of needing to notify Sammy that the lies weren't going to get covered anymore. But it maybe wasn't as bad as the tension of knowing it needed to be done and not having a plan.

They got out of the car, with a very proud Beagle on the end of her leash. They spent the requisite three hours drawing stares from passersby. Brandy wondered if anyone who actually knew sign had seen their pitiful attempts at it. If they had, they hadn't said anything. However, three different people had asked about the dogs and Brandy had handled all of them, making sure that Ash never opened his mouth.

She handed out cards for Jade River Sanctuary. They had the number and address, and on the back, Roz had put information on how to qualify for government grants to get a trained dog from Jade River. Hopefully if these people knew anyone who needed a service dog, they would pass it along. If not, then she figured her goal was to build goodwill with the locals and be an ambassador while she was in town.

Curie had performed like a champ. Though she'd been distracted by the first three people who tried to pet her, Ash had given a gentle correction and she hadn't messed it up again. They worked on crossing the street. Though deaf people didn't need help with that, it was a great way to start training Curie to alert to loud or alarming noises. And because she couldn't be a hindrance, she had to know how and when to cross the street for herself.

Roz would be meeting with a worker from one of the backing charities next Monday. Hopefully by the end of the week they would have Curie, Katherine, Norgay, and Sidney matched to their future humans. Their people still wouldn't arrive until after Thanksgiving, but the lead time gave them a chance to celebrate being chosen and make plans to be away from home for several weeks.

They put Curie through her paces, even clicking the beeper on the car and working with her to lead them to the sound. Then, with Curie secured in her carrier in the back seat, Brandy and Ash climbed in, still not allowed to fully communicate.

Again, they stayed quiet the whole way back. They had a great time in town, though their conversation was stilted—not because it was ASL, but because they were so bad at it.

Brandy was still calculating how much she could improve before Curie's person arrived at the Sanctuary. It would be embarrassing to not be able to communicate. Ash took the road back up to the Sanctuary, the long winding drive signaling the end of their silence.

"Okay, that was fun."

"You're breaking the rules!" she protested out loud, thinking that making him focus on her hands could make him run them off the road. That was a bad idea on mountain drives.

"I can't deal with it anymore." He sighed. "I hope you had a good time."

It wasn't a date. It was work, but, "I did."

"Come out with me this weekend. We'll find a bar and some live band?"

"That sounds wonderful." She was already exhausted and had planned to sleep the entire weekend away. But she couldn't tell him no, not when he was looking at her that way again, not when she wanted to go and have him pull her into his arms to some slow song.

She couldn't help but grin as they pulled into the parking lot at the Sanctuary. Brandy turned her head, peeking through the trees to the Jade River below. She didn't mind the extra hours, but she minded losing the extra time to sit on the rock outcroppings and just stare down at the valley below.

But as Brandy looked up, she saw a small sports car, clean and too-shiny in the parking lot.

"Who would even drive a sports car up a mountain?"

Brandy knew, and her heart stopped.

CHAPTER FORTY

Ash reached out and slid his hand into Brandy's. *Something was wrong*, but he didn't know what.

Whatever it was had hit her suddenly, too. "Are you okay?"

"Sure." She answered far too quickly.

Ash laced their fingers together and squeezed. He didn't even call her on the lie. "Tell me what you need."

It took her a moment of just sitting there breathing in and out, looking down at where their fingers were joined. She glanced out the front window again before she finally said, "I probably need a few minutes alone."

"Okay." But he didn't really believe what she said either. "Do you want me to take care of Curie?"

"Please." She still didn't look at him, just stared straight forward at the lodge as she put her hand on the door handle but didn't pull it. She wasn't quite ready to step out of the car. Whatever had stopped her, it was between here and the building.

The car in the parking lot—Ash wondered *had she recognized it?*

He watched as her eyes darted back and forth, finally

landing on the taillights as if they meant something. That had to be it.

He waited with her, though he'd volunteered to take care of Curie. He wouldn't move until Brandy did. Then, in a flurry of motion, as if she had suddenly found the strength, she popped open the door. Her feet were out and on the ground. The door slammed almost before he could move in response.

She'd asked for a few minutes alone, so he didn't follow her. Instead, Ash opened his own door, trying to turn his attention to the dog in the back. She'd been doing a great job, sitting quietly and waiting for their conversation to be over.

Trying to keep his thoughts on his own business, Ash told himself the training was good—Curie had to learn to stay calm in a tense situation. There was no way to fake that level of concern. The dog had done well even if the conversation had been a vocal one, rather than signed.

They desperately needed someone fluent in ASL and preferably before Curie's human got here. But Ash knew that the Sanctuary didn't have the extra budget for that. He and Brandy and Beck would do their best, and Lynzee would probably still be the one who wound up with most of Curie's sign training.

He stepped around to open the back door and unclip the dog, trying to keep his focus there, but he couldn't help but notice a tall, dark-haired, dark-skinned man stepping out onto the front porch. The man wore suit pants and a casually buttoned, pressed white shirt—a stark contrast to the rest of the sanctuary.

Ash's heart dropped. He'd suspected whose car that might be. Whose would Brandy even recognize on sight? Except perhaps her little sister's. For whatever reason, Ash simply hadn't thought the slick little sports car would be Sammy's.

He'd been right. It wasn't.

He was talking to Curie, trying to stay calm and motioning

her to jump down out of the car, the other end of her leash in his hand. Ready to go, she heeled like a champ. If only he could keep himself together as well.

Though Brandy and her tension had left the car, she'd left Ash with more than his own share. If Curie felt it, she was holding it together and being a perfect support dog. There was no better way to test it than this, but Ash still didn't like it.

"Brandy," the man said literally unbuttoning his cuffs and rolling up his sleeves as he said it.

Though Ash was giving a command to Curie, and technically not paying attention, he couldn't help but hear Brandy answer back.

"Theo. What are you doing here?"

Just like that, any hope he'd held out that he was wrong crumbled. Suddenly, all the dreams he hadn't admitted that he had began to wash away.

CHAPTER FORTY-ONE

"What are you doing here?" Brandy asked Theo. Everything in her felt twisted and gnarled.

Why was he here at the sanctuary?

It was supposed to be *exactly that* for her—a *sanctuary*. They weren't supposed to let in the things that hurt them. Yet here he was. He'd already been inside the lodge. Had he seen her cabin? There was something that felt as if he'd violated a trust simply by coming here.

Not that she had any trust left with this man.

Roz stepped out behind him. "Brandy, you see you have a visitor?"

Brandy almost snapped back, *I can see that.* But, instead, she nodded, feeling her face tighten and her lips press together.

"Can we talk?" Theo asked.

"About *what?*" *What was left to say?*

Though, honestly, they'd never *said* anything. She'd overheard him and Sammy. And it had been clear when she called off the wedding, they knew that she knew.

So, what was there to talk about?

"Everything," he said. "I'm so sorry. And I'd like to explain."

She wanted to cry out, *"Explain what? That you cheated on me with my sister? That you got her pregnant?"* But she only sighed. She held all the accusations in even though she'd told herself so many times that it was his shame and not hers.

Still, the very idea of blurting out what he'd done to everyone here would feel so justified, so righteous, so good. But she didn't quite have that in her because shit like that would somehow bounce back onto her.

Things never stuck to Theo. For a long time, Brandy had believed it was because they shouldn't. Bad things didn't stick because Theo was good and decent. Now she realized he was simply slick.

"Please, Brandy?" he asked, his eyes looking sincere.

She felt bad. *Why did she feel bad for him?*

But what if there *was* something to explain? She asked herself even as her other little voice reminded her, *How would he possibly explain away what he'd done?*

"Anything you have to tell me, you can tell me here," she said, knowing full well that Ash was right behind her at the car with the dog. Roz was standing in the doorway of the lodge. Beck, Casey, and Lynzee might not be in earshot, but they were supposed to be here today.

Let Theo tell them all.

He didn't explain though. Then Ash walked by with Curie perfectly at his side. Her leash hung with a dip, indicating that she didn't tug at it—that it was just a backup measure and not what guided her. Perfect.

Theo looked around the open space, as if to ask, *Did she really want to do this here?*

Brandy crossed her arms. She was busy. She had things to do. She had left Theo behind; he should have stayed behind. She didn't say yes, just tipped her head up at him, letting him know that if he wanted to do this, he would have to do it here.

Roz nodded at her. She didn't quite wave but ducked back in and closed the lodge door behind her. Ash walked Curie straight past Theo. Brandy was almost surprised he didn't shoulder-check her ex, though that would have been funny.

He led the dog up to and through the door Roz had just shut, probably through the building, as the dogs all needed to be trained for indoor and outdoor companionship, and then the door closed behind him, too. Somehow, like always, Theo had managed to get a semblance of the privacy he'd asked for.

"I called you and messaged you for two weeks after the wedding."

"It wasn't a wedding," Brandy reminded him and that wasn't information. She hadn't answered him except for one last time to tell him to quit trying to contact her.

"I called you the other day, hoping that you . . ." He was smart enough to pause before he said, *calmed down enough.* Good, because she would have walked right up and punched him across the jaw. "Hoping that you were maybe ready to hear what happened."

Sadly, she had no audience for his shame, but she answered him. "I know what happened. You slept with my sister. And you got her pregnant. Now you're not even following through, because she's told my mother—who still adores you, by the way, and thinks the sun rises and sets out of your ass—that the father is just someone who's not around anymore. So please, *do explain what I don't understand.*"

He didn't even address the accusations. "Will you tell me what you overheard?"

"No!" Brandy uttered back, fast, sharp, and loud. She was not handing him all her evidence so he could work it around to what he wanted. He was in finance and the friends he had in finance had always been so slick, manipulating everything to mean whatever they wanted it to. She'd always stupidly thought that *Theo wasn't like that.* He certainly wasn't like that with *her.*

She should have judged him more by the friends he kept. It would have helped.

"I know you heard that Sammy's pregnant."

Brandy nodded.

"And I know you heard her telling me I'm responsible."

Brandy nodded again.

"And I did lie to you."

Well, well, well, but she also didn't say this out loud. But she quit nodding and let him go on.

"But I didn't sleep with Sammy."

He didn't? How was he going to spin that? She tipped her head, as if that would shake around the exact words of the conversation and make it make sense.

She'd heard Sammy saying *this is your fault* and asking him what he was going to do about it. Had her sister said *This is your child?* Had she said that they had actually slept together?

Brandy tried not to let her face show that she was actively analyzing her memories and mining for what he'd said, what Sammy had told her. But Theo wasn't willing to let the space hang empty.

"I set her up with Curtis."

One of the guys at the office. Brandy hated him. He was such a fucking ass. They all were.

"They dated for a while—"

"And you just didn't tell me this?" She finally interrupted, unfolding her arms and putting her hands up as if to show him that he made no sense. She had no time for his shit.

"I know you don't like Curtis."

Of course not. Curtis was a piece of shit playboy.

"He and Sammy met one night when we were out. We all ran into her at a bar."

Brandy obviously hadn't been there. She would have remembered.

"They started dating—"

"Sammy didn't tell me this." She interrupted him again.

Had Sammy actually told her that Theo was the father? Why were there cracks in the solid wall she had built?

It crumbled down around her.

CHAPTER FORTY-TWO

S he looked at Theo as his eyes darted away.

Was it because he was lying? Or was it because he was ashamed?

She should have taken courses in psychology. Too late now, though.

He was talking again, and Brandy scrambled to keep up. "Sammy probably didn't tell you about Curtis because she knew you didn't like him."

"I'm still not sure how this is your fault." There, that was a missing piece. She latched onto it as the information flew past, causing her to unravel the tapestry she'd woven and re-examine every strand.

Theo sighed, his head hung down. Was it a game?

"I knew that Sammy was seeing Curtis exclusively. That she thought it was serious and mutual. I also knew that Curtis was seeing a handful of other people and hooking up whenever he felt like it. I knew he didn't feel the way about Sammy that she did about him. I didn't think it was my place to tell either of them what was going on with the other."

Brandy crossed her arms again. It was a fitting tale.

Unfortunately, it worked with what she had heard. Fuck. "This doesn't change that you and Sammy both lied to me."

It might change her giving Sammy an ultimatum about telling their mom that Theo was the father of her child, though. It would mean that Sammy had lied to her about who she was seeing, but that was hardly the betrayal Brandy had believed it to be.

"I didn't do what you think I did," Theo said, his final protest that Brandy was unfair to him.

"And you didn't tell me this before now?"

"I tried!" he protested, his anger finally coming to the surface. Did he have a right to it? It didn't matter, he was still going.

"I was sitting in the bathtub in my wedding dress drinking a beer." She didn't add that she was clutching the penny—her escape route.

"I messaged and called, but you wouldn't listen to me," he protested again, clearly trying to keep himself calm. She didn't call him on that, though she did wonder . . .

How could she not have listened? She couldn't have avoided it had he and Sammy yelled it through the bathroom door, had he actually put this information in a text. She would have been a prisoner to the words coming at her, but they hadn't done it. Had they?

He visibly got himself together, his expression contrite again as he stepped forward. He held his hands out as if to envelop her in a hug.

Did he think everything was all right? It had been *months.*

"It's been so long," he said, as if he heard what she thought. "I miss you so much. Everyone asks what happened? Why you left me."

"What do you tell them?" she asked, not moving. Brandy found for the first time she was genuinely curious.

"Only that you heard something that made me look bad."

She felt her eyebrows raise. That sounded a lot like Theo throwing her under the bus.

He quickly added, "Also that I had done something, and I deserved it."

She took a moment to process, trying to put all the pieces together. She couldn't help but wonder about the dark haired, blue eyed man who was now surely out of the lodge on the other side.

He would have put Curie into her kennel. Where would he go next? To the vet clinic? To his cabin?

Would he come back through the lodge and stand beside her?

She'd asked him for several minutes to herself. Maybe he was granting them, and he wouldn't come back and be a silent wall beside her. She didn't need him to fight her battles, but the quiet support would be nice.

The door to the lodge didn't budge.

She had no idea about either man right now.

Though she and Ash had blown up and only slowly found their way back to each other, she'd honestly apologized for her mistake with him. But were they really on the same page?

They hadn't done the work. What they had done was told themselves it was casual, and that they didn't need to invest.

But, to Brandy, they had history. They had been *real*. Or Brandy believed they were real—whether or not she was right about it.

Clearly, she shouldn't trust that. She'd believed she and Theo were real enough to put on a white dress and invite all her family for vows and canapes and cake.

"Please come home with me," Theo begged. "We can start over if you want."

If he suggested that they start planning the wedding again, she would smack him into next Tuesday.

For all his explanation, if every second of it was true, she still couldn't be away from him for two and a half months and just walk right back into the relationship. She couldn't button up her wedding dress, slide her feet into the pumps, and be ready to marry him again.

"Theo," she protested, her voice softer, her arms at her side now and surely her indecision showed. *How could it not?* "I can't come home and just start over. I'm on leave from my job. I'm here. I have a contract."

"Then maybe just for a week?" he asked. "Back to Los Angeles. See your family, I know they all miss you terribly. Let us start again. Then, if you still need to come back here and finish this . . . we'll deal with it."

He sounded so reasonable, and she'd loved him once.

She'd walked into the church on their wedding morning, her eyes glowing and dewy. All her thoughts had been on this man and the life they were going to have together.

"The condo sold last week," she blurted out, as if the change of subject would protect her from old feelings. The real estate agent said they'd gotten an offer and Brandy had accepted it.

"It hasn't closed escrow yet," he told her, "We can still back out."

Brandy shook her head. They would be getting out with a bit of a financial gain for all the work and money they'd put into it. And she wasn't going to be that client.

Seeing she wasn't going to give him an answer right now, Theo nodded at her as if he'd made a decision himself. "I'm going to go, but I'd love to come back tonight and take you out to dinner. We should at least discuss this."

Brandy looked off to the side, into the trees and the blue, blue sky beyond. Clean air, dogs barking from the back of the compound, a voice—probably Casey.

How could she say no to Theo? How could she say yes?

The way her heart had jumped when she saw him, that she hadn't quite known if it was fear or a little bit of excitement . . .

She still didn't quite know now, if she should forgive him and go back to Los Angeles. Not even for a week, maybe for a couple of days, or maybe not.

He'd told her that whatever they had, it might not be what it was, but it certainly wasn't finished.

Slowly she nodded. "All right."

"I'll be back at seven," he told her. Walking toward her, he smiled, straight white teeth gleaming, eyes sparkling as if she couldn't possibly have given him a better present than to say yes.

He leaned forward, kissing her on the cheek, the ever-present five o'clock shadow brushing against her skin, the way it always had.

Brandy closed her eyes, savoring the feeling and wondering what that savor meant. She stood, taking deep breaths, listening to the sound of his nice shoes on the gravel of the parking lot. The door to his car shut.

Only then did she take one last breath and open her eyes to see Ash standing in the doorway to the lodge.

CHAPTER FORTY-THREE

Ash could tell from the look on Brandy's face that she'd agreed to have dinner with Theo.

He'd waited on the other side of the lodge door like a lovesick fool before he told himself he'd given her the few minutes she'd wanted, and he wasn't about to get caught here like he was eavesdropping. So, he'd opened the door slowly, not making a sound.

He stood, leaning in the door jamb, where he would appear to be in open space for anyone to see. But all he saw was Theo's back and a wisp of red ponytail beyond the man's shoulder.

Brandy couldn't see him, and Theo had his back to him. Ash listened in. And it wasn't shameless.

He shouldn't have done it. It wasn't his to hear.

The center of his chest hardened like it was in a vise grip as he'd heard her tone. Even if he couldn't hear any words, he knew she was agreeing to dinner. Theo was everything that Ash wasn't—slick suit wearing, rich, stable.

Brandy saw him now and he had to react as she offered a small half grin. Her shoulder shrugged, palms coming up as if to say *what could she even do?*

She could have told him *no!*

Instead, she'd said yes, and Ash watched as Theo climbed into his expensive little sports car and backed out of the parking lot. The low, wide tires churned the gravel as he went, and Ash saw the moment that those eyes connected with his. This man understood that Ash was not an innocent bystander in all of this.

Something in Theo's eyes hardened, letting Ash know that he would not go down without a fight.

Did it matter? He already seemed to have won round one.

Brandy had agreed. Whatever the fight would be, it wouldn't be decided by him and Theo, it would be decided by Brandy. And she'd already taken that first, important step toward her ex.

Still, Ash couldn't make those pieces fit together. Not with the Brandy that he knew. So as Theo turned around, waving to Brandy, but only getting her back, Ash was the only one who saw it. He didn't wave back.

Ash and Brandy both stood there, a few feet and miles between them, unmoving until the taillights were down the drive.

"You agreed to go out with him." He didn't mean for it to sound like an accusation, but he already knew the answer.

"Just for dinner tonight."

Ash had also heard him invite her back to Los Angeles. While she hadn't said yes, she hadn't said no either. But he didn't bring that up. Instead, he let all his feelings fly, messy and hot all over the space between them. "He slept with your sister before your wedding! What are you even doing with him?"

"It turns out he didn't," Brandy said, though she didn't look as if she were fully buying it.

Still, that was rich. Ash had no words to go with it. "You were wrong all this time? You were mad at him for something that wasn't even true?"

"It looks that way." The tone in her voice conceding whatever ground she'd gained in the past few months.

He didn't like it. "He let you believe something so horrible—"

"I shut him out." That much was true.

"It's not on you," Ash said, wondering what he was doing even as he did it. Why was he here fighting when he'd so obviously lost? How could she have been so wrong? "Seems like it'd be very difficult to blow up your entire wedding on a mistake."

But right now, Brandy was conceding that she had done just that.

Though Ash couldn't make all the pieces go together, he knew he wasn't seeing anything clearly. But he nodded at her, almost saying *Have fun tonight* or whatever was appropriate as you watched your almost-girlfriend go out with her ex fiancé.

Instead, he turned, almost rolling backward as his feet didn't want to catch the ground. He closed the lodge door behind him, the click of the lock unsatisfying. He walked woodenly right out the back, heading toward the clinic. The place he'd built the way he wanted.

As he passed through the front door, he didn't find the solace he'd expected. It was empty. The clinic wasn't what it was if it wasn't full. It was just a room with a table and some equipment, lonely when it only held a dream.

There were only six dogs here to care for, including Shadow and Astra. And none of them needed him right now. Ash walked right out the back door and headed toward the old barn at the back of the property.

Roz hadn't even begun to make her way back here. They couldn't afford to do anything with it yet. She'd converted only the parts she needed. Ash conceded that, as long as no one wandered back here, they would never know the old monstrosity lingered, original cobwebs still clinging, door hanging slightly crooked.

No one touched it, and Ash knew it would be a quiet place to sit with his horrible thoughts.

CHAPTER FORTY-FOUR

A sh shouldn't be in here. The old barn wasn't safe and would probably fall down around him while he sat here stewing in his own irritation at himself. He could die in a heap of splintered wood and barn dust.

He didn't care. It probably would fall down as some point, unless they fixed it. But so far, they hadn't touched it. Luckily, the chances that it would fall in the next hour or two were relatively slim and Ash needed to be somewhere where he could just sit with no interruptions to his own ugly thoughts.

Even though he plopped down on a hay bale and his vision glazed over, he still couldn't quite seem to grasp what exactly felt like the knife in his back. Solid ideas flitted past him. He reached out but couldn't hold on tightly. They rolled around him while he sat there.

Theo was here now, and Ash didn't see any way that he could win this.

Brandy had been about to marry the guy—not just *about* to marry him, but in the dress and the veil and the church.

Ash tried for a moment and failed to figure out how they

would tell the guests. Would Brandy just say, *Oops. I thought he screwed my sister, but I was wrong. We're getting married again.*

He couldn't make that work. But Ash also didn't know how Brandy wouldn't give Theo a second chance. Not when the infraction was actually as small as it was.

Another set of thoughts whirled by him—that he shouldn't have listened in to the conversation in the parking lot. Exploiting a loophole wasn't his usual style, but this time he hadn't been able to resist. She'd said she needed a few minutes, so he'd come back.

As if she might need his help. Clearly, she hadn't.

Now that he knew what he knew, he wondered if he could sit out here until darkness fell. Until well after Brandy left at seven.

Ash looked up at the light coming in through the cracks in the wood. The sounds of the woods around him were starting to seep in. The place wasn't soundproof, or lightproof or weatherproof.

He sighed. Theo was good looking and charming. And he himself was . . . smart, but full of boundaries. Boundaries he'd needed but that didn't change that they were there, that they were tall and hard to scale.

Ash was Blue Ridge Mountains now. Theo was Los Angeles. Home for Brandy.

He told himself that it was for the best.

In an effort to convince himself that he was right, he stood up and paced. The straw that had been on the floor had been blown up against the walls. The dirt was hard packed under his feet. But he still couldn't see beyond the haze in his vision.

He felt he was realizing only too late that Brandy meant more than he'd given her credit for. It didn't matter now.

Someone better would come along. Even if he couldn't right now imagine what better might possibly look like than red hair, round curves, and freckles.

He plopped down on a different hay bale, let himself lean forward, and put his head in his hands. Fingers squeezing his own scalp, he felt the pressure as if it could make the pain go away.

The uncertainty was more than he could deal with. He couldn't control anything in this situation—what Theo said, what Brandy did, who she chose.

Ash could drop his heart at her feet. He probably should. But he had to admit the odds weren't in his favor. He wasn't quite willing to cut it out of his own chest for numbers that low.

The Jade River Sanctuary must have once abutted a farm on the other side. The barn's existence made him wonder who would have horses way up here? Then again, what a ride.

He sat there, quiet in his own anxiety, letting random thoughts carry him away. Quiet now, he heard the noises seeping in around him. Rustles in the hay were most likely mice or rats. He didn't have any revulsion to the idea. This was their home, he'd barged in. Besides, rats made great pets and everything carried disease.

In the loft, more noises shuffled. A hoot let him know that an owl was up there. If he remembered correctly, it might even be a Great Barn Owl. He appreciated the irony of finding one actually in a barn and decided he'd have to check out their region.

He was starting to stand up when something prompted him to turn and look around behind him. Only as he spotted it, the tiny kitten mewed at him.

"What are you doing here, buddy?" he asked. It only took a glance to see that it was small. And thin. Ribs were showing between orange stripes.

"*Meeeewwww!*"

The second time the cry was long and wailing. A third plaintive cry had Ash making his way around the large hay bale he'd been sitting on to see if he could scoop the creature up.

Being young and scrawny wasn't enough to slow it down. The kitten darted out the barn door. The cracks were too small for Ash, but certainly big enough for the little guy to squeeze right through.

With two hands and his feet planted, Ash tried to slide the door. He didn't actually manage it but got it to swing outward enough to make a gap he could push through.

Sure enough, the little guy stood there waiting, looking over his shoulder at Ash.

"*Mew!*"

"Coming." He chuckled at himself. He was talking to a kitten, but he was a vet and wasn't he supposed to do that?

The tiny thing led him a good quarter mile—a great distance on such tiny legs. Sure enough, when Ash got close enough, the mama cat didn't hiss or try to scare him away.

She didn't move at all.

His heart sank. She was gone. Probably for more than a day.

From the cuts on her side, it seemed she'd gotten in a tangle with something and made it home but hadn't won the battle. Around her body, three kittens—an orange tabby like the little guy and two more calicoes—huddled close. Mom was no longer warm, and their little cries reflected the chill of the evening and their empty bellies.

Ash let out a breath and accepted that he had a task now. Something, finally, that he could take control of.

CHAPTER FORTY-FIVE

"You look beautiful," Theo told her for maybe the third time.

Brandy smiled, sitting across from him at the table set with several layers of plates, multiple forks and knives. Dessert spoons were placed across the top of each setting. The service was impeccable.

She hadn't known there was a Michelin starred restaurant in Charlottesville but leave it to Theo to make sure they had a table at it. On such late notice, she was willing to bet he'd reserved it before he showed up at the Sanctuary.

"Thank you," she said, her hands in her lap between courses. Then she laughed and let it spill out. "These are about the only heels I packed. It's the only skirt and only blouse I have."

"I saw you wearing hiking boots and jeans, hmm."

"It suits the work here." She wondered why she felt a need to defend it.

"What exactly is the work?"

Shouldn't he know? He'd come across the country to follow her here. How hard would it have been to just search the name *"Jade River Sanctuary"*?

Brandy knew the website popped right up and explained everything. Theo must not have bothered to look.

"I'm learning ASL," she told him instead.

"Whatever will you use that for?"

"I'm already using it. We're training a hearing ear dog." Her skirt felt tight, a little uncomfortable. Had she gained weight? She'd almost definitely gained muscle.

Though in her usual job she'd lifted and carried things as needed, she certainly hadn't built a fence or kennels.

"I would not have pegged you as a dog trainer." Theo twirled the wine glass by its stem, running it smoothly through his fingers. He looked at her with a curious eye, as if trying to reconcile what she told him with what he knew.

"I wouldn't have either. It was a temporary gig . . . and far from home." The expression on her face would let him know that that had been a primary attractor—being away from him and away from all the others.

He seemed to sense her irritation and reached out, taking her hand and squeezing her fingers as the next course arrived. He waited until the server left before he spoke. "I'm so sorry that you misunderstood. I thought . . ."

He paused and she let him fill in the space.

"I knew you were mad."

"But what did you *think* I was mad about?" she asked. "I wasn't speaking to you. I didn't want to speak to you. Yet, you claim I had it all wrong."

He looked down at his plate for a moment. Maybe he'd heard that she said 'claim' because she believed him, but little thoughts kept popping up at the back of her brain.

"I thought I figured out what you had thought," he said. "How you must have interpreted it. Thinking back on what Sammy and I had said—it made sense. Of course, we heard you on the other side of the door, right as soon as Sammy accused me of being responsible for her problems."

Brandy nodded. They had nearly chased her down the hall, Theo the only one able to move with any speed as she and Sammy had been in their wedding heels.

"I just kept believing you'd reach out."

She shrugged and shook her head. Maybe he hadn't counted on her being as stubborn as she was. If he hadn't counted on that, if he hadn't known that about her, maybe they weren't as good of a match as she thought.

He smiled and apologized, and she found she couldn't forget that she'd been with him for five years. That had to count for something.

Squeezing his fingers back, she smiled back. It should count for a lot.

The conversation moved to easier things, Theo asking questions about the dogs and listening as she had animatedly explained how she'd gotten to name the inaugural class.

"They graduate? Do they get little caps and gowns?"

"Don't be ridiculous." Brandy grinned. "They get their official vests that don't say *in training* anymore. And they get to go home with their people."

She thought about Buzz for a moment and Theo must have caught the expression on her face.

"What is it that's bothering you?"

"We were supposed to have five, but one of our dogs washed out. So, we only get to make four people's lives better right now."

"It's still four who are going to be better than before," Theo reminded her as he squeezed her hand again and pushed the dessert menu her way. He tapped his finger on a listing for a berry pie the chef had thought up.

"Oh, that looks fantastic."

"Get it. I'm getting the lemon." He didn't share desserts with her. They'd never quite had the same tastes foodwise.

He waited until dessert showed up, until she plunged her

spoon down into the whipped confection and pulled out strawberries and raspberries and popped them in her mouth, until her eyes had closed in sugary ecstasy.

"Come back with me. Stay for a week." Her face must have twitched. He walked it back. "Three days. Whatever you can spare. See your mom. It sounds like you've been at odds with her."

"I haven't been at odds with her," Brandy protested. "She just doesn't know what's going on. And I wasn't willing to rat out Sammy."

"Probably a good thing you didn't." He grinned.

Brandy wasn't quite sure what to make of it. Had she ratted out Sammy this all could have been cleared up much earlier.

"You can make friends with Sammy again. And if you stay, you stay." He shrugged.

"I'll come back here." She was firm in her commitments. Why would he think she wasn't? He'd even said once that he loved that about her. "They're counting on me."

"They can't find another dog trainer?" He waved his hands around, gesturing as though one must be sitting at one of the other tables.

"No, they can't. I know this class of dogs. I know the specifics of what we are training. So even someone who's much better at it than me would have a lot to catch up just to get to where we are."

"Fine then."

Why did he sound petulant? Had he thought he'd just say she was wrong, and she'd crawl back home?

"I've got seats on a flight for tomorrow for us." He announced it casually as if it weren't a big deal.

"You already booked it?"

He leaned back, holding his hands up as if her words were an accusation. She wasn't quite sure they weren't.

"The prices would change. The seats might not be available

if I hadn't booked them when I did. If you don't want it, say so. I'll eat the cost."

Of course, he would, Brandy thought. That was always Theo's response: He would eat the cost of whatever it was. Most people felt guilty and went along.

But she did want to see her mother. As she needed to sort things out with Sammy. She'd been so mad for so long . . . and, apparently, she had been wrong about all of it.

He reached out and gently took her hand again. Brandy pulled her fingers away. "I still don't know yet if I can go. I have to ask Roz."

"They can't do without you for a week?"

"Three days," she countered. "And no, I don't know if they can."

When she plunged her spoon into the desert again. It didn't taste quite as sweet.

CHAPTER FORTY-SIX

A sh settled two of the four kittens into his pockets. Poor things were small enough to fit even if they weren't quite pleased with the move.

But he had only two pockets big enough. The two others he tried to hold onto, but their tiny claws were out. They clung tightly to him, seeming to realize that Mama wasn't going to be able to take care of them anymore and their best bet was with the stranger.

The sun had set while he tried to scoop them up. "Come with me babies. I'm alive. I'm warm and I can feed you."

The tiny mews came now, long and sad, from all sides. They changed as he started walking around and checking the area. Some of the sounds became angry, some scared. A few hisses sounded right next to his ear.

"It's okay, be spicy. I've got you." He tried to sound reassuring, but Ash had been here before and it broke his heart every time. He'd never toughened up to the idea of a dead mother cat.

He was almost in tears over it. She'd tried so hard. If he'd found her yesterday, maybe he could have saved her. They'd had a guest lecture about that in school, he remembered. You can't save them all, and you can't be responsible for the ones you didn't know about.

Still, he'd seen the cuts. Deep slices on her side that had tried to heal, but they had just been too big. He wondered what she'd tangled with. Most likely a much larger cat.

Whatever she'd done, she had made it home to her babies— that maternal drive that seemed to override everything else in the animal kingdom. Ash wondered, was it his own fault that his drive told him to protect his heart rather than put himself out there for a woman who was already pulling away?

He didn't know. He just appreciated that he had a task now to focus on.

Though he'd looked around as best he could, there were no more kittens. Hopefully, the litter had only been four. The one he cradled in his hands was smaller than the others, a tiny calico whose still-blue eyes belied their young age.

"I've got you." He turned around to head back to the clinic, only then realizing he'd followed a kitten out here.

Ash didn't know where *out here* was.

His eyes had been on the tiny orange stick of a tail. He'd followed along knowing that the kitten was too young to have made it as far as he did.

"You pulled off a bit of a miracle there, dude." Ash told the little guy. Then he had a thought and turned the kitten over, despite hearty protests.

"Apologies. Not a dude." He tucked the kitten up under his jacket. They needed all the heat they could get. "You can be Miracle."

Exhausted from her long journey, her head curled against his chest and she fell quickly asleep. It had to be the best feeling in the world, being trusted by something so small and needy.

She had chosen him, and she seemed to feel the safest of the four. Or maybe she was just the most tired.

It took him a while to locate the top corner of the barn through the trees, but once he did, Ash simply aimed himself that direction. The sun was almost gone, only stray light from the colorful clouds as it set beyond the next mountain range helped him find his way. If he was down in the valley, it might already be dark.

It was probably a bad decision to be out in the woods now. Not only that, but he was covered in four tiny, furry, adorable pieces of bait.

They made it back without attracting the attention of anything dangerous. Ash fished in his pocket for his keys, having to disturb the kitten sleeping in it. Tiny protests let him know it was okay.

He pushed his way into the clinic, tiny eyes opening and blinking at the lights as he flipped them on. Ash thought about lining up the little guys on the exam table but didn't think they would like the cold metal very well.

He had them in the incubator in no time, popped a can of kitten formula and managed to get bottles into two of them at the same time. They slurped hungrily while the other two wailed at having to wait.

He considered calling the front to see if anyone was available, but he was still too raw for company. If there had been six kittens, he would have had to ask for help, but four he could handle.

He fed the smallest two first, happy as their little bellies grew round and concerned by the quantity of fleas that he saw on them. When they had drunk their fill, ears ticking along as they suckled, they basically fell off and rolled over. Their bellies were too big to stand up around. Good. He gave the bottles to the other two.

The tension inside him wound him up like a spring. Just the idea of Brandy and Theo already out at dinner . . . He wondered what they were talking about. If it was like old times.

He'd seen the clock. He knew she was making a decision now and that her decision would probably take her far away from here.

It lingered under the surface. But if Brandy didn't need him, these kittens did, and the time heavy task of caring for babies was exactly what he needed tonight.

He was at the work until almost midnight. He administered baths, de-flea-ing them and then warming them. It was time and attention heavy and he was grateful he didn't feel every tick of the damned clock.

With the baths, he discovered he had three girls and one boy. Merry—short for Miracle—was already named, but the other three he called Bourbon, Whiskey, and Jaeger. Then he realized he'd been far too obvious naming them things like "Brandy." But fuck it. It wasn't like no one knew.

He cradled each one close, trying to make up for the loss of their mother. Their lives would be very different now and he wondered if he could—later, when they were ready—convince Lynzee to use her skills to find them homes.

Feeding them again was a huge task in itself. He made a box with a warming blanket, something that he could carry back to his cabin. Casey saw him on the way, and it was impossible to miss the crying sounds coming from the box.

"You found kittens?"

"You know it." Ash held the box up for the future vet to look in. He motioned around with his head. They were on a mountain top and the barn wasn't the only abandoned building up here. "Had to happen sooner or later."

Casey offered to help feed and take care of them, and Ash accepted.

When he made it to his own front door, he balanced the box on one knee, so he could grab the knob. Though he told himself not to, he looked over at Brandy's cabin and saw no light filtering through the trees.

Had she brought Theo back with her? Did the man know that Ash had been in that bed just last night?

CHAPTER FORTY-SEVEN

R oz sat at her desk and listened to the door quickly shut behind Brandy.

It was late, far too late for her to be here. Far too late for anyone to need anything from her. But Roz was still in the office and Brandy had seen the light was on.

And wasn't that what she wanted?

She'd smiled and said *Of course.* Of course, Brandy could have three days off. After all, they were down to four dogs. Being down an employee shouldn't hurt that much, right?

She hated herself for it, but she thought about lowered food costs for three days. One less mouth to feed. A slightly lower electric bill, since everything but the fridge would be off at Brandy's place for three whole days.

Should she have told her employee to take the whole week? But she was still paying Brandy for the time she was gone. It would be really bad form to suggest the time off then suggest she dock her pay.

Roz hated the idea of it. She hated the idea of all of it. It wasn't supposed to be like this.

Every muscle grew tense every time she thought about it.

Beck had sold his car and given the money to the Sanctuary. Roz had noted the money like a loan, calculating interest from day one. Even though Beck had refused interest and only suggested she pay it back when she could.

Still, she'd worked her schedule around him needing her car. That had been the agreement. The Sanctuary needed the money, so she happily handed over her car keys. Even once for an overnight, though she wondered who he was visiting.

She knew he had a friend in town—Liam, she thought—that he'd mentioned once. Unless Beck swung an entirely different direction than she'd thought, it wasn't Liam he'd stayed overnight with. She reminded herself, it wasn't any of her business. But would she have been so curious if it had been Ash? Then again Ash was with Brandy, so she knew who he was staying with. Or at least he had been until Theo had showed up.

When Brandy had interviewed, something had struck Roz about the woman—she looked like she needed the escape. Roz hadn't been able to say no.

But now? She should have been ready for this, too. She'd been there. She knew the awful drama these relationships could bring. She just hadn't factored in the time for the back and forth bullshit—necessary bullshit, she knew—when she gave Brandy the job.

Maybe she hadn't been ready to help anyone else. Maybe she should have just hired the people who could help *her*. Too late now.

When Theo had arrived here, he'd knocked on the door and come into the lodge. Roz had had an overly polite conversation with him for about forty-five minutes before Brandy showed up. Not once had the man asked if she had the time to spare. She thought about it while she sat there, discussing the weather and the view from the ridge, because she didn't have it. But she stayed.

He was openly charming and perfect, with a straight nose

and straighter teeth. Roz didn't like him. It had taken a long time and a lot of reading to know that his not asking if she had the time was an assumption that he was the most important thing in the room.

He hadn't said anything out loud, but everything about him casually oozed money. She had offered him a soft drink from the small fridge that sat in the corner of her office. He'd refused, so she hadn't gotten one for herself either, getting the impression that a can was maybe beneath him.

Just thinking about him left a taste in her mouth and she headed over and pulled out a canned soda. She could have it now. Pulling the cheap soda from the fridge, she reminded herself she could no longer afford to get the good stuff anymore. Well, apparently, she couldn't ever afford it, she just hadn't known that until a few weeks ago.

She sat back down, admitting that the money from Beck's car was going to run out before they got the grant money from the dogs. And that was assuming that the state paid quickly.

She heard footsteps outside her door again. As she popped the top on her soda, savoring the hiss and the fizz, she could only hope that it was Brandy coming back to say that she wasn't leaving after all.

In a moment the heavier footsteps made it clear who they belonged to. When the light knock came, she said, "Come on in, Beck." Quickly followed by, "Why are you up this late?"

To which he only grinned at her, crossed his arms and repeated it back in the exact same tone she'd used. "Why are you up this late?"

"I think you know why I am."

He stood for a moment as if contemplating the universe, while she took a few sips of the soda until she finally set it down on the desk and told him, "Say it. Ask me what you want to ask."

His expression got a little more grim as he settled into the chair across from her and leaned forward, fingers laced. He'd seen the books. He was the only one who had. He'd volunteered to sell the car and give her the money. *A loan!* She reminded herself.

It had made a difference. But it was an older car, and it certainly wasn't the same as if she could have, say, gotten Theo to volunteer the sale of his sports car.

"How did it get this bad?" Beck asked.

Roz sighed. "I know. It looks like I'm a shitty businesswoman who had no idea what I was getting into."

Beck nodded along. *Lovely.* He could have at least been decent enough to disagree with her.

"It does look that way."

Ouch.

"But I've been working with you, and I know you're smarter than that. I've seen things pop up around here. Is that all it was? Was there no buffer for that?"

"I got stupid a little early on," she admitted. "I bought the van because it was an excellent deal."

"It really was," he agreed. "I don't think I would have passed it up either."

That at least made her feel better. How often did one find a conversion van already outfitted to travel with dogs? "It would have cost so much more to get it made and we use it. All the time."

"Agreed. It's needed."

"Exactly." Then she told him, "You weren't here the first day. Ash actually arrived slightly before I did. The pictures when I bought it . . ." She explained about the trash on the side of the building. The places that looked like the pictures actually looked fine but needed restorative work.

Those were things the appraiser had told her about. She'd been ready.

"There were things we found only when we went inside. The inspector did everything right. He told me it would need some minor repairs, which was true. But it's not his job to say the place is filthy, and it's going to take a *lot* of money to clean a place of this size."

Frustrated with herself and her situation, Roz waved her hands around. She thought about the maid she had paid when she lived in Houston. Thought about what it had cost to clean that house. As grand as it was it was nothing compared to the size of this property. "The Sanctuary didn't need to be *dusted*! It needed to be scrubbed with bleach and have trash hauled away with a dumpster I had to rent!"

It had been so much to get that up here. *"Up here"* had been a problem that cost her a lot that she hadn't budgeted for. "I actually looked up the costs of things . . . but . . . Getting it on a mountain top seems to double every estimate."

"Had you not seen the place before you bought it?" Beck asked.

And this was the truly stupid part. "No. I was in Texas. I thought I was saving money by not traveling just to visit. I had pictures of everything! I also got stupid in that I applied for six different grants and told myself I would get at least one or two of them."

"And you didn't get any," he filled in.

"I got *one*. But I got a secondary version of it, not the main gift, and it was much, much smaller. It was gone in seconds."

He nodded along. "Are we going to make it to graduation?"

She did the only thing she could and assured him, "Yes."

They would. Then she let him tell her *good night* and politely responded before she hit the keyboard, calling up her computer screen.

The message was still there. The one she had avoided all day. Roz clicked it now.

Great to hear from you.

Was it?

I've been doing great. I opened a charter company recently.

Of course, he had. He always loved planes and what else would someone like him do? He'd never had the ability to buckle down and do the work to learn to fly them. So, the answer, instead, was to own them.

She wanted to ask for the money now. But she couldn't. It would look so bad. She would only be able to hold out for a little while more. She would just sleep better once she had it, because right now, he could still say *no*.

She wrote back. *That's wonderful. I've opened an animal shelter.*

She wasn't quite willing to give him information about where she was. Roz offered a few more sentences befitting of their stilted relationship and hit send.

Then she calculated just how much longer they could make it before she would have to ask.

CHAPTER FORTY-EIGHT

I t wasn't quite until she stepped out of the airport into the Los Angeles air that Brandy felt it. It was drier and warmer here. There was more wind and less breeze.

People were everywhere—a crowd that she navigated easily from motor memory. Only now, for the first time, did she really notice it. She'd traveled plenty for her job, but couldn't remember how long it had been since she'd actually lived somewhere else. Had she ever lived anywhere with the clean air of the mountains? Because she loved Los Angeles, but right now, she could feel the pollution in the air.

Theo grabbed her hand, tugging her along, her little suitcase bouncing behind her. This she was used to. She climbed into his car as the valet brought it around. It was so much like the one he'd rented in Virginia. She'd seen the looks from Casey and even Lynzee. Who would feel the need to show off their sports car at a lodge?

Brandy had never thought of Theo as showing off. These were just the things he liked, and he worked hard to afford them. Somehow, now, everything was tinged with a different light.

"I'm sorry, I'm hungry," she told him and then rattled off her favorite burger joint.

"Is that what you want?"

"Is it too lowbrow for Mr. I'm Wearing A Suit?" she teased. "Take off your jacket and come inside and have a burger and chili fries with me."

She was trying to stay light-hearted but couldn't help but wonder if he seemed snobby. Had he always? She'd always loved Fatburger, but had they ever gone together?

"Are you trying to avoid seeing your mother and sister?" he asked, but he did pull into the parking lot.

"No. I do really want to see them. But I'm really hungry and I haven't had one of these in so long."

"That's your own fault," he chided.

She ordered, thinking he was right, but did he have to point it out?

She savored the food, wondering if he was looking at her because she was eating more than usual or maybe for some other reason? She was eating more than usual. She'd been doing far more physical labor than she was used to. Though maybe not for the next couple of days.

She'd thought through the logistics. She had the things she'd packed but being here with Theo was a stark contrast to the jeans and the heels that sat unused in her closet. Most of her things were in storage near her old apartment. She'd sublet the unit, but Brandy could get to the storage easily enough if she needed.

She'd also left a few outfits at her mother's house for easy access. When she'd left, she'd had no idea what she was getting into or what she would come back to. It had all been such a scramble. Looking back now, Brandy knew she hadn't been seeing straight.

Back in the car, she watched the road as he took the turn away from her mother's. "Where are we headed?"

"To my place to drop off your stuff?"

Had Theo really thought she would stay with him? "I want to stay at my mother's."

She heard the words, disappointed that her tone was not as forceful as she'd intended. Why should she be meek around him? She didn't know. Maybe she was just reverting to her old state, and she hadn't realized quite how much her new state was different.

Or was she just in a situation that had her confused? She was plenty confident at her job—either of them these days. But . . . what was she doing here? She needed to find out and she only had a short while to do it.

"Is that what you really want?" He sounded surprised.

Reminding herself to stick to her guns, she only said, "Yes."

How could it not be? Did he think she would just head over to his apartment and sleep with him? Had he thought telling her what had really happened would erase everything?

It occurred to her then, as she laced her fingers together and pointedly looked out the window so that he couldn't see her expression, that he might not know that she had been sleeping with Ash Cooper.

Hell, she might have been doing more than sleeping with him.

Had he not been with anybody during their break-up? Was she the one who'd actually cheated on the relationship now? At least it wasn't really cheating. They'd been in entirely separate states and fully broken up. Did he think she would wait for a man that she had believed had slept with her sister? And why hadn't he just told her the truth?

It was all so confusing, certainly far too confusing to stay at his apartment with him. He turned the car around and hopped on a different freeway, heading the right direction. At least he didn't have a fit about it.

Pulling out her phone, Brandy checked all the messages that

had popped up since she landed. Then she tapped out a new one letting her mother know that she was almost home. Sure enough, when she climbed out of the car, Mom bolted across the front lawn embracing her in the biggest hug.

A hug Brandy knew she needed, and she leaned into it, holding on tight. Only barely noticing that Theo headed right past her with her suitcase, dropping it onto the front porch.

As Brandy let go of her mother, Theo stepped forward. "Mrs. Blackwell, take good care of her." He nodded to Brandy as he gave her mother a hug. Her mother's huge smile at the gesture was telling.

There was no animosity toward Theo here.

Then again, if he hadn't slept with Sammy, should there be?

Brandy still felt a shudder of revulsion. She'd believed for too long that her ex fiancé would be the father of her mother's first grandchild, but not with her.

Her mother's voice was warm with friendship and gratitude. "Oh, Theo, thank you so much for convincing her to come home."

Was Theo getting credit for her visit? Did it matter? Brandy told herself it didn't. The fact was he had flown all the way across the country to get her, and she wouldn't have come home if he hadn't. Not yet anyway.

Then Theo was telling them goodbye climbing back into his car as Brandy's mother steered her inside. Her parents had raised their daughters to be anything, but her mother had always taken a more traditional route. Mrs. Blackwell had stayed home with the kids, cooked, and cleaned and been content being a housewife. Brandy tried not to stop and think how that would have changed had anything happened to her dad before all the kids were mostly grown.

So Brandy wasn't surprised when her mother shoved food at her. She should have known. "I just ate, Mom. I'm so sorry. I was starving when I got off the plane. I wasn't even going to make it here."

"No big deal." Her mother put the food away. Brandy at least knew that her mother meant what she said. "How about tea, though?"

"That sounds great." Even though she wasn't normally a tea drinker, it was how her mother handled difficult conversations. Brandy felt the sheer normality of it all as her mother waited out the screaming of the pot, offered her several varieties of tea bags, and then poured their steaming cups before leading her into the main room.

Sitting on the couch, her mother patted at the spot next to her. It was a summons Brandy knew not to ignore.

"I've missed you so much, baby."

"I missed you too, mom."

"Maybe you can help because I just didn't understand . . ."

Brandy knew what was coming.

"Why did you leave your own wedding?"

It was past time to spill the tea.

CHAPTER FORTY-NINE

It had felt good yesterday, telling her mother everything. How she'd made a mistake but found more. What she had at Jade River was unique and she wouldn't have gotten anything like that in her life without something spurring her on.

"You're going to go back and finish the contract, aren't you?" Her mother said now as they prepped for dinner.

It wasn't really a question. Her mom seemed to understand by then what the job and the place and the people meant. Even if she still didn't fully grasp it. "If I wasn't doing it for myself, I couldn't leave the people in a lurch."

"Good for you." Her mother patted her hand.

Brandy tried to hold onto the sensation. She would need it for what was coming up.

Sammy hadn't been available yesterday, but she'd be here any minute for the big family dinner her mother was serving. Still, she'd promised to get here after lunch, and she was already a good hour-plus late.

McKayla and Dakota had been all over the place. Though they'd had to go to school, they were as exuberant as ever. Best friends, conspirators, co-captains of varsity cheer. Their senior year of high school had just started and the always-on-the-go twins were now even more so.

In fact, Brandy wasn't convinced they weren't going to pick up their old hijinks of trying to trade places. Though it had never worked on their family, they'd managed to pull it off a couple of times at school and once in the local theater.

She was cutting veggies, anxious, when she heard the car pull up in the driveway.

Her mother motioned for her to go, and Brandy wiped her hands and headed toward the front of the house. Sammy had taken the afternoon off, probably because she—like Brandy—hadn't wanted to have this discussion with the whole family sitting around the dinner table. She was finally here, but there wasn't much time left before the twins got home from school.

Her sister walked tentatively in the front door, small belly leading the way. Sammy was now noticeably pregnant.

Brandy just kept heading forward. Sammy wasn't going to be the one to make the first move. So, Brandy enveloped her younger sister, shorter by four inches, in a long overdue bear hug. "I'm so sorry for everything!"

So often she had felt like a second mom for Sammy. Now she realized that was a mistake, even though she couldn't quite stop doing it. But Sammy, for having taken her afternoon off work, still didn't want to confront the issue head on. She pulled awkwardly out of the hug and stepped away.

"Did you enjoy your time in the mountains?" Her sister headed directly into the kitchen, past their mother, and straight into the pantry. She found a bag of chips and pulled out a bowl, pouring herself a portion.

She was eating them before she seemed to realize what she had done. Holding the bowl out to Brandy, she asked, "Do you want any?"

"No, I'm good." Brandy waved a hand, motioning the chips

away. How long had it been since she'd had potato chips? It was an odd thought. She was usually a fan.

Right now, Sammy couldn't seem to eat them fast enough. Probably because she was pregnant.

"The mountains have been fantastic," Brandy answered, "but I am going back."

"You're training dogs." Sammy said it between chips, but her tone was clearly asking *why?*

Brandy found herself explaining all over again. She kept her words to the work though and not necessarily why she'd made the decision, hopefully that would speak for itself. Even so, aside from the apology and the hug, Sammy kept the conversation on stilted ground until the twins ran in through the door.

Their conversation at least was animated. They had none of the need to hold back that the older family members did, and they were going on about some Derek and Jason. Though Brandy had no idea what they were talking about, Sammy jumped directly in.

Before Brandy knew it, her father was coming home from work and her mother was asking for help in the kitchen again. It was an odd sensation, knowing this dance, knowing that she'd fit into it just a handful of months ago. But the last time she'd sat at this dinner table the conversation had been sad and stilted. Theo's absence had been felt like a missing person. Brandy's insistence had been that he not be invited to dinners anymore. It shouldn't have felt like she'd clipped out one of her siblings, but it had.

She still hadn't been able to bring up any of the things she needed to say. Sammy had made it near impossible being her usual late self.

Brandy had too many experiences with bad dinners in the past months. Starting with after she'd left the wedding. Then when Ash had blown up at her, and they had done the same thing at the sanctuary.

No more, she thought. She decided that dinner would be fine as she set out plates and silverware all around the large table. She had a part in the dance, but she didn't quite fit into it now.

Sammy brought napkins and serving utensils as their mom called Brandy back to help with the salad. She knew to dice the tomatoes rather than slice them. She knew to grate the carrots the way her mother liked and where on the fridge door the salad dressings could be found.

She was putting the large bowl onto the table when the front door opened again. Rick Jr. walked in, Brandy's own grin naturally growing wide at the sight of her brother. But right behind him, came Theo.

Looking down at the table, Brandy felt foolish. The number of places that had been set should have told her. Had she just not thought about the extra place because she was so used to Theo joining them for dinners before the wedding?

"Rick!" she called out, heading over to hug her brother. She was going to be happy at dinner, no matter what anyone did.

Rick lived an hour away, so this was the first she had seen of him. After she hugged her brother, Theo reached out to hug her.

It was an odd place to be, finding herself in his embrace. She wouldn't have hugged him herself. She didn't quite know where she stood. She had stayed here with her family, not reaching out to him. But she also wasn't in a place where she would say no and refuse the gesture.

"I'm so glad you could make it, Theo!" Her mother came out of the kitchen, answering the question Brandy hadn't yet asked, and probably wouldn't have drummed up the courage to. *Who had invited him?*

Brandy had to ask herself a second question: *Why did she feel that way?*

She'd come home to see her family. To explain to her mother

what had gone wrong. To apologize to Sammy. And to see if the old spark was there with Theo.

The problem was she saw everything, now. The sleek looks, the wide smile, the suits that oozed class. The car was the same one they'd driven out to check the wedding venue in. He upgraded often, but he hadn't gotten a new car since she'd been gone.

Maybe she'd just felt so bad about him for so long that it was difficult to swing back the other direction. Whatever it was, she didn't want to sit next to him. So she manipulated the seating to put him across the table, but not near Sammy. *Ugh.*

She passed the food and participated in the conversation but didn't do much more than that. So much for deciding she wouldn't let the company change things.

Brandy just didn't have anything to add. The family moved around her . . . and so did Theo. *As if he had been here all along.*

When the meal was done, and the pies her mother had made were half gone, the family slowly disbanded. Theo took her hand, pulling her outside.

"Come home with me tonight." It wasn't really a question. She didn't answer and he leaned in for a soft, slow kiss.

Brandy didn't know what she felt. "I can't. I told my mother I'd go to breakfast with her in the morning before I leave."

It was true. She'd already anticipated Theo's objection. He would drive her back here in the morning. She knew he would do it, too. She shook her head and stepped back, releasing his fingers from hers and reclaiming her own space.

"I'm going to stay here tonight." She could tell he was disappointed.

He'd paid for a flight. Had he thought he was going to get laid?

As they stood there in the yard, searching for the next thing to say, the front door opened behind them. Sammy came out into the warm night air, her bag over her shoulder, one hand going almost protectively toward her belly.

Maybe it was suggesting something? There was a move that made Brandy think Sammy was making a point, but she wasn't sure what that point was . . .

Reaching out, Sammy hugged Brandy one-armed around her side. "Night, sis."

Then she looked at Theo and only glared at him as she walked by.

CHAPTER FIFTY

"Tomorrow?" Her mother looked upset last night when Brandy reminded her she was flying out at noon. "I thought you had three days off. It's the weekend, you should have two more days?"

"We work weekends. I get different days off." Despite her repeated explanations, no one seemed to understand. "We train all the time. They're living creatures—almost like children—we can't just not feed them on the weekends."

She would fly out on a flight that Theo had booked and paid for. She wanted to offer to pay him back. While she could scrape the funds together, last-minute cross-country flights weren't something she wanted to hit her account with. And the house hadn't yet closed escrow. And she wasn't making that much at the sanctuary. And Theo always seemed to like to pay for things anyway.

She'd decided she'd pay it if he asked, and he certainly had too much class to ask.

She'd had breakfast with her mother but then requested to use the car. She had an errand to run. She just didn't say what.

Something about Sammy's reaction to Theo as she left the

night before had Brandy coming here to her sister's office. She hadn't ever come to see Sammy at her job before. She should have! Sammy had gotten the job after she'd finished her thesis but before she officially graduated. Brandy had been too busy, planning her wedding . . .

Sammy had been right. Her own celebrations had been shadowed by Brandy's and they shouldn't have been.

So now Brandy found herself looking up at the front of the tall downtown building. Luckily, corporate logos were scattered across the front, and she saw the marketing company that Sammy had been hired by. Sammy seemed to like the work fine but had suggested she would move on when the opportunity presented itself.

Brandy wondered now if the baby would keep her locked into a job that paid well but wasn't exactly what she wanted to do.

She hadn't told her sister she was coming, and she felt a little bit like shit about doing it. By the same token, the visit and the lack of warning felt absolutely necessary.

Something was still up.

The elevator up to Sammy's floor was empty at mid-morning. Down the hallway, Brandy found the glass door that led to the tiny front office. She listened with a smile and a thank you as the young man behind the desk called her sister.

Sammy came out front, her pace brisk on her high heels, looking every bit the marketing executive.

"You look fantastic!" Brandy told her but Sammy was talking over her.

"Is everyone alright?"

"I'm sorry, it's *fine*. I just wanted to come see you. Do you have a few minutes?" Shit, of course her sister was worried. But Sammy nodded and calmed down quickly once she realized nothing was wrong.

"Sure. Give me a second." She had to go back into her office and gather her bag, then tell the front desk that she would be out for a little bit. The next thing Brandy knew they were standing in line at the coffee shop at the base of the building.

"I'm so sorry, Sammy. I really am."

"You didn't startle me that bad. I just leapt to conclusions."

"No, I'm sorry about everything. Everything since the wedding. I am just trying to put all the pieces together here. And last night it seemed—"

Sammy snorted as she took the cup of hot coffee from the barista.

She had added extra shots and Brandy desperately wanted to ask if that was okay for the baby. But she knew better. Her sister wouldn't hurt her child. Brandy took her own cup and headed toward the corner table where Sammy was already making a spot for them.

She tried again. "I'm really sorry I misjudged you."

Brandy had to hope it would lead to a better discussion. The one that she thought they could have yesterday afternoon. Maybe she shouldn't apologize for showing up at her sister's work. This might be done if Sammy hadn't been late enough to derail the whole talk yesterday. But Brandy was trying.

"I thought you slept with Theo. I thought this was Theo's baby." She pointed at her sister's belly even though she couldn't quite see it below the edge of the table. She took a sip of her coffee. "But he told me what happened."

Sammy sat quietly sipping her drink, not nodding or shaking her head. She looked at the barista making the next drink, out the front window, at the generic paintings on the walls.

Not a good sign. But Brandy didn't have anything else to contribute but to keep going. "He told me about Curtis."

"Curtis. Hmm." It was the first words Sammy had said. The first time she looked at her older sister.

"You're frowning." Brandy continued. "But it was Theo's

fault for not telling me about Curtis." She wasn't going to put it all on Sammy.

As she watched, her little sister set her cup down, her eyes looked up at the ceiling, wetness rimming the edges. Her mouth pulled into a bewildered grimace. It seemed as though she made a decision.

"Is that what he told you?"

Brandy felt her heart harden in the center of her chest. She looked at the time and realized she was going to miss her plane.

CHAPTER FIFTY-ONE

"I didn't figure you for a kitten guy." Ash watched as Beck cradled the tiny creature in his hands. Jaeger, of course, curled up against the big guy, seeming to know that he was safe.

Ash lived by the adage of trusting the people the animals trusted. Beck, still scratching the tiny head as the creature began to purr like an old diesel motor, looked at Ash with a frown on his face. "I may be a hardened criminal," he looked down at the kitten, "but no one can say no to a cat. Certainly not a cutie like this one."

Ash grinned as he watched Whiskey and Bourbon crawl around on the metal tabletop. He put each kitten on the scale and recorded how much weight they'd gained. He'd even hiked back out to the spot in the daylight—though it had taken forever to find—hoping to find any extras from the litter that might have been missed the first time.

Though he found mama, still in the same spot, no new babies had appeared. He could only hope he had gotten them all. Then, hands in his pockets, he looked down at what remained of the mama cat and said softly, "You did good. They're safe now."

Now, little Merry jumped onto his T shirt, claws digging in. Ash's face pulled to one side in a grimace. He could feel each tiny needle claw as it pushed with her weight. She made her way to his shoulder. He would have to train that out of them, and quickly.

Everyone had been stopping by to visit and help with daytime feedings, which he appreciated beyond measure. "It's time," he told Beck and handed the man a tiny bottle watching it disappear behind the tattooed fingers.

The tattoos looked a little blurry to Ash, and at last he caught on. "Were you getting laser removal?"

He picked up Bourbon, watching her little paws cycle until she managed to get the bottle into her tiny pink mouth. Ash had no great love for human babies but a kitten or a puppy, even a baby squirrel, got him every time.

"I was," Beck looked up at him, half a grin on his face.

Ash was proud for a moment that he'd guessed. Then he caught on. "You *were?*"

Beck sighed. "I stopped going a few weeks ago."

"You have to keep going." Ash held the bottle up, only occasionally looking to Beck, but the man was doing everything right.

"Of course." Beck shrugged without disturbing Jaeger. "I ran out of funding."

"You sold your car back." Ash didn't quite ask it, but Beck nodded at that too. Not wanting to push any further warred with his innate curiosity.

It seemed odd. Ash thought he had a good idea of what Roz was paying people. And with room and board included . . . Beck should be able to afford it. But then again, what did he know? He still had student loans to pay. And who knew what an ex-con might owe to various places. He didn't push further.

"What about you, Ashley? You got any ink."

"I do." Ash responded, Merry squirming on his shoulder,

little claws digging in as she did it. Bourbon's ears twitched as she happily sucked down her bottle. Whiskey, still wandering the table, was attempting to climb Beck.

"Tramp Stamp?" Beck grinned.

"No. And don't call me Ashley."

Beck almost guffawed at him. "I saw your intake forms, Ashley Vaughn Cooper."

Ash rolled his eyes. He'd always hated the names his mother had given all three of them—as if she could make them better with classic monikers.

But Beck was already going. "Sounds really highbrow, you know. To be *Ashley*. You should be sipping juleps on a wide front porch somewhere."

If the very sound of the name *Ashley* didn't twist him inside, he would have laughed. "I haven't been Ashley since third grade."

Jaeger finished his bottle and Beck held the lone male kitten up, showing off the now round belly, swollen like an avocado. "Do I need to burp him?"

Ash finally laughed. "No. But Whiskey wants her fair share."

He pointed at the small calico who had her hind feet on the table, but her front two paws hooked into Beck's belt. As the man looked down at her she wailed at him.

Ash nudged one of the two remaining bottles toward the man as Beck clearly caved and picked up the tiny beastie.

"She's got your number."

"Definitely. You're coming to the fire pit tonight." He rubbed his nose on the kitten's head. The kitten seemed to agree.

"Only with leashes," Ash added. He couldn't handle the heartache if one got lost in the dark.

Beck didn't even look up. Just picked up Whiskey and got her nursing. But he wasn't about to let the rest of it go. "So, what happened in third grade?"

Ash didn't know if he'd ever told the story, he'd hated it so much at the time. But looking back with distance, maybe it wasn't so bad. "There was this girl . . ."

"Isn't there always?" Beck asked.

Ash had to laugh. It felt good to have a friend. It felt good to laugh, because somewhere in the very core of him, he was wound so tight that he wondered if he'd ever be normal again.

Brandy was due back tonight and he didn't want to face her. He didn't want to have those conversations. Ash held out stupid hope that it could work out, but he knew that chance was beyond slim. He knew what he needed to do.

So right now, he appreciated the laugh. "It was elementary school, and she was new. Belinda Johnson. Looking back, it's pretty clear she had a crush on me—"

"But you didn't return the feelings?" Beck filled in.

"Well, we were eight and I didn't realize it was a crush back then. I just thought she was torturing me. She would run across the playground calling out for me or come into the classroom and call out a personal greeting to me every morning."

"Not seeing the problem here." Beck adjusted Whiskey in his hand, the tiny cat dwarfed by the large fingers.

"The problem is she had a lisp—"

Beck frowned. "You were making fun of a disabled kid?"

"No." Ash wondered how it had come out like that. "The problem is she yelled across the playground *Ass-Lee, Ass-Lee!*"

All four kittens jumped, Merry digging her claws into Ash's shoulders as Beck threw his head back and laughed loud enough to ring off the clinic walls. "She called you *Assley!*"

Was he red? Ash wondered. He could feel all the muscles in his face and maybe the embarrassment creeping up through his veins too. "She did this multiple times daily—loudly—for all of third grade and sometimes the whole schoolbus to hear."

"Oh man. That's harsh, Assley," Beck replied, a wide grin and sparkling eyes as he tried not to laugh so hard that he disturbed the kittens again.

"Listen up, Benji—" Ash faked his own harsh frown at his friend. If Benjamin Becker wanted to play that game, then he could get as good as he gave.

"Oh, I think I can handle Benji in return for getting to call you Assley."

Ash wanted to threaten *"I'll kick your ass"* but that was not a tangle he wanted to get into. What he replied instead was, "I will murder you in your sleep and make it look like a suicide."

Beck still laughed at him.

At least it wasn't quite as embarrassing as it had been in the third grade. Damn Beck if he called out *Assley* for everyone to hear. Still, it was better to have a friend than just a job.

And, Ash told himself, he had enough friends here now that he could survive anything.

Even Brandy.

CHAPTER FIFTY-TWO

The alarm had gone off at two am and, though he'd gone to bed early to be ready for it, it was still too much.

Ash had fed the kittens at ten and then immediately fallen asleep after feeding them. The six am feeding he could handle. It was the getting up in the middle of the night that killed him.

The good news was that it would only last a few weeks. Though there were only two other people here at the sanctuary overnight, they'd said they were willing to relieve him and take the kittens overnight if he could prep them. He just hadn't done it yet.

Maybe tomorrow when he was exhausted, he'd find the drive to make everything into a kit and hand them off so he could sleep.

He worked hard to make sure he wasn't shirking his other duties but, like many a new parent, he was definitely lacking on sleep. Also, the crew was one shy with Brandy gone for several days. There just weren't enough hands to distribute the extra work to without noticing. It figured, he'd gone and found some very needy creatures to add to the mix.

As he popped a can of kitten formula, their cries intensified.

It had taken them about two feedings to learn what that sound meant. Kitten formula wasn't cheap. He'd drained the supply he kept on hand in the clinic for emergencies the first day. Then he'd had to head into Charlottesville and get it. Jade River had one clinic and they were running low and were almost three times as expensive. Ash would use them only as a backup.

He'd had to get enough to keep four kittens fed until they could be moved to mush, then kitten kibble. Kittens cost a pretty penny and a couple of hours of direct attention per day. And that didn't begin to count all the hours they distracted everyone just by being cute.

So now he let the kittens stay upright with their front paws against the box as he held a bottle in one hand, feeding two of them at the same time, struggling to stay awake himself. As hungry as they were, they had no issues with getting fed this way.

This time, Merry and Bourbon went first. Jaeger and Whiskey cried and circled their siblings who were already eating.

As tired as he was, Ash still tried to comfort them. "You guys know you're going to get fed next, right? I'm not a cat mama. I can't feed four of you at once."

"Wahhhhh," Whiskey replied. It was angry and pitiful and adorable. Surely kittens had evolved to be cute, because it got them taken care of. It was working on him now, even if he could barely keep his eyes open.

He got the first two fed and traded out the bottles for the next two. Merry and Bourbon waddled to the other side of the box now with round bellies. Merry only made it a few steps before falling over mid stride and simply giving up. She'd licked her tiny paws and started to put herself to sleep.

Must be nice, Ash thought as he watched Merry's siblings' ears twitch as they tried to suck down formula as fast as possible. He'd been lucky that none of them had any health problems so far. They hadn't come from the best situation.

Jaeger looked away, and Ash had to prod the little boy back with the tip of the bottle. Sure enough, as soon as he got the kitten drinking again, a knock came at the door.

Ash's eyes fell closed. His heart plummeted through his body in a never-ending spiral, and he could only hope that it was Roz or Beck. But he knew it wouldn't be.

He'd gone to bed early and Brandy still hadn't been home. She'd left her car here at the sanctuary. Ash didn't know who was supposed to pick her up at the airport and he liked that he didn't know. He told himself he didn't care.

A knock at his door shouldn't have made dark adrenaline flood every cell. He sucked in a deep breath. "Come in."

He did not want to do this now. He wanted to go back to sleep. However, he also didn't want to do this later. He'd learned from too many painful letdowns in the past that he wouldn't go back to sleep—the anxiety of not knowing would be too much.

The pain of knowing of a final conclusion would also be too much. But at least he could start getting through it if he knew. At least that's what he told himself.

He heard the knob turn and the slide of the well-oiled hinges, ones he'd oiled himself. Turning his head, he saw the jeans and the cute little sneakers that wouldn't last long up here. Had they not trained him out of it, Sidney would have stepped on them and left muddy prints on the white shoes.

"Kittens?" she asked, her face lighting up. "Can I help?"

He shook his head, no. He didn't move from where he was perched, feeding two kittens at once, his hands anchored on the side of the box as he looked down and saw Whiskey and Jaeger were close to the ends of their bottles. He almost wished there was more to drink, something that would keep him occupied for longer.

"I just got in," she told him, as if he cared, as if it were important. "I missed my original flight and ended up catching a later one."

He nodded along because that would be polite and wondered why this was important for him to know.

"I saw your light on," she added as though that might prod him into conversation.

Obviously, it was about feeding kittens. He wasn't waiting up for her. He didn't know what to say. Should he ask her if it went well? What would that even mean? He should simply say, *Are you back together with Theo?*

As much as Ash knew it'd be the right thing to do—information he desperately needed—he didn't quite have the guts to pull it off. He chickened out. "How are things with your mom? Did you make up with Sammy?"

Brandy sat down on the edge of his bed, and he almost told her *don't get comfortable.*

"We had a huge talk. We got everything out in the open."

"That's good." It was all he could think of. She was here in his room at two a.m. and he loved it and hated it at the same time.

He tried again. Still not hitting the target but getting closer. "Are you just getting your things before you head back to Los Angeles? Or are you staying through the end of your contract?"

As the words came out of his mouth, Ash realized that no matter what the answer was, at most, she would be around for just a few more months. And there was nothing he could do about it.

No matter how this ended she would break him.

CHAPTER FIFTY-THREE

Ash didn't ask about Theo, Brandy noticed, but she still needed to tell him why she'd come here at two in the morning.

Leaving her little suitcase on the porch of her tiny cabin had been so different from life in Los Angeles. The feeling that she could simply leave her luggage outside and walk away and know that it would be there when she got back made her feel more like herself. She could have fished out her keys so she could set it inside the door, but she hadn't even bothered.

She'd come straight here because Ash was the one person she'd wanted to talk to. She'd held out a foolish hope that she would run right into his arms. So many things had become clear while she was gone. As much as the trip had sucked, and as much as many of the things she'd learned had been knives in her gut, one truth had emerged from all the crap.

She loved Ash Cooper.

Brandy had thought of nothing quite as much as she thought of coming home to the tiny cabin up in the mountains. Coming back to the dogs and the work. She'd dreamed of it enough to make her wonder what she would do at the end of her contract.

Theo no longer waited for her in Los Angeles. Los Angeles no longer waited for her. It no longer called the way that it had in the past.

The clean mountain air beckoned her and swaddled her in feelings of home. Though she wasn't sure she was going to throw away a civil engineering degree and all her years of experience to become a dog trainer, she did know that the life she had led and the road she'd been on had simply been the path of least resistance.

Not the best one.

She waited, but Ash hadn't asked the most important question.

Sitting quietly on the end of the bed, Brandy laced her fingers together and looked down. She started to pick at her fingernails, a thing she knew she did when she was avoiding something. She forced herself to stop and look up as Ash removed one of the bottles, the kitten was apparently done nursing.

She forced herself to say the words out loud. "Theo and I aren't together."

Ash nodded, but he didn't come to her, he didn't kiss her, his expression didn't even change. Was that it?

She thought about asking him, *What do you want? What do we have?*

Because for all that she had realized she was in love with Ash, he'd said no such thing to her. In fact, the things they *had* said were that they were only going to be casual. What they had was simple and they could walk away at any time.

She'd changed the game and it wasn't fair of her to do that. She'd changed herself. She didn't want simple and unattached— not with Ash. Brandy wasn't quite sure how she should declare her undying love when she'd been the one who just walked away.

She tried to do it, but what came out wasn't quite the

declaration she'd intended. Instead, she gushed the story to her best friend. "It was all a lie, Ash!"

"What was a lie?"

Suddenly he was in the conversation. Ash had been listening when Theo told her that she had misheard. She was trying to pick up the thread at the right point for him when he said, "Wait, the part where you didn't understand? That was a lie?"

Brandy nodded. "Sammy's baby *is* Theo's."

She squeezed her eyes shut against the pressure that strained each time she thought it. It hurt fresh but she told Ash that, too. "You know, I thought I was getting over the fact that my sister had betrayed me with the man I was fifteen minutes from marrying. Then I believed I had it all wrong—that I had vilified her because of my own mistake."

She sucked in a breath, not realizing she'd lost it until her body forced her to. "I didn't think I could be more angry, but I am."

"Of course, you are," Ash said. She watched as his hand moved away from the box, the last kitten finally having finished with his bottle. He set it aside, still not quite looking at her.

Reaching down in, he petted the tiny creatures. She could just hear a few little motors purring. "He not only lied to you, he lied to you about lying to you."

She sucked in a breath. Ash was right.

"And then after doing one of the most heinous things one person can do to another—"

Brandy wasn't sure about that. Maybe murder was higher on the list, but Ash was usually right.

"—he tried to make you believe it was *your* fault."

Brandy frowned. "He didn't say it was *my* fault."

"Sure, he did. Theo's too slick to say that to your face, to actually put the blame directly on you. But by making it an issue that you had misheard, and that you ruined your whole wedding because you failed to get the story correct . . . he made you pick up the guilt yourself. It's a smooth move. A dick move, but a smooth one."

Her mouth hung open. *Yes, Ash was right.*

The horrible feeling of having been played for a fool settled over her. "I wonder how long he's been lying to me."

"Since he started sleeping with Sammy?" Ash asked her, but he still didn't come sit on the bed next to her. His hand stayed down in the box, petting the kittens.

Brandy wondered. Despite the ease of the conversation, the ease of throwing Theo under the bus he deserved to be crushed by, was Ash taking care of the kittens because it was necessary, or because it was merely a distraction for him?

"No, it just occurred to me," she sighed out the words on a huff of shame and regret. "I'm so stupid because I've just taken so long processing this pile of shit that I've been handed. But it only just now occurred to me that Sammy probably wasn't the first."

Ash looked over his shoulders at her, his blue eyes widening. Slowly, he shook his head at her, but it was a move of agreement. "You're probably right."

He probably thought the same as her. Someone who would lie to her and then try to make her feel bad about his own lies, certainly wouldn't have just started recently. He certainly wouldn't have just done it once.

She leaned back on the bed, hands behind her, supporting her. Her head fell back. She tried to open her chest, but she couldn't. She couldn't breathe.

All her life Brandy had believed she was smart. Everyone told her so. She struggled in English classes but being the best in her math and physics courses had made up for it. She'd tried at the stuff that was hard but brushed the rest aside. She knew what she was good at.

She'd met Theo and they were good together, so good. They got engaged and bought a condo and overhauled it. He gave her a nice car as an engagement gift, and she thought she had everything.

She should have looked at her life more closely and she wondered if she'd ever be able to forgive herself the costly mistake. But then she looked across the room at the beautiful man with the hard edges and the hands that softly handled delicate tiny creatures and big dogs alike, and she realized that she was lucky.

It was so much easier to forgive herself her stupidity when she could see exactly where her mistakes had led her. And just how amazing this man was. How much better off she was now, despite all the pain.

They still hadn't said anything about them. Brandy felt too broken and torn, too stupid and too brave all at the same time to do anything the right way. So, she asked, "Can I stay here tonight?"

Ash froze. He finally pulled his hand out of the box, and she didn't hear the kittens protest. They were probably long since asleep, letting Brandy know that his movements had only been a distraction. They'd been about her being here.

He stood up straight and turned to face her, her best friend morphing into a steely stranger. He moved no closer and when he looked at her, she felt it like an arctic wind. Still she prayed she was reading him wrong, this man that she knew so well.

"No, you can't stay. I can't keep loving people who don't choose me."

CHAPTER FIFTY-FOUR

Roz's stomach churned. She looked through all the mail in her hand and peeked into the empty post office box again just in case it had gotten stuck.

But it wasn't there.

Though the mail did actually deliver up onto the mountaintop—a fact for which she was supremely grateful—she had the post office box in Charlottesville for business. It was where she'd asked for the check to be sent.

It was too far away to check in daily but the acid eating her up inside told her it was worth the drive. Sadly, none of that mattered if it wasn't here.

Closing the door, she locked it shut and sorted through what she had again, just in case. She had a few pieces of spam mail and a couple of bills. The van had needed a three-thousand-dollar repair. But, as Beck had pointed out, it was still a bargain.

A bargain she didn't have the money to take advantage of, but it was too late.

She put the service on a credit card with an enormously high rate, her stomach churning the whole time. It had been tempting to leave the van at the shop and simply decide that she would repair it later when she had the money. The sanctuary could make do without it. Honestly, she'd not figured she'd have that kind of van until the place was much better established. But when the opportunity had popped up she hadn't been this deep underwater and she hadn't said no.

Now, even leaving it at the dealer wasn't an option, as they had a daily storage charge. Then, the mechanic had warned her, a vehicle left sitting would develop more problems. By the time she got to it, Roz would have three or four more things to repair from lack of use.

It felt as if she was always in a damned if she did and damned if she didn't scenario. She shouldn't have opened the sanctuary. She'd thought she was ready, but she wasn't. Still, it had been her dream and she had reached for it.

If she folded now, would she ever be able to start a service dog facility at all in the future? Or would this failure become a failure forever?

She decided to be grateful for the PO box. Even though it was another charge, it was too small to make or break her. So, she kept it, glad that she'd been able to give an address for him to send the money to a place she didn't live.

Not that she would be too difficult to find.

Brandy had come back and decided to stay out the duration of her contract. While Roz was personally more than happy to have her there, she'd mistakenly calculated what she could have saved if Brandy had quit more than once. Each time, she told herself it was working out for the best.

It had to be.

Casey had gone off to veterinary school. One less salary, she told herself. At least she was happy for Casey, off living his dream. She was allowed to be happy for one less mouth to feed.

Beck had stayed up with her more than one late night trying to figure out where they could squeeze the money from. She'd eventually given up and shown him all of her accounts. He'd pulled out a piece of mail he had saved—a crappy spam credit card with abysmal rates.

He'd waved it in her face though. "It has zero percent interest for the first year. You transfer the others onto here. You save a lot in interest and you get usable space on the others."

Beck had shuffled everything around for her. They'd called up and accepted the card at midnight. Roz thought it wasn't a good sign that there were operators on twenty-four-seven, but she couldn't be picky.

Beck calculated it all out. They could cover salaries from what was in the bank. Everything else went on a card. When the grant money came in, she'd be at zero.

Initially, Roz had talked herself in and out of her misgivings about hiring an ex-con. What a fool. He was the best hire she'd made.

She'd never been able to bring herself to ask what he'd been in for. Now she found she'd be disappointed whatever the answer was.

Swinging the front door of the post office in an angry arc, she tried to avoid spreading her irritation and blatant anger onto the people she passed. She'd hoped to turn right and head the few blocks down to the bank and deposit a cashier's check.

It had hurt enough asking for the money! She'd swallowed enough pride to want to barf it all back up. But he'd agreed. *So why wasn't the check here yet?*

With nothing left to do in Charlottesville, she headed back on a drive that should have been pretty. It should have been everything she dreamed and wanted. She was going back to *her sanctuary.* She had four dogs already matched to applicants. The government had approved the matches and would pay her when the humans took ownership of the dogs. She'd even gotten word that it would come through within a week of transfer.

She just had to make it until then.

Maybe they didn't need the money. Maybe Beck's shuffling

would be enough. There was simply no margin for error or accident or even a small incident.

She held her breath as she drove back to her favorite place on earth. Back to the people she loved, and had basically lied to by telling them everything would be okay when she knew full well she could lose it all. Every day she got closer to the edge.

She headed back to the four kittens that Lynzee had been advertising. They'd gotten a handful of adoption applications. Ash was letting Lynzee help choose prospective kitten parents and it looked like they were going to get the kittens adopted as pairs so they could stay together. Roz thought about paper and ink to print flyers for the parks. She thought about . . .

Ash had covered most all of it. Her part had been negligible. Had he figured out she didn't even have enough for a lost litter of kittens? At a place called *Sanctuary*?

What had she come to?

Maybe she just needed Lynzee to do a fundraiser for her. *Could they do a fucking bake sale for her dog training facility? She sure felt like a charity case right now.*

Hell, she was ready to try anything.

Driving by rote memory, she missed all the views of the Jade River on the way back. Did she really think she could come up with something that would save the day? It had been several months now that she'd been almost dead in the water. Each month she'd scraped by.

Could she scrape by again? And again? And then again one more time?

If the government money didn't come through fast enough, she could lose it all anyway. That would be the worst—to succeed but ultimately to fail, simply because of a time lag.

She was at the gravel parking lot facing the lodge before she even realized she had made it home.

Home, she thought. *Home for however long she had it.* Roz savored the thought for a moment, before she was jarred back into reality by the sight of a strange car in the parking lot.

Another slick, low slung vehicle that didn't belong here.

At first, she thought Theo had come back. Brandy had told them all the story after returning. She and Ash managed to be on elbow bumping terms, but not much more. They were cordial enough at dinner, but Roz knew she wasn't the only one who could feel the tension.

But that car . . . she stopped breathing. All movements ceased.

It wasn't Theo's. For all his slick showmanship, Theo didn't have this kind of money. Roz knew several people who did. None of them would be good.

She tried to swallow but couldn't. She should have known better than to sit in the car. She *had to* get up and take action. Sitting idly by had put her in the hospital more than once.

Still, she didn't react fast enough. The front door of the lodge opened and Calvin Westin Jr. stepped out the front door. His suit made Theo's look like he'd found it at the Goodwill. Calvin's movements bore every hallmark of one born to excessive wealth.

Roz opened the door, thinking that she should say *it's good to see you*, or some kind of trite platitude. Instead, she stopped where she was, feet planted, and said, "I didn't expect to see you here."

CHAPTER FIFTY-FIVE

Ash was operating at half steam, and he knew it. He had been since Brandy went back to LA. Her being at the Sanctuary again hadn't changed anything . . . except now he noticed that only four to six people were here on any given day. It made her a huge part of his life, whether he wanted her to be or not.

It made her that much harder to get over.

At least that's what he told himself. He warred with himself constantly. If what they'd had was truly casual, he should have been over it. Then again, he reminded himself he might still not be tangled up so tightly if she didn't live one cabin over from him and wasn't one fourth of his basic human interaction most days. Maybe it really was because he was a red-blooded man living on a mountaintop with only Beck, Roz, occasionally Lynzee, and some dogs to talk to. It didn't mean that he'd fallen as hard as he might have.

The sad answer was, he *had* fallen that hard and it was insanely difficult to dig himself out from under the crushing defeat.

Still, he had promised himself this time that his boundaries couldn't be just about his mother. If his brother and sister couldn't understand, then he would limit his interactions with them too. It had to include everyone who wasn't good for him. At least for a while.

He'd been here before.

How many times, he wondered, *had he fallen for a woman who couldn't love him back?*

Looking back, he operated as if getting just one of these women to actually love him would prove that he was worthy. Well, he hadn't proved it yet. And he was fucking tired of breaking his own heart by picking people who would break it for him.

Looking down into the box of kittens in his hands, he saw they'd grown. It was what kittens did—the passage of time was clear with a baby that grew this fast. It had been a few weeks and a full pound each per kitten since Brandy had returned.

Now their paws and faces reached up over the edge of the box. They mewed excitedly at him, knowing they were headed to the lodge to play. They were almost seven weeks old by his estimate. Time to get adopted out.

They were also big enough to get out of the box if they wanted to. They seemed to stay in until he set it down, but Ash was seriously contemplating getting some kind of a lid for it. If they jumped out, they could just run away. They'd been born on the trails. It'd be so easy for them to go back. He worried they might come to the same bad end as their mother had. If they stuck with him, they could be someone's well-fed and pampered babies.

He taught Lynzee how to assist him with them. Her ads for families insisted that the kittens have proper enrichment and the right kinds of toys, so they didn't get bored. They were also set for spay and neuter, which he and Lynzee would do during the week. He would have loved to have had Casey on it, but honestly Lynzee was going to be fantastic.

266

Heading toward the back of the lodge, he emerged from the trail and cut past the dog training facilities. He'd taken to letting the kittens run free in the lodge—even sometimes with the dogs, as it was good training. He always put a sign on the door that read: LOOSE KITTENS! So everyone would know not to mistakenly let one escape.

He'd managed to provide them with enough toys that they hadn't destroyed the furniture. So far. He was near the kennels when the back door opened suddenly, Beck swinging it wide.

Ash almost grinned knowing that Beck was sure to call out *"Assley"* as loud as he could. Ash at least always replied with a good *Benji*. He was opening his mouth to ask what his friend needed before the dreaded name rang across the mountain, but he caught the look on Beck's face.

Something was wrong.

Ash couldn't run. He was carrying baby animals. Still, he picked up his pace and saw Beck coming across the yard to him. It was only as Beck got close, that Ash began to wonder if maybe it was about him. *Had he done something? Not done something?*

Beck was already talking. "There's someone here and it's not good."

Ash shook his head in reply, though Beck had pointed and was steering Ash across the compound, but not toward the lodge. Ash didn't have enough information.

Was someone repossessing one of the cars? Or, hell, the whole sanctuary? Was there a fight? Just some asshole being harassing?

Beck was already explaining, and Ash had to keep up. "A younger man, rich. Concerning." Beck said the last as if he couldn't quite find the right way to describe the situation, so he was simply throwing words at it.

Taking the box of kittens from Ash, Beck startled him. "We can't put them in the lodge. I wouldn't trust this guy near babies. We should take them back to the clinic."

Ash followed along as he still didn't know what was going on.

"This guy knows Roz. I don't like the way he's talking to her." Beck hovered at the door, waiting for Ash to pull out his keys. Moving in quickly, he set the box down in one of the exam rooms where the babies would be safe.

Pulling the door closed behind them, Ash tried to work out everything that could go wrong. Though this should be like leaving them in his cabin. They had just been fed and should be pretty sleepy for a while. Still, he added a sign to the door so someone wouldn't open it and not realize that the wee beasties would be freed.

Then the two men headed back toward the lodge almost at a run.

At the back door, Beck paused, taking a breath to gather himself and startling Ash.

"What's going on?" Ash reached out and put his hand on Beck's arm, holding him back.

"That's just it. I don't know. But we need to back her up." There was a pause. "Whoever he is, he knows Roz, and something is *wrong*."

Together, they opened the back door, Beck stepping through first, Ash right behind him. He could already hear the voice of the stranger.

"So, you own this little place?"

Were his decisions colored by Beck's warning? Ash wondered. Because he already didn't like the sound of the guy. Even the phrasing was condescending.

"Yes," Roz replied, monosyllabic and without tone. *Not like her.*

Beck motioned him to creep forward, down the hallway toward the front room where the conversation was echoing.

"I checked your financials," the man said, "when you asked for the money."

Checked her financials?

No, he hadn't imagined the condescension. He'd read it quite clearly the first time.

"You *what?*" Roz sounded surprised, and then resigned. "Never mind. I'm sure you just know someone at the bank who can get that information for you."

Beck turned and looked at Ash mouthing, "Isn't that illegal?"

Ash was pretty sure that it was, but he didn't know for sure, so he shrugged.

Then the man laughed.

Beck and Ash scooted forward, enough to see the back of him. Ash understood Beck's concern. Even from here, this guy seemed just a little oily. Just a little *off.* Something in the way he stood—though Ash had no training and absolutely no skill—made him wonder if maybe the man was a sociopath.

"You didn't even want to write to me, did you?" Then he answered his own question. "Yes, that's what it was. You wrote to me to butter me up to ask for the money."

Ash turned to Beck, frowning, and trying to figure it all out. *Roz had asked this person for money?* It was obviously someone she knew.

Beck tipped his head back and his eyes rolled, letting Ash know that the fact that Roz needed money wasn't a surprise to him.

Son of a bitch. What had he been missing?

At the next words, Beck's eyes flew open wide, as did Ash's.

The two of them stepped boldly into the back of the room as Roz darted her gaze around, barely acknowledging them.

Instead, she looked at the man whose back was all Ash could see.

Then the man said, "Don't worry. I brought your check, *mother.*"

CHAPTER FIFTY-SIX

B randy stood waiting at the kennels. All four dogs were out, sitting and waiting for their commands.

When no one else showed up, she started to wonder. Beck was supposed to be running training with her today. Two of them to four dogs, making sure that the pups paid attention, even if the attention wasn't always on them.

Then they were supposed to work with Curie's dangerous noises training—things like trains, alarms, and more. She'd also need specific alerts for doorbells and such. Sidney was learning how to turn lights off and on, to hit elevator buttons and recognize up and down. He also needed to learn to fetch a variety of items. Like Curie, he would train to specifics for his human once they arrived at the Sanctuary.

Katherine was doing very well with her seeing-eye harness. Though they were still weeks before the people came, she was learning to cross streets and lightly bark warnings. Norgay was learning to sniff various scents they had, indicating a patient was in distress—his young companion would need to be alerted to high or dangerously low glucose levels.

It seemed so long before their people would arrive, and yet the time was truly so short, Brandy knew.

So where was Beck? She messaged him a third time, growing worried at his failure to respond. Anyone who came back to the kennel area could see her, so it was unlikely he didn't know she was waiting.

Then she realized she couldn't see anyone.

Her phone pinged. Beck.

—At lodge. Get here quick.

That was not good. She motioned with one finger to the pups and all four dogs immediately returned to their homes. They'd come out and sat and waited for nothing. She hoped it was at least good training.

Closing each door with the little latch, Brandy moved quickly toward the lodge. But something tickled at the back of her brain. Something she didn't like, even if she couldn't put her finger on it. Why was no one else out?

She began to bolt, coming in through the back door, throwing it wide, her mouth open to call out.

Ash stepped quickly into her space, making her draw up short. He meant to stop her from yelling with a finger to his lips. She could smell him and feel the sensation of having him so close. But she couldn't enjoy it. His expression was alarming.

What was possibly going on?

Turning, he looked over her shoulder and motioned for someone to come on.

Brandy looked back and saw Lynzee, a scowl on her own face, blond hair pulled back, eyes ringed with dark eyeliner. She liked to make sure everyone knew she was not happy but, even from this distance, Brandy could see her expression now was worried.

Ash motioned again for Lynzee, who picked up her pace. As much as she had sullen teenager vibes, she had grown into the work. Whatever was going on now required speed and Lynzee gave it.

"What?" the young woman asked quietly, as Ash held his finger to his lips again.

"Roz's son is here."

Roz had a son. How had they not known?

Brandy watched as Ash shook his head at them. So that wasn't even the most important thing. Whatever it was about the son, it wasn't good.

"He makes Theo look like he's playing with Monopoly money."

Brandy shook her head again, as though that might make the pieces of her brain fall into place and work. But Ash was still explaining. Beck stood at the end of the hallway in the open arch, blocking most of her view into the main room.

"Apparently he came because she asked him for money." Ash motioned them forward.

So, they were all going to go join the conversation. Brandy wasn't sure why.

She had no idea that Roz even had a son. From the looks on their faces, neither had Ash or Lynzee.

Then again, what did she really know of Roz's life? Still, she'd thought she had an idea, and it wasn't that she had a wealthy grown son and was asking him for money.

Brandy and Lynzee trailed Ash quietly down the hall to where the three of them lined up behind Beck. They stood like sentinels in the large archway that connected the open lounge area to the hall that led to all the smaller rooms at the back of the lodge.

Brandy could hear the conversation clearly now.

"I can give you the money, but this is going to fail. You know that." He waved a hand at the lodge.

Wow. What a dick.

It turned out she didn't even know the worst of it.

"I'll have to keep bailing you out. You know you're not very good at this kind of thing, mother."

Though Roz didn't disagree with him, she didn't agree with him either. Their boss stood firm, her mouth looking as though it wanted to pinch tight, but she fought the urge and mostly won.

Her eyes flicked to the back of the room, clear that she saw all four of her employees lined up there. For a moment, Brandy read deep, deep embarrassment before Roz covered it up, crossed her arms, and said, "Not this time."

"Obviously this time, too." He laughed, the sound too practiced and yet still grating.

Apparently, Beck had had enough. He took one simple step forward and said, "She's doing fine."

Whoever this prick was, he turned around. He was blond— radically different from Roz's own pitch black. His eyes were the same shape. She could see Roz in them, though his slate gray lacked the sparkle Roz's hazel eyes held sometimes.

If they were black, they would have looked completely lifeless.

He offered Beck a visual pat on the head. "You haven't seen her financials."

Fuck! Brandy thought. Another asshole who spoke in terms of *financials*. But also, she realized, whatever this douchecanoe was talking about, there *were* problems with the Sanctuary.

She had gotten the impression all along that Roz didn't have extra money to throw around. But that didn't mean there were problems, it meant the business was a startup.

"I have seen them," Beck assured the asshole in front of him.

Though he was shorter than the newcomer—Roz's *son*—he managed to fill up more of the space. Brandy wanted to tell him exactly what she thought of him. She thought, *Please excuse me Roz because I know he's your son*. But this shitwidget looked at Beck and seemed to understand that he was completely outmatched.

Then Brandy finally processed what Beck had said.

Ash turned to look at her and they shared their surprise.

Beck had seen the financials.

Brandy lifted a finger as if to point to Ash, to say, *I thought you were second in command here.*

Ash offered the tiniest move of his shoulders and twitch of his lips, but it clearly said, *I thought so, too.*

CHAPTER FIFTY-SEVEN

Roz hated this. She squeezed her fists until her nails bit into her palms. Her jaw hurt from holding back the rage-scream that wanted to emerge.

This was the moment when the hero understood that they'd been defeated. When all the bad luck and poor decisions came crashing down.

As she looked at it now, she could see that the poor decisions weren't the things like buying the van, like making dinner for everyone, or expanding the play area. It had been taking possession of the Sanctuary when it wasn't what she'd been sold.

Even though, she'd done a good job bartering down the cost once she'd seen it. She'd done it even after she'd signed all the papers, because the place had been badly misrepresented.

Still, that bartering hadn't yielded all the fruits it should have. The cost to bring in the lawyer to make the threats, to make the price come down, had taken a large chunk of the windfall she'd secured. The sellers had refused to cover the cleaning and clearing costs. By that time, she'd run out of time to hold out for the deal she wanted . . . the one she really had *needed*.

Her grant money stipulated that she had to deliver the dogs by a certain date. Waiting any longer would make the timeframe too tight and nearly guarantee failure. She'd taken the deal in front of her because it was that or walk away completely— which she wasn't sure she could do. She couldn't be sure the sellers wouldn't drag her through a countersuit.

It would also scrub the grant money waiting for her and, in doing so, maybe kill her chances to ever qualify for it again.

No, she thought looking over the four of them standing there in the back of the room. She couldn't regret the choices she'd made. They were all so different and yet so wonderful. Still, she'd screwed them over by not telling them what the situation was, by thinking that she could dig all of them out of this on her own. By thinking that Calvin wouldn't come *here*.

She'd so stupidly believed that he would just send her the money. *Of course not*.

Roz tried not to think about the obvious ramifications of Calvin finding her here, because they were harsh and horrifying. At no point had she believed she was truly hidden from her ex and her son—she had hoped it wasn't necessary. She'd stupidly believed that they had let her go.

This was on her. She'd been so wrong to think that, and *she* was the one who had reached back out.

Still, Calvin was always his father's boy and now anyone could drive up on top of this mountain and find her. Maybe Jade River Sanctuary wasn't much of a sanctuary anymore. Calvin's appearance here had completely blown her naive beliefs apart.

She would not cry no matter how much she hated admitting all of this to her team. She hated that Calvin had fucking forced her hand. That she had to do this in front of him. Then again, they were her mistakes and maybe she deserved it.

"My intent," she told them between cold breaths as her world crumbled, "is to return every penny to him, unused. We don't necessarily need it. But . . . if the grant money from the dogs is slow to come in, or if something else breaks, or if we have to restock the veterinary supply. . ." Roz waved her hand around aimlessly indicating each of these things passing. She shrugged as if that would convey the tangle of sick emotions she felt. "It could kill us."

Calvin turned then, addressing her crew directly. Roz wanted to step forward and slap him across his smug face. He had no right to speak to her people. No matter what she had done.

He grinned and held his hands palm out as if to show he had nothing to hide. She could see only the side of his face, but that was enough.

"I'm so sorry my mother got you into this. She does this periodically—tries to do something, start a business, learn rock climbing—" Her heart froze at the memory, and she couldn't hide the breath she sucked in, "—and she just fails at it."

"No." She was too quiet. Not forceful enough, but he didn't know her anymore. She told herself her team wasn't here to sabotage her, to tell her that she was bad at it, to withhold the very information that would have made her a success.

Yet, here Calvin was, doing exactly that. She shook her head to her employees. Hell, she thought, they weren't her *employees*. They were her *family* now.

She looked at Beck, Ash, Brandy, and Lynzee and simply shook her head as if to say *no, he's not right*.

Still that fucker kept going. A woman shouldn't feel this way about her own son. But holy fucking hell. He actually turned and said to them, "Did she tell you? We've had to place her on a psych hold more than once."

The problem was, assholes like him had an uncanny ability to know just where to hit. While they always used lies to construct whatever story they needed, they built them on pillars of the truth.

She'd never *needed* a psych hold, as evidenced by the fact that the doctor always let her out after seventy-two hours with no follow up. But Calvin Sr and Calvin Jr had certainly put her there more than once.

"You know what, Calvin?" she said now, too angry to think straight. Too fucking mad to remember why she'd sold her soul for cash. "I think I'll fail before I take your money. I don't need this."

Her heart broke as she stood there and told him where he could fucking stick it. She saw the man and thought of the baby she'd once held in her arms. She'd once had such high hopes for him. Even though she'd known the house she was raising him in would be harsh and cruel, she had stupidly believed she would be able to change him.

Here he stood, her greatest failure.

In a smooth move, he grabbed the front of his suit jacket, opened it and reached inside. He produced a cashier's check with a grin and almost no flourish, but as smooth as a magician. "I made it out for twice as much as you asked for, Mother."

The way he said *mother*, as if he were mocking her . . . she hated him as much as she loved him. As much as she knew things could change, she knew they never would.

Roz was shocked, but too frozen to respond as Brandy stormed forward, fast enough that Calvin didn't even catch it. He was too busy paying attention to her, waiting for Roz to crack.

Brandy plucked the check from his hand and—to Roz's great surprise—ripped it into tiny shreds and dropped them like trash to the floor. She simply said, "No."

Then she moved to Roz and took her hands. "The house Theo and I bought just closed escrow last week. I've got this. I'll cover it."

One by one, as Roz watched, they all did the same.

Ash moved forward. "I'm good. I've been saving most of my salary. You can either have it back or stop paying me."

Beck said, "You know you have whatever you need from me."

Lynzee even stepped up, maybe shocking Roz most of all. The dark eyeliner ringed eyes that were no longer sulking, but suddenly determined. In fact, she clumped forward on her heavy black boots, and body checked Calvin out of her way.

Roz almost laughed.

"Give me a cabin and dinner. That's all I need." Lynzee crossed her arms and sucked in a determined breath, before adding, "You don't need this asshole. And neither do we."

Roz watched as Brandy, Beck, and Ash, all with their arms crossed slowly smiled together.

The room hung silent for a moment.

Calvin's disdain showing in his every expression, but it was Ash who grabbed him by his shoulders and manhandled him out the front door. His own limit had been reached and it stung in every word. "That was your cue, Asshole. You missed it. You can leave now."

"You're not needed." Beck called out.

Ash did all but shove Calvin down the front steps and Roz should have told him not to, but she couldn't quite bring herself to do it. Her heart was too busy breaking. Always, *always*, when she saw Calvin, her heart broke. It broke for everything she knew he could have been, everything that she'd simply failed at.

Brandy was right on Ash's heels, as if together they would simply block the door. "You're not welcome back, either."

They all stood, unmoving, unspeaking, as they watched Calvin straighten his jacket as though he'd never been treated so badly! He climbed into his car, lowered the top-opening door, and drove away without so much as a wave.

Then Roz turned back, looking at the shredded cashier's

check on the floor, and faced her four employees—her family—who desperately deserved some explanations.

CHAPTER FIFTY-EIGHT

Brandy listened intently, trying to process all the information Roz was throwing at them.

After they'd all made sure Calvin was far down the driveway, Beck had muttered, "I should have placed a fucking tracker on his car."

Sadly, it was too late for anything like that.

Roz gathered them around the dining table, folded her hands, and started with an apology. "I'm trying to tell you everything. So that you can make reasonable decisions. If you decide you don't want to stay, I won't hold it against you."

Brandy didn't see herself leaving. Then again, she always *had* seen herself leaving. Her contract was up right before Christmas, so her decision wasn't as important as everyone else's. Still, she wasn't going to walk out now. Not when she'd just loaned this woman all her savings.

Roz explained how and why she'd bought the place sight unseen and who she had trusted by mistake.

Reaching out for Roz's hand, Brandy offered a quick squeeze of reassurance. "Don't worry about me. I'm not going to blame anybody for trusting the wrong people."

Roz offered a half smile at that. "Thank you."

Then, she explained, "My options were to either close everything down—destroy any future chances of getting a grant for training service dogs and call all of you and tell you that you didn't have a job. Or I could try to give it a go with the money I did have."

This woman she admired took a deep breath and Brandy felt it in her own bones. "Obviously, I decided to try. I thought we could run on a shoestring and it would be okay. There was still, at that time, a little bit of buffer."

"Buffer doesn't last long when you're starting a business," Ash commented softly.

"Don't I know that," Roz looked up at the ceiling. "Please understand. I'm not trying to tell you that I made the right decisions or excuse what I did. I'm just trying to explain why I made the choices I did. I was *biased* and completely based decisions on the fact that this is my dream. I was trying so hard to make it fly."

This time it was Beck who reached out. "It is still flying."

Brandy thought she saw tears form at the edge of Roz's eyes.

But the woman was still going. "I lied by omission. Things just slowly got tighter and tighter. Each time, something saved me. Once, it was Beck."

As Brandy watched, Roz squeezed the man's hand, then seemed to realize she was still holding it.

Interesting. But Brandy turned first to Roz, then looked around the table, addressing the rest of the group. "I'm sorry. I know he's your son, but he made me so mad. The good news is that—though Theo is a lying bastard—he's also a whiz with money. Nine months ago, we bought an older condo which we started to fix up so that it would be ready when we came back from our honeymoon."

She sighed, understanding Roz's desire to hold onto a

dream, no matter how misplaced. It wasn't like Brandy's stupid idea of a future would employ anyone.

She kept going. "All of the upgrades had been done by the time I walked out on my wedding. I told Theo to make the payments on it."

She was glad to see Ash across the table grinning at her as a way of offering his support for her vindictive decision.

"Then, when we sold it, we split the profits. We basically did a nine-month flip on this condo. It's not quite exactly what Calvin's check was worth, but I have the majority of it." Brandy rattled off a number.

Roz looked at her with tears in her eyes. "I asked for more than I hoped I needed . . . because I didn't want to ask twice. And the check he held was for double what I asked for."

Then it should more than get them through. Brandy smiled. "Well, it's yours. I believe in this place."

"It's a *loan*." Roz emphasized the last word. "Not a gift. It will get repaid—every penny—and my hope is to hand most of it back to you as soon as the government grant money comes in."

Brandy looked around the table as if to explain. "It was a windfall."

"It was payment for bullshit," Roz muttered.

Brandy laughed and Beck added, "If we got adequately paid for bullshit, none of us would be in this position."

Roz laughed too hard for a moment. As if it was all a little too much.

Brandy continued. "That's true. I got lucky. I considered it karma for the shit that went down with Theo."

At Lynzee's confused look, Brandy told the whole table about how she'd locked herself in the bathroom fifteen minutes before she was supposed to walk down the aisle. About how Theo had slept with her sister and then lied about not doing it and had even bribed Sammy to get her on board. Eventually though, Sammy had caved.

The others seemed to have already known most of it. Well, Ash knew all of it. Beck and Roz seemed to have picked up pieces here and there. But Lynzee's mouth fell open. "He did that?"

"All of it," Brandy admitted, feeling a rank fool and thinking she had a smidgeon of understanding how Roz had felt with her son here, actively belittling her. Theo at least hadn't done that.

Then she turned to Roz again. "What if it's not a loan?"

She looked at the rest of them. "I mean, I'd like to have a fraction of it back." She rattled off a number. "I'd eventually love to have that in my savings. Maybe use it as a down payment on my own place."

"Of course," Roz assured her again. "I'll gladly pay every penny of it back. I don't want charity."

Brandy thought about the small part she wanted back. She was thinking she wanted to stay here, but her feelings on that might be contingent on whether or not she could get Ash back.

She couldn't help it. Her eyes darted across the table to him, catching the blue of his that seemed to have been deeper these past few weeks.

She'd *heard* him. She knew she could never undo going back to LA with Theo. But maybe she could convince him that what they had was real. Maybe there was a way forward.

She turned to Roz and asked more clearly, "What if it's an investment?"

CHAPTER FIFTY-NINE

It was a week later that Ash noticed the mood around the dinner table. It had been better since Calvin left. Since Brandy offered up her money, and Roz said she didn't even need anyone's salary.

It was true that money couldn't buy happiness, but it certainly could change unhappiness. Roz's underlying tension was gone. She had never explained, and no one had asked what Calvin had said about her failing at previous businesses or being put on psych hold. As far as Ash was concerned, whatever it might be, if she had it under control, then she had it under control and it wasn't his place to ask.

He wouldn't begrudge any kind of recovering addict either and, honestly, the number of times that he'd left his family and then went back years later made him feel like a relapsed addict himself. So, no, he would not judge Roz.

She was lighter, it was obvious. The smiles crinkled at the corners of her eyes more than they had before. The food even got a little bit better. Whether that was because there was a little money to go around, or simply because the people weren't quite under the stress of the shoestring budget, he couldn't tell. Hell,

Roz and Beck had shared the stress of knowing that it wasn't a *shoestring* budget, but a *thread* already starting to fray.

Though everyone around him was doing better—even Lynzee was present and participating, already moved into the fourth cabin—Ash didn't feel any better.

Roz refused to speak about business at the dinner table, but now they were each eating with a dog sitting at their side, waiting patiently. They were taking them back to their cabins in the evenings and training them to live in a room with a person.

Beck even had them waking up in the middle of the night and faking needing help. Ash wouldn't miss when that ended, but he did find he liked having a companion.

He missed the kittens, and he missed Brandy.

They'd had a class about the incoming humans with Roz showing pictures of who the dogs were being matched to. Ash had gone so far as to show the pictures to the dogs. Graduation would happen without the underlying fear that one thing going wrong could tank the whole sanctuary.

Only, the underlying tension in him hadn't changed. He knew what it was, too.

Shouldn't he be getting over her by now? Shouldn't something give? Shouldn't he feel better about the decision that he'd made?

If he compared it to any other big decision in his life, it didn't feel the same. When he had broken up with Rena all he'd felt was overwhelming relief. Each time he decided to cut off his mother, he felt freer. Yet here he was—he'd cut Brandy off. Not as a friend, not as a coworker, but as whatever they had been.

Everything was fine—or so he told himself. He no longer had a lover. He stopped himself when he wanted to run to tell her something. He no longer had his falsely inflated hopes to curl up with at night.

Ash didn't feel lighter. He felt heavier.

"I will be here with the dogs for Thanksgiving," Roz

announced, a big grin on her face. No one asked if she was going to have Thanksgiving with her son. In fact, probably no one wanted to.

The subject of Calvin had not been brought up again or the fact that Calvin had a different last name than the boss lady.

"I can handle all the dogs by myself," she said, "so you're all free to go for the weekend. Does Wednesday through Saturday sound good?"

"It sounds really good," Beck perked up. "I have plans for Thanksgiving Day. Is it okay if I take the car out overnight?"

He was the last one Ash had expected to have plans. They all knew now that he'd sold his car to fund the Sanctuary. He was using Roz's car where he could.

"However you need it." She said it with confidence, as though she didn't even calculate for her being stuck on the mountain without it. Ash guessed she had the van if she really needed it.

Not having any family he was willing to spend the day with, Ash expected to be here himself. He volunteered.

"I'm staying, too." Brandy said. "I just went home and visited, and I'll be glad to not have to deal with the travel again."

Lynzee curled one lip. "My mom is expecting me. But it's close, so I'll just be out for the day on Thursday."

The conversation moved as though there was a small wall between him and Brandy. Everything else flowed freely. If anyone else noticed it, they didn't say anything.

"I know we aren't supposed to talk business at dinner. But I had a question," Brandy asked. When Roz shot her the stink eye, she added with a polite smile, "So please tell me when dinner is officially over, and I can ask."

A while later, when the plates were empty and they started to stand to carry the dishes back, Roz told her she could ask.

"Why are we still operating on a threadbare budget?"

They all looked at her like she was crazy.

She defended the choice. "I think we should spend some of the money on converting the other rooms."

Roz looked at her, "I don't want to overspend. I want to use it wisely."

"I totally agree. I am absolutely a silent partner here. Not even a partner! My investment is miniscule. And obviously, I'm sucking at being silent. However, I'm just throwing it out there." She stood with a dish in each hand and looked at each one of them in turn. It had become far more of a democracy once the floodgates had been opened.

"Look, I don't have many good things to say about Theo, but he did teach me about investing and managing money. We know that startup businesses perform better in the long run—much less likely to fail—if they're well-funded at the start. Operating on a shoestring budget can be penny wise and pound foolish."

Roz started to open her mouth and Brandy waved her one dish at her to ward her off. "I know that's not what you did. *Penny wise and pound foolish* refers to when you actually have pounds to invest. You were making the best decisions based on what you had at the time. However, that's not the case anymore. I think it's worth considering what kinds of things would get this business running better, faster."

Ash looked to Roz then Beck. Then he caught Lynzee looking around, too. She might be young, and she might be hourly, but she'd volunteered her salary, too. She deserved a voice. He also had to admit that Brandy might be right.

They'd been thinking under old constraints that didn't exist anymore.

"How many dogs can we train in the next round?"

"Five," Roz answered quickly.

"But you want to train more per round, right?"

Roz nodded, the look on her face told Ash she wasn't dismissing the idea out of hand.

"What's limiting that?" Brandy asked.

"We have kennels for more than five. So, it's not that." Beck pointed out. "And graduating more in the second class gets more money in faster."

Brandy nodded and let him run with it.

"The staff now has a much better idea of what they're doing," he set down the stack of plates he'd been taking into the kitchen, his eyes off in the corner of the room as he calculated. "If we train two dogs of the same skill set, we could train almost double the number of dogs for very little extra effort. What limits us is the number of rooms to put people in when they come to graduate."

Roz loaded dishes directly into the industrial dishwasher that they never seemed to quite fill. "That's a really valid point. But maybe we can still save the money. The rooms are useless when empty—we heat and pay for this place every day regardless. So maybe we can stagger the graduations."

Ash jumped into the conversation now. They were hitting his forte. "That would mean staggering the costs of testing incoming dogs and getting shelter fees or grants again. It would mean we don't take such a big hit if a dog washes out."

He was comfortable with the idea, though he wasn't saying it directly to Brandy. Even if it was her idea to start. Even if he wanted to tell *her*.

He also knew he hated the idea that it was *Theo* who was helping them out. But it wasn't, it was Brandy, simply using the things she could from the bad situation she'd been in. At least she got something out of it.

Beck added more in. "Staggering the graduations should be fine. It does mean probably a couple of weeks between because the dogs who are in the second round will get less time and attention while the others do their specific trainings with their human, and they won't get quite as much training then."

"Also, just to give ourselves a buffer should something go . . . less than smooth," Ash added, and they all nodded.

Lynzee spoke, her voice soft. "It also depends on you having the same amount of staff that you have right now."

Nobody seemed to follow. But Ash did. So, he said it. "Brandy's leaving after the first graduation. Which means that we lose an experienced dog trainer. We can hire someone, but they won't know exactly what Jade River Sanctuary does."

They'd have to take time to train the new person. He was looking to Beck, wondering what the man thought, but Roz turned to Brandy.

"He's got a very valid point with that. That might be where the money needs to go—training your replacement. Unless?" Roz waited a beat and asked it out loud. "You'd like to stay for another cycle?"

His heart broke yet again, and he hated himself for waiting on her answer.

CHAPTER SIXTY

I f Brandy had expected a subdued Thanksgiving, she was in
for a surprise.

Roz had shooed her out of the kitchen early Thursday
morning but, from the produce, cans, and assorted items on the
counter, it was clear that she had plans.

However, as she pushed Brandy out the door and closed it
behind her, her boss warned her. "I'm only a decent chef, but I
want to do what I can."

Brandy had been unceremoniously plopped into the hallway,
the kitchen door clicked firmly behind her. She turned and
found Ash looking at her.

"Clearly any attempts to enter the kitchen are not going to
fly today," he told her. His tone was a bit jovial. Had he softened
toward her?

"Strictly verboten!" she answered with a smile.

Something clattered to the floor and Roz called out quickly,
"Everything is *fine!*"

"What's happening in there?" Ash asked conspiratorially, as
she had actually managed to see inside, and he hadn't.

Brandy could only shrug. She had no real idea. Roz hadn't let her look long enough to put any of the pieces together. "Just the usual traditional stuff?"

Roz had been clear that they were taking the day off—no training. She'd fed the dogs in the morning and played with them already.

Without being able to help in the kitchen, and no assigned tasks, Brandy didn't know what to do. Her cabin was warm, but tiny. The grounds outside were wide open, but chilly.

With a tip of his head, Ash turned and walked away. Even though they weren't training today, he'd said something about the clinic yesterday. As Brandy inadvertently followed along, thinking she might take the dogs out in the yard and throw the ball or find a stick, Ash was already ahead of her.

Everything to do was already covered or called off.

Wherever she went, it was going to be lonely. She headed back to the cabin for a little bit, enjoying the warmth that enveloped her as she headed inside. The mountaintop had grown as cold as the space between her and Ash. It had been far too long, but not long enough for her heart to get over him.

She scrounged her way through her own tiny kitchen and put together an egg sandwich. She ate it at her table, scrolling through social media, grateful that Roz had made sure there was adequate signal on the mountain top.

As she chewed, Brandy wondered *had she made the wrong decision?* Should she have gone home for the holiday?

Her family was large. Her mom had told her Rick had to work today and wouldn't make it until Friday. But everyone else would be there. For a disturbing moment, Brandy wondered if Theo was included, as he was now confirmed as the father of their first grandchild. Still, Brandy thought, she would have been around family.

She turned the phone the other direction and started tapping at it, waiting while it rang and enjoying her mother's exuberant, "Brandy! It's so good to hear from you."

"I just wanted to check in and wish everybody a happy Thanksgiving."

"Right now, I'm in the middle of cutting apples for the pie." Oh, just the thought of a good Blackwell apple pie made her mouth water. "Let me hand you over to your father."

Brandy didn't tell her no, even though she fully understood that getting handed over to her father meant getting handed off one by one to everyone else. Maybe she could shut that down. But her father kept her on the line for a few minutes to himself. "How is the dog training going?"

"The training is really good. We are on track to graduate all four remaining dogs on time!" She paused and thought through something she'd learned. "I liked my regular job, but there's something really cool about seeing the names and faces of the people who will get these dogs. It's *direct good* if that makes sense."

"It does!" he agreed and asked, "Are there enough people left behind to make Thanksgiving worthwhile?"

"Only three of us today and I just got booted from the kitchen. From the looks of it, we're getting a full multi-course meal tonight."

Her dad next handed her off to Gary Jr, then to the twins. Then, without any irony at all, he took the phone back and sadly informed her that Sammy had not yet arrived. "You'll miss the chance to talk to your sister, unless you call back later. Or I can tell her to call you!"

"Just tell her I said Happy Thanksgiving," Brandy said as politely as possible before she hung up. Had her father remained that clueless or was he simply that optimistic? Probably a combination of both.

Though Sammy had finally had enough of Theo, it wasn't enough to set things right. Brandy was grateful her sister saved her from playing the fool for any longer. But that didn't change that her dirty ex fiancé had talked Sammy into accepting money to say it was Curtis's baby. Or that Sammy had slept with him in the first place!

Grabbing a book, Brandy headed into the lodge where at least she could be inside and be warm, but the four walls would be different. At the back door, she was greeted by six exuberant dogs. Not only were Shadow and Astra loose in the main area, but so were all four training dogs. Brandy was glad they were just getting to be regular puppies today.

She settled into one of the big leather chairs, thinking that she would be on hand if anything dropped, shattered, or caught on fire in the kitchen. Though there were a series of noises, each time something clattered, Roz called out "I'm fine! Everything's fine!"

Brandy read until she was hungry again, at which point she forced her way into the kitchen, demanding some level of food from Roz.

Pushing a metal baking bowl at her, Roz pointed inside to the puffs there. Brandy popped one into her mouth before she recognized it. "Oh, these are delicious."

"I hope it's okay . . . that I made them." Roz turned back to the apple pie she was putting together. Brandy would get some anyway and try not to compare it to her family's recipe.

"Why would it not be okay that you made them?" Brandy grabbed a second one, the savory sausage and cheese flavor melting on her tongue.

"Good point," Roz replied as though Brandy had said something profound. She popped one into her own mouth. "I've been snacking on them all day." But then her expression grew wistful as she looped back to where she'd started. "I was told for years not to make them. That they were poor or trashy."

"They're delicious." Brandy said, "Sausage puffs, right? I know I've had a version of these before."

"Yes." Roz turned back to a second, empty pie crust, and

Brandy wondered if the three of them were expected to eat all this food. "We'll set the table in an hour."

Brandy stayed put, popping a few more puffs into her mouth until Roz pushed the whole bowl at her. Accepting the offer, Brandy cradled it in her arm and headed back to the front lounge of the lobby and her book.

She curled back into the chair that she now knew Ash and Roz had reclaimed. She tried not to think about what might have lived in the cushions before her, but probably nothing. It was in good shape, and it was clean now.

When the table was set with ten different dishes, she asked Roz jokingly, "Is it enough?"

"I want to have enough leftovers for Lynzee and Beck tomorrow," Roz told her.

Ash came through the door then and they settled in. Dinner was an exuberant affair, impressive given that there were just the three of them at it. And given that two of the three were barely managing to talk like normal people most days.

When they were all stuffed, and the pumpkin pie and whipped cream was taking center court, Roz shoved them out of the way, insisting on doing the dishes herself.

Ash thanked her and stood up to leave. Knowing she wouldn't get many chances with the Sanctuary this quiet, Brandy followed. This was her shot.

CHAPTER SIXTY-ONE

"Are you following me?" Ash asked but didn't turn around to face her.

Brandy had expected to make it all the way back to his cabin and knock on his door. She didn't think he even noticed she was back here. But if they were doing this here in the open in the cold, then she was willing.

She didn't think she could hold out much longer. "Yes. Will you talk to me?"

"I talk to you all the time."

"You know what I mean." She pulled her thick jacket tighter around her. Maybe this would work, but maybe not if he was pushing her away already. She'd thought they were doing better these last few days. Perhaps it wasn't the sign she'd read it as.

"I was concerned," she started, "when I was lonely today. I was lonely for most of the day. Thinking that I should have gone home, that I should have battled the crowds and dealt with the travel and been there."

He still hadn't turned around. "Maybe you should have."

She ignored him. "Then I realized it would have been lonely there, too."

It felt like she was slicing a knife into her own chest, ready to cut out her heart. She was prepared to hold it out to him into the chilly night, but it seemed he didn't respond at all to her pain.

"I miss you." She dug the blade a little deeper.

"I miss you too." Hope swelled hot and heavy in her chest. She couldn't tamp it down, but his next words did that for her. "I just don't think it changes anything."

He still hadn't moved from where he stood at the edge of the open space, looking over the outdoor training area of Jade River Sanctuary.

Brandy looked at his back, at the broad shoulders that she had once been allowed to touch. At the dark hair she'd run her fingers through, holding him closer to her. At the jacket she would have gladly peeled off him . . . but he now seemed so, so far away.

Was he looking through the trees at the sky beyond?

Not good enough, she thought. Brandy took several steps forward, her feet warm in her boots. It was her fingers that were exposed, chilly in the biting night air. She stepped sideways, walked a small semicircle, and planted herself directly in front of him, facing the man she loved. If he wouldn't look at her, she would make him. "You said you couldn't keep loving people who didn't choose you."

He nodded slowly and barely blinked, only giving her credit for being correct and nothing more.

She dug the knife a little deeper into her chest, reached in and held out her own heart, right there between them. "Does that mean that you love me?"

He didn't answer. The silence grew heavy. Her heart grew cold. She didn't think it could hurt any more than it already did, yet somehow it always seemed to. She tried a little harder. "Because I love you. I still love you and I know that I screwed up, but I need to know if there is any second chance for us."

He looked away, then down at the ground near his feet and she didn't know what it meant.

"I've been here before." His words were soft but firm. Too firm. "You chose what you chose, and I'm sorry that it didn't work out for you."

"That's not what it was—"

"It doesn't matter what it was." He cut her off. "It's what you chose. What you chose wasn't *me*. And yes, I loved you."

The past tense wasn't lost on her.

Brandy wished she could put her cold heart back into her chest and it would start beating again. It felt now as if she had ripped it out forever.

He was so calm, standing there in front of her, his face not moving. Could he not see that she was dying? Maybe he did. Maybe he just didn't care.

She called him on it. "You loved me, but you don't anymore?"

"I'm trying not to," he told her and this time he took a firm step to the side, clearly moving around her before continuing to his cabin.

She stood still for a moment staring blankly back at the lodge, then up at the sky. Only then did she realize the wetness on her face wasn't tears.

She should be crying. She should be bawling. She should be worried that Roz was watching out the kitchen window and seeing her epic failure. But it wasn't any of that. She was too numb. She was too cold. There were no tears to come.

As she felt the flakes on her face, she looked up and realized that it had begun to snow.

CHAPTER SIXTY-TWO

He'd gone back to his cabin, walking carefully so as not to reveal just how mad her words made him.

She loved him? *Now?*

Ash was glad the kittens were all safely in their new homes. The fumes of anger coming off him likely lit up the whole place.

Maybe Brandy didn't know what love was. It sure as hell wasn't going back to your ex to try to work things out. It wasn't *"he's a liar but not as bad of a liar as I thought."*

And it sure fucking wasn't *"I went back to my ex and that didn't work out so I guess I love you now."*

He knew better.

So why did he still have these feelings for her?

Even being around her all the time, he should have been over it. He'd done it before—forced his heart to comply with his head. He knew the old adage that *We don't choose who we love* was true. But he also knew that reminding himself what Rena had done to him had helped him see her in a different light, a truer light. And he had fallen out of love with her.

He'd *learned*. He'd understood that the woman he'd loved for two years didn't exist other than in his mind. Telling himself who the real Rena was, over and over, had gotten him out of that loop. It had saved him when she came back around, thinking she could hook her claws into him again.

So why wasn't that working now?

Brandy hadn't chosen him.

He didn't even taken off his coat. He was starting to overheat, pacing angrily around the cabin, stomping from one side of the bed to the other in a concerning U. She couldn't do that to him.

He flung open the door, barely catching it before it slammed the wall and pulling it shut behind him. He was at her door before he knew what he was doing.

Ash didn't even bother to knock, just turned the knob, unsurprised to find she hadn't locked it.

Brandy was doing something on the bedside table, and she turned, startled, her eyes softening when she saw it was him. "Ash!"

Her voice was breathy, a sweet shot to his heart.

"You can't do that!"

"Come inside. It's cold."

He closed the door but didn't take his jacket off. "You can't tell me you love me. It's not okay."

"I do, though." She paused, now standing at the foot of the bed, only a few feet away in the tiny space. "Why can't I say what's true?"

"Because it's not true!" He wasn't rational. Ash knew that. But he was never going to be rational—to be *okay*—again, if he didn't put a stop to this.

"It is true."

He shook his head. "I get that you think it is, but it's not. So you can't say things like that to me."

The air waited between them. She took a step forward.

He almost retreated, but the door was at his back, and he refused to give ground.

"It shouldn't matter what I say if you don't still have feelings for me." She almost whispered it and it tugged at every cell in him. As if she were a magnet whose pull he could not resist.

She had him. He couldn't say he didn't have feelings for her. But that was the problem.

He looked at her, really looked. Her red hair was down out of its usual ponytail. She was in a T shirt, her cabin unusually warm. The cotton hugged at the curves he remembered the feel of. Her mouth was full, and her breasts moved with the depth of her breathing—the only thing giving away that she was as affected as he was.

The hazel of her eyes was the deep, mossy green that he remembered from being inside her. He was lost.

Her hands reached up to his shoulders and he felt his eyes shut—as if by not looking she couldn't have an effect on him. Her touch caressed his shoulders, pushing the coat back even as she spoke, her breath whispering in his ear. "Take your jacket off, you'll overheat."

He was already overheating.

He heard the jacket hit the ground at his feet. Her fingers never left him. They slid softly, seductively down his shoulders to his waist. She grabbed at his shirt, taking fistfuls of it. The flannel had no give and she tugged him forward.

As if the flannel was the problem here.

No, he was.

Ash was under her spell again.

He knew better. He wanted to be free of her. But he so desperately wanted this, too. He needed her touch, the soft words. He needed to believe that she did love him, that she could.

He felt her lips touch his.

CHAPTER SIXTY-THREE

Brandy kissed him for all she was worth. Could this one touch alone make him see that she did love him? That it was real. That it was good—good for both of them.

She tugged him down and brushed her lips against his, but he didn't respond.

He didn't pull away, either.

Still holding him close with fistfuls of his shirt, she pushed up onto her toes. Her whole body pressed to his, her breasts feeling the hard planes of his chest, her hips against his, the pressure there belying his aloofness.

He wanted her.

She kissed him with everything she had. Open mouth, tongue reaching for his, breathing from his breath. She tilted her head, fitting them together, kissing a man who wasn't leaving, but still wasn't kissing her back.

Then she ground her hips into his.

The whole game changed.

His arms came around her, holding her closer than she thought possible. One hand reached into her hair, tangling through the waves and controlling her head. His other hand reached down around her ass, pulling her up against the hard ridge of him as he ground his hips against hers.

She almost didn't notice.

He was kissing her as if she were his. As if she were all that he ever needed.

Brandy wanted to be that for him.

He needed that from her.

Ash was half lifting her, half walking her backwards, and Brandy didn't fight it. It was only three, maybe four, steps before the back of her legs hit the end of the bed and she tumbled onto it, but Ash stayed plastered to her. His weight pushed her down onto the comforter.

The bed smelled clean . . . but now it would smell like him.

She wrapped her legs around him, keeping him close, kissing him as if the world would end if she stopped. And maybe it would.

Maybe it would end because his hand slipped under the edge of her shirt, sliding up along her ribs, fire tracing his touch. He tugged at her bra strap, pulling the fabric down until his fingertips touched her nipple under the cotton of her shirt.

She arched her back, wanting more of his touch, pressing harder into his hand. Surprise rushed through her like wildfire when he growled and bent down to take her into his mouth through the shirt.

His touch was mind-numbing. She was a needful ball of want, writhing to get closer to him, though they were already pressed together. When he stopped, he held himself above her, breathing heavily and looking down at her, blue eyes deeper than she'd ever seen them.

Something in him was torn.

She wanted to mend it.

Grabbing at the hem of his shirt, she pulled it up and over his head, awkwardly pinning his arms for a moment, and taking

303

advantage of that to lay a fiery streak of kisses across his pecs. She bit and nibbled, eliciting groans and sighs.

The sound of Ash's voice, rumbling in pleasure, in her room, again . . . it was all that she needed. Or so she told herself. This was her whole world right now. There was nothing beyond the four close walls of the tiny cabin. No cold wind, no snow coming down, no change of seasons, no new people at the sanctuary. Just the heat and need that filled this one space.

He lifted one hand, then the other, peeling the tangled shirt she'd left behind and leaving it on the bed next to them. Grabbing her head, he pulled her from her downward path and stared at her for a moment as if he were deciding what to do.

Brandy couldn't let him decide. She decided for them. With every muscle in her core on fire already, she lifted herself up, peeled her own shirt from where one large breast already peeked free. Then, while he watched, mesmerized, she pulled the bra off and dropped it over the edge of the bed. She wrapped her arms around him, pulled him closer, skin to skin, and kissed him.

He couldn't seem to really hear her when she spoke, so maybe he would hear her now. Locking her legs around him, she moved her hips against his. She heard his breath hiss in as she did it.

Or was it hers?

They kissed like that for an eternity, but when Ash didn't move to take the rest of their clothing off, Brandy did. Her fingers found the button on the front of his jeans, popped it open and pushed at the waist band.

She ran her hands under the denim and over his ass, grabbing and pulling him closer, enjoying the sound of his groan at her touch. The sound of a man who had given in.

His mouth covered hers again, and he tasted her, greedy for more. She was willing to give it. But she was on autopilot, her conscious thought gone, driven only by the primal need to feel him inside her.

Her fingers moved between them, reaching for him—

Then, suddenly, everything went cold.

Ash pulled back, his blue eyes icy. His hand reached down and circled her wrist before she could touch him.

"We can't."

"But—" But they already *were*. Her mouth was open, her breasts heaving with the movement of her heavy breathing. It matched his.

He was turned on. He *wanted* this as much as she did.

But his hand gripped hers tightly and he said it again, "We can't. *I* can't."

CHAPTER SIXTY-FOUR

B randy watched as Abby's mother hugged her goodbye. Abby was eighteen. Brandy recognized all the people coming for the dogs from the pictures Roz had been circulating. Abby would be getting Katherine, the seeing eye dog.

"Welcome, Abby," Brandy called out. She'd spent the last week trying to forget her night with Ash. It was her own fault. She knew that, but she hadn't quite shaken the guilt or managed to turn off the hot dreams that taunted her since.

Abby turned around to face Brandy and Roz on the porch, her cane out in front of her, ready to tap at the ground. Behind her, her mother motioned, pointing at her daughter, making sure the staff knew that Abby was important.

They knew the story. Abby was heading off to college the following fall. Her parents wanted their blind daughter to go with a companion.

Abby made it two steps before she stopped, her expression growing cross. "Mom! Stop motioning behind my back! I'll be fine."

Brandy tried to suppress a laugh, grateful for the moment of levity. She'd needed it.

Next to her, Roz grinned as the mom sighed and called out, "Busted," before adding, "Take good care of her."

"They will!" Abby said before continuing forward, leaving her mother behind. "Brandy? Roz? Lynzee?" she asked. "I only hear two people."

"I'm Brandy." Brandy stepped forward not surprised that Abby had great ears.

"I'm Roz." Her boss moved next as Abby made her way competently up the ramp they'd installed for their wheelchair user and shook Abby's hand as she held it out to her.

"Lynzee is in the back with the dogs and our first arrival. If you'd like to go through, you can start to meet everyone."

"I've been paired with Katherine?" Abby asked.

"Yes. We named all our dogs after famous firsts. You're more than allowed to change her name, but she's currently on the records as Katherine Switzer—the first woman to run the marathon."

Abby's face lit up. "Then she shall stay Katherine. I think Katherine and I should run a marathon together!"

"It's ambitious. But hey, go for it," Brandy said. "Shall we go meet her?"

"Absolutely. She's part Greyhound, right?"

"Perfect for running," Brandy agreed. "Are you a runner already?"

Brandy was talking like a normal person. But for a full week she'd been replaying her night with Ash in her head. Her conversations happened over the memories and useless analysis.

Brandy looked at Abby's build, she was athletic. So she wasn't surprised when Abby replied, "Oh yes. I ran distance in high school, and I struggled to find humans who could keep up with me as a pacer."

Brandy opened the door to the lodge, thinking about Ash grabbing her hand and holding her. He'd told her, "I can't." But she'd stared him in the eyes and reached down, grabbing his cock anyway, stroking him from base to tip until his eyes closed and his head fell back.

In the real world, she heard another car pull up behind them. Though Brandy and Roz turned to face it, Abby's head merely tipped in that direction as she listened. Her blond braids barely moving.

The car door opened, and a tall, blond man stepped out, green eyes sparkling. His build was worthy of a model, and he ran a hand through his hair, as if he might know he looked like a photo shoot in the jeans and green T shirt.

Brandy would have wondered just what this man was doing here, except she'd already seen his picture. Devin James.

Brandy heard nothing but wasn't surprised. He waved. Devin was getting matched to Curie, the hearing ear dog.

Roz was already signing *Hello*, though none of them was quite fluent yet. The Boss awkwardly fingerspelled *Devin?* And he nodded, then pointed to himself and made a D at his forehead, moving it slightly away.

"One second," Brandy told Abby. "Devin is here." She tried to sign it and say it at the same time and found that was also a skill she had not mastered. Turning she signed, "Hi, I'm Brandy," spelling out her own name.

"I know," Devin answered. "I saw your pictures."

"This is Abby."

Devin nodded, and Roz took over his introductions as Brandy and Abby once again headed through the lodge toward the back.

The last person, a twelve-year-old named Jeff would be arriving with his parents the next day.

Brandy walked slightly ahead and beside Abby, letting Abby use her cane and listen to Brandy's footsteps. She didn't need a guide or an arm or anything and moved handily through the new space, following perfectly as Brandy headed down the ramp they'd installed on the back steps.

Brandy called out, "Hi Lynzee." Then, when she added, "Hi Ash," for Abby's sake she flashed back to the feel of Ash giving in. How he'd felt, hard and hot and heavy in her palm. How he'd pressed into her touch for a few moments.

He looked at her across the open space, Katherine and Curie sitting perfectly beside him waiting to meet their people. Was the flash of heat in his gaze his own? Or just an answer to hers?

Maybe it was good that Abby was blind. Though she hadn't missed anything so far.

Brandy tried to add a bit of narration for her new companion. "Talia is here, too, with her new companion Sidney. It looks like the two of you are getting along really well."

Talia's dark hair gleamed in the cold air, her chair—fitted with all-terrain tires—moved smoothly over the leveled ground. Sidney was already sitting in her lap. "Oh, we are already best friends."

Abby leaned a little closer, asking, "Sidney's trained to help someone in a wheelchair. Correct?"

"Yes," Brandy replied. "Shall we meet Katherine?"

The greyhound mix was clearly anxious, as was Curie, each one seated on one side of Ash, waiting as he did. Katherine was ready, her trainee jacket and seeing eye harness already on.

Though she could have operated perfectly from hand signals alone, Abby wouldn't be able to hear that, and she wouldn't likely use it much, though they would teach her.

Brandy leaned close to Abby, and said, "Just lean down a little and pat your thighs. Like you would call any dog."

When Abby did it, Ash said the words, "Katherine. Go."

Katherine bounded forward, stopping in a perfect sit right in front of her new person. Brandy beamed up at Ash, thinking *we did it*.

Once again, she found herself remembering what they had

done. How he'd torn at her clothing, stripping her naked and let her strip him. How he'd needed her, how he wanted her. Even if he hadn't wanted to want her.

Forcing herself back to the world as it was, Brandy watched as Abby held out a hand and found the dog's smooth head. She was scratching behind the ears in an instant. "Hello, Katherine. We're going to be great friends."

Brandy stayed next to Abby, giving her small words of encouragement, letting her know she could play with the dog and get to know her. "You're not responsible for any commands, not yet."

Then she thought of the command she'd given Ash when they were both fully naked, when there was no turning back. She'd demanded, "Now."

He'd pushed into her, and she'd cried out at finally feeling him again. She'd held him close and screamed out his name and only later wondered if they'd heard her at the lodge.

No one had said anything.

Did they figure it out? Did they know she'd begged him for more? Did they realize that he gave her everything?

That he came apart in her arms and for one shining moment they were exactly as they were supposed to be.

Then he'd gotten up and said, "This didn't mean anything. And it can't happen again."

He was gone, leaving the heat that had suffused through her to harden into ice and crack. She'd been cold the whole week.

Now, as she looked up across the space, Brandy caught Ash's gaze for just a moment. There was unadulterated joy in his grin. There was a flash of heat at seeing her before he shut it all down.

CHAPTER SIXTY-FIVE

R oz could barely contain herself. The rooms in the lodge were finally full.

Jeff and his parents had arrived the previous evening. They met Tensing Norgay and immediately fell in love with the dog. *Though*, Roz thought, *Who wouldn't?*

Jeff also quickly asked about renaming him, and thus Norgay was now going by Haku.

"He's my favorite dragon from my favorite movie," Jeff had grinned.

"That sounds like a great name," Roz had grinned as Jeff's dad put his hand on his son's head for just a moment. Something that it appeared he wasn't going to be able to do much longer, the kid was going to grow quickly. Haku would be great for him.

His dad added, "Haku the dragon also transforms into a boy."

"It's perfect." Roz offered her support.

Jeff had type one diabetes. His parents were used to waking up in the middle of the night and checking his blood sugar while Jeff slept through it. But as he became older and more independent, yet not quite adult enough to constantly keep track of his own blood sugar, a dog like Norgay—now Haku—was going to make his life radically better.

Tonight, Roz had left all the dogs for the first time, in their rooms with their new people. So far, it was all going as well as she could have hoped. Even having Buzz wash out of the program meant that Jeff and Haku had one room and his parents had a separate room right next door.

After seeing everyone settled, Roz headed to the clinic where the others were standing around one of the exam tables. Roz had called them all here, not quite knowing where else to do this. She hadn't thought through it before now.

Though all the guests were staying on the ground floor of the lodge, Roz wasn't sure how soundproof the upper rooms would be. Plus, aside from her own suite, the rooms remained empty and unfurnished.

The dining room didn't have doors that closed, and she'd told everyone they had free access to the kitchen and the food there. So now the five of them stuffed themselves around a room in a tighter fit than was generally expected. Brandy was mushed in next to Ash and Roz could see the war in their eyes.

She reminded herself it wasn't her battle.

"There's nothing to talk about that's bad," she told them, watching as everyone visibly relaxed. "I'm sorry if I stressed you out. I just didn't want anyone hearing us assign them out like work."

"Well, we know Devin wouldn't hear us," Brandy shrugged. Next to her, Ash's eyes flashed.

Jealousy? Roz couldn't have that. Her staff was too small. But damn, she wouldn't get in the middle either. She distracted them by diving in. "Ash, your major job tomorrow is to bring each pair to the clinic, one at a time and discuss the dog's capabilities and proper medical care."

They'd already made a list of special things like shoes for hot pavement—as there wasn't an option with a service dog to simply not walk with them during the hottest parts of the day, or to only take them into grassy areas. There were notes on when veterinary checkups should occur, which was more often than for a standard pet. It was necessary to keep the dogs in peak health and make sure they were functioning at their best. Though the lists would go home with them, it wasn't enough to just hand out a paper. Plus, each dog had slightly different, personal, needs.

"That's all good," Ash agreed, but then glanced around the room. "My only concern is Devin. My ability to communicate at a veterinary level isn't solid in ASL."

"Understood," Roz told him. None of them were fully fluent yet and interacting with Devin had quickly taught them they weren't even as good as they thought they were. She told Ash, and the others, "We'll all be adding text and writing wherever necessary."

She got a nod of agreement from each of the four. It wasn't news, and it wasn't the best option, but it was what they had.

"I'll interpret wherever I can," Lynzee offered. Though she kept a straight face, it was clear that she didn't mind spending extra time in the good-looking man's company.

"Wherever it helps," Roz told her. Because, the fact was, Lynzee was the one who picked up the language like a pro.

Though Roz had liked the girl's initial employment application, she'd had several that she thought would be a good fit. Now, she could fully admit that she'd hired Lynzee on a bit of a bleeding-heart whim. After interviewing with her, it appeared the girl needed something—more support than she was getting, a place she could thrive. Roz didn't know what it was, but she had sensed a bit of a wounded spirit, or at least a kindred one.

Looking around the room now, she could see that Ash and Casey were her only hires where her emotions hadn't come into play. But she was grateful now for each of them and she regretted nothing.

"Brandy, I'm moving you over to work with Jeff and his family."

"I thought I was with Talia."

"You were, but Jeff's mother seems to really like you. And she *listens* to you."

Brandy nodded. It wasn't a surprise. Though Jeff's father seemed open to anything they said, his mother wasn't.

"She's full of research," Roz added. "It's valuable, so listen to her, too. Feel free to incorporate the things that she says," Roz told Brandy. "In fact, try to do it. It will probably make her more open to the things we can't budge on."

Brandy nodded along. "She's definitely more knowledgeable about type one diabetes than we are."

"True, but remember, you're the dog expert," Roz told her with a conviction she wished Brandy would carry.

"Oh, the irony," Brandy said, carrying out her usual self-concern about her time on the job. She likely had no doubt that her almost six months shouldn't qualify her as an expert.

Roz stared her down, "You've got six months ahead of her, and you know Haku better than she does. Stand firm."

Feeling like Brandy would do her best, and hopefully show the woman that she was more than competent, Roz turned to Beck. "You've got Katherine and Abby. They're doing great."

"But they need to work together the most closely," he filled in.

"Exactly." They knew what they were doing. She was proud of this group. They had another week and a half to go before they could declare round one a success, but she could almost taste it. Calvin Sr, Calvin Jr and her history be damned.

When the meeting was finished and everyone was up to speed on their assignments for the next day, they all headed different directions, back to their cabins as she made her way back toward the lodge.

Her heart was full. The dogs were going to be good. There were no apparent problems in the matches. She had not expected any, but she'd braced herself for the possibilities.

Soon, this place would feel empty, and she would give her trainers a full week of vacation. She would also pay Beck back for his car, with interest. To a certain extent, she hoped he would buy a new car for himself. He'd been flitting off here and there, even doing overnight visits, with her car. She didn't mind, but she felt she knew too much and not enough of where her car was going. She told herself she wasn't curious and that it wasn't her business.

Him not having to use her car to do any of it would help ease the curiosity that ate at her. Now if she could just get Ash to . . .

What?

The fact was even she didn't know what he needed.

She didn't need to play matchmaker for him and Brandy. Maybe the week off would get him far enough away to sort out his head. But she couldn't give them that space until the end of the program. There simply weren't enough employees at the Sanctuary to make that happen—money or not.

Brandy's heartache was obvious. She would either get over Ash or she wouldn't.

And Ash? Roz had no idea how he was going to react when she told him.

CHAPTER SIXTY-SIX

Ash was becoming less and less of a fan of Jeff and his mother.

"Mom, stop!" Jeff squirmed away from her touch.

She immediately responded, "No," and continued messing with his hair.

Though the more Ash thought about it, the more he realized the things he didn't like about the kid were simply Jeff's reaction to an overbearing mother.

At least the dad stepped in. "No one cares about his hair here, honey."

She looked around to the rest of them, and finally quit interfering with her child while he was learning to work with his dog.

"Can I do this myself today?" Jeff asked Ash directly. There was a clear plea in the child's eyes and Ash figured it was the only way he'd ever figure out what the kid could do.

"I think that's a great idea." Ash saw that Brandy was about to answer, but he spoke first, cutting everyone off. The more he thought about it, the more Ash believed the dog and the kid needed this. Ash looked to Mr. And Mrs. Turner. "Haku will be spending the bulk of his time with Jeff, and often with Jeff alone. He should probably be working on his own here, too."

The mother threw up her hands, but his dad turned her away, saying, "I think it's a great idea."

Brandy stepped in then, smoothing things over. "Obviously, you'll all need to work with Haku and all have the training, but we do need to see how Jeff handles him on his own."

Mr. Turner agreed and told his son, "Jeff, please remember, you're the youngest one here, but you'll need to act like an adult and show them that you can earn Haku's trust."

What a great way of putting it. Ash tucked that away for later as Jeff nodded, and said, "Okay," already sounding more adult. The kid didn't watch his parents leave the area, but stood at attention, with one quick hand signal to Haku, re-asking the dog to stay, even though Haku was already doing his job.

Abby, still looking straight ahead, tried to help. "Don't worry Jeff, my mom also applied for my dog, and she tried to come with me."

Jeff kept looking forward but giggled just a little.

Lynzee was standing next to Ash at the front of their open-air classroom today and serving as interpreter for Devin. So, a moment later, Devin laughed, too, and signed—which Lynzee voiced—"My mom applied for my dog, too."

Jeff grinned wider and Talia looked around the group from where she stood. Today she was up and out of the chair for a while, getting Sidney used to blocking things that might bump her.

Abby was eighteen, Jeff twelve. She and Devin were supposed to be the two adults here. "Am I the only one who applied for my own dog?"

"Looks that way." Ash lifted his shoulders at her.

Jeff was smiling, glad to finally be part of the group for real.

Talia sighed, "I did apply for myself, but my firefighter fiancé really pushed me to do this."

Talia had been in Redemption, Nebraska with him when the floods had come, and she had almost lost her life.

"Rex Roma, right?" Ash asked. The firefighter had been part of a crew that helped save Ash and a handful of abandoned dogs during that same flood.

"Yes." The light in her eyes confirmed that they were as good of a match as Ash had originally thought. "Rex just wanted me to have a companion, That way if anything went wrong, I wouldn't be on my own again."

"He's smart. Are you going to make us cupcakes while you're here?" Ash pushed. Talia owned Baby Cakes back in Nebraska and her cupcakes were legendary.

"Oh, now I'm baking for you all?" But her eyes lit up and Devin's head turned.

"You can teach *me* how to make cupcakes. My mom loves them." Lynzee voiced his signs, but Ash was proud that he caught most of it himself. There was something in the man's eyes that said there was more to the story than simply a woman who loved cupcakes. Ash didn't push, they needed to finish this training before the day faded.

Lynzee, Brandy, and Roz joined in, helping individually with corrections, reframing hands for signals, or repeating words or phrases the dogs had been trained to. Until they were all in need of a break.

Beck announced, "Our next training is in a car and around town."

Getting the dogs used to riding in something other than the van was important, so they split up, taking cars and teaching the new owners how to safely harness their companion for a trip.

Ash wound up in the SUV with Roz, trying not to be jealous that Devin was with Lynzee in Brandy's car, the three of them already smiling and laughing like old friends.

This jealousy had no place. He was the one who'd let her go. Brandy had come back to him and, though he'd fucked her, he'd made it clear he didn't want her. This feeling shouldn't even be possible, because he told himself he wasn't in love with her.

But the *shouldn'ts* didn't matter.

He began to wonder if maybe there could be a second chance after all. But as they arrived in Charlottesville, he watched Brandy and Devin close together—the man easily reaching out and touching her hands to correct her signs—Ash realized he might already be too late for second chances.

CHAPTER SIXTY-SEVEN

The large dinner table was full, and Brandy felt the energy in the room. Everyone who worked at the sanctuary signed as they spoke and tried to sign for the others who didn't.

Though Jeff's mother had taken it upon herself to try to learn ASL she was only passable. At least it was keeping her out of other people's hair. Jeff, his dad, and the rest of the staff had managed to convince her that not only could Jeff be capable of handling Haku himself, but that he needed to be.

"Can you pass the broccoli?" Brandy tried to ask with both her voice and her hands, still not quite used to being unable to talk while she held things.

Lynzee sat opposite Devin and tried to interpret for those who didn't sign at all.

The bowl was passed to her, and Brandy tried to be polite, offering it first to Devin, next to her. He politely refused and pointed toward the end of the table, where a batch of freshly made cupcakes of three varieties waited in a lovely arrangement.

Earlier in the day, Talia had taught them all how to make and decorate the cupcakes. It was Beck who had turned the baking lesson into a training session as well. Talia was, after all, a baker and Sidney would have to understand how to be a dog in a kitchen with her. For the others, it was yet another experience that they could practice their good behavior in a new setting. There was no way to give the dogs every possible experience before they left the Sanctuary, so every new one was appreciated.

Brandy, looking at the cupcakes for herself, turned back to Devin and signed, "I understand." Then she looked at the broccoli again and set it down on the table without taking any, making Devin laugh.

Abby looked confused and Ash tried to hide the fact that he was glaring at Brandy, though she didn't know why. Was it because of Devin? But Ash didn't want her. Brandy tried to ignore him, but she couldn't. Even if she didn't look, she was tuned into his every reaction.

The dogs all lay at their owners' sides and the food had stopped moving. The sounds had turned to conversation less than silverware clicking against the china.

"If we're about done," Beck announced, "Then let's try a dog test."

He gave them instructions and each of the dog owners, one by one, faked losing a piece of food over the edge of the table. Then, one by one, they waited, watching as the dogs saw the food and clearly wanted it. None moved. They were well enough trained to not go for it.

After a time with the owners clearly not even paying attention, he told them, "They did good. Pick the food up."

Brandy signed the instructions for Devin, repeating Beck's words. "Put it on your plate and we'll take it to the kitchen."

"They don't get to eat it?" Jeff asked.

"We can't train them that every time we drop food they eventually get to eat it. So sometimes they can, but sometimes they shouldn't. Remember, some foods are dangerous for dogs."

"He can have a little piece of hamburger, though. Can't he?" Jeff asked, looking up at his parents.

"You have to be very careful about table scraps." Beck, once again, launched into his discussion of how mushrooms could harm dogs. So could chocolate. They'd all heard it before, but clearly Jeff needed it again. He was doing well, but he was also twelve.

They put all the dogs on *stay* and filed their way through the kitchen, scraped plates as Roz loaded them into the dishwasher.

Soon enough they were back in the dining room all gathered at the end of the table looking at the cupcakes with big eyes. Until Talia told them, "Go ahead. They were meant to be eaten."

Hands reached out, choosing between cream cheese filled pumpkin spice, chocolate ganache drizzled chocolate ones with frosting piled high on top, and birthday cake with confetti baked into the cake specifically for Jeff.

Talia waited at the back of the group. "I like them all and I eat them all the time. You can choose first."

Devin picked one up and signed one handed. "I have to try the chocolate for my mom." He proceeded to take a huge bite and Brandy watched, remembering he'd said that it was his mother's favorite and the one he was most needing to learn how to make.

Brandy had seen Devin in a new light after that bit of information. He'd been raised by a single mother who had him at age sixteen. Brandy was stunned and horrified by the thought, remembering her own sixteen-year-old self. Then as a teenager his mother had discovered that her baby was deaf, and she hadn't known what to do. Somehow, she'd given him everything.

So now that she needed him, Devin had moved back to the area, quitting his job and finding work closer to home. He'd also appeased his mother by getting a companion dog.

Brandy knew it wasn't her place to ask more than he'd said,

so she picked up one of the pumpkin cupcakes, biting deeply into it. It was heavenly, but she didn't manage it well. She could feel the frosting she'd mushed onto her face.

Devin pointed and awkwardly tried to politely tell her what she'd done.

"I know," she signed, her mouth full. Again, she felt bad for leaving Abby out of the conversation. Sadly, her skills at eating cupcakes, speaking, and signing all at the same time were clearly not up to snuff.

Ash had somehow been grumpy enough to refuse a cupcake and announced to the group at large that he had things to do at the clinic and headed out the back door with polite good-byes.

Would it be worse if he was acting normal? Brandy wondered. Was this grumpiness a sign that something was still there? Or was it just that he was mad at her?

If that was the case, *if there was never going to be anything between them again,* then she should probably go back and tell Roz *No.* Because maybe she just made the biggest mistake of her life.

CHAPTER SIXTY-EIGHT

R oz stood on the wide front porch of the lodge, lined up next to her four employees. Beck stood on her left with Lynzee on the other side of him, and on her right Ash watched with Brandy in the last spot. They all waved as the Turner family drove down the long gravel drive, Haku secured in the backseat, leaving for his forever home to be with his people.

Tears threatened at the edge of her eyes. She'd held it together until now. Roz didn't know if she'd ever been happier than at this exact moment. Four dogs had gone to four good homes. Four people now had service animals who would help them every day. Four dogs who loved having a job were off and being useful.

Even the day that Calvin had been born hadn't been like this. It hadn't been unadulterated. She'd loved her baby more than anything, but so many worries and so many fears crept in at the corners, even then.

As the car disappeared, Roz turned to face her people. *She had people!*

"All right, guys. We've got a debrief and an update and then Brandy, Ash, and Lynzee are all on vacation for a week."

"You're not going on vacation?" Lynzee asked Beck.

"Nope. Roz and I are staying." He answered the group at large. "We're expecting questions when they get home, things that come up that weren't anticipated that they'll need help training. God forbid, anybody gets home and decides they need to bring their dog back, or hopefully just come back and do more training, someone has to be here."

Roz laughed, "Apparently, he's also going to whip Shadow and Astra into shape."

"They're very lazy compared to the other dogs," Beck said as though everyone knew this.

They weren't working dogs, but they could stand a little bit better obedience. They did look particularly unruly compared to the others.

This time when they headed back inside, she sat them around the dinner table. It felt a little empty, compared to having all the seats filled. But she started by asking each of them what went poorly. Then what they would do next round if they were in charge.

Ash started when no one else dove in. "I'd pay more attention to dog size for different kinds of training."

Lynzee held her hand up.

Roz didn't chide her shyness, just motioned for her to speak.

"If we do multiple graduations, we might group the same kind of trainings rather than one of each. Do several seeing eye dogs, several hearing ear dogs, several diabetes dogs, and so on." When they all seemed to like the idea, Lynzee continued, her voice a little stronger. "I think we overused Beck. He was running from one specific training to another. When he showed the Turners how to use Jeff's socks to train Haku what different glucose levels smelled like, he could have taught multiple people at once. Then they'll all benefit from the questions the others ask."

Roz nodded, making a physical note of the idea and a mental one that Lynzee was coming into her own.

Brandy piped up. "I think Lynzee is right. I noticed having Abby and Devin at the same table made communication really difficult. At one point I was trying to sign and speak and eat dinner all at the same time."

Roz made more notes. Beck had ideas about applying additional tests during the initial shelter run. Ash had a question about the clinic.

When they had gone around the table several times, and she had a full page of fantastic ideas, she threw out several of her own, waiting to see what the others thought. In more than one case, somebody pushed back, and the idea was molded and reformed until it worked.

At last, she put the pen down. "In about ten minutes, vacation starts. You start work again a week from Saturday, in the morning. You're welcome to stay here—it's your home—but your time is completely your own. On Saturday and Sunday, we get ready, and on Monday we hit a different shelter in Charlottesville." She smiled with pride. She couldn't help it. "I have a grant for ten dogs this time."

Though she beamed with her news, Lynzee and Ash looked confused. Beck had come to her late at night again and managed to weasel this secret out of her. So he already knew. Before anyone could ask how they would handle ten, she added, "I'm pleased to announce that for the next round of training, all of you are returning."

Lynzee looked surprised this time, but Ash's eyes immediately flipped to Brandy.

Yes, everybody. Roz made her point. "Beck and Ash were already signed to multi-year contracts, but Lynzee has agreed to stay." The girl was getting a raise—something the new grant money allowed for. Roz was so proud that Lynzee had earned it and she could provide it. "So has Brandy."

Lynzee staying wasn't a surprise, Roz knew. Nobody figured the girl would go out and simply get a different job and move away. It was Brandy who'd been intending to leave.

"You're staying?" Ash asked incredulously and maybe a little rudely but voicing what everyone else wanted to know.

Brandy nodded. "I officially quit my job in Los Angeles. At the end of the next term here, I think I'll start looking for something in civil engineering. But I like the area."

Clearly, Brandy hadn't seen her life going this way. Then again, Roz hadn't seen hers going this way either. She owed her sanity to an emotional support dog. She owed some of her own recovery to a trainer who'd helped her out. Now she was making far better decisions for herself and choosing a path she wanted rather than following the one in front of her.

She was glad that this one had opened up. She was glad for a life that included this beautiful place, and all the people in front of her.

Beck caught her gaze as she swept around the table. He frowned, clearly wanting to ask something, but Roz couldn't read his mind.

What he said instead was, "Are we good for ten dogs with this many people?"

"No." Roz grinned. "I've been looking for one more and as of this morning, I officially hired him."

Four expectant faces turned to her. Roz knew her announcement would create friction. A small tight knit group like this operated one way. They'd lost Casey when he went off to school, but to just add someone in? It would be odd.

She told them, "You already know him. I hired Devin James."

"You hired *Devin?*" Brandy asked.

Roz looked around the table, gauging the reactions. Lynzee lit up. Beck seemed surprised. Ash's eyes narrowed. *Oh.*

"Devin already knows the facility and he knows what we do here. He's clearly fluent in sign, so he can train dogs for the

Deaf, which we had intended to do more of in the next round anyway."

Most of them were shaking their heads as they thought it through, then nodded along, understanding the wisdom of her decision.

"I thought he already had a job. He moved out to be closer to his mom," Brandy said.

Once again, Ash's features pinched as though the information bothered him. Or maybe it was just that Brandy had that kind of information that bothered him.

"Apparently, he started it, and it didn't work out."

"What happened?" Lynzee leaned forward, clearly curious.

"I didn't ask." Roz held her hands up. "I just counted myself lucky. Do you know what he's trained as?"

They all shook their heads, except for Brandy, who'd spent enough time with the man. Her mouth fell open as she put it together. "He's a grant writer!"

Again, all eyes opened wider in shock.

"Exactly," Roz said. "He's already set me up with ten other places that he thinks we can go to get more money into the Sanctuary." They could get more units, they could get money for upgrades, some of the things she'd done on little budget or no budget could get run the way they should be. Devin James could be a Godsend.

"Well, that's wonderful," Beck said. "When does he start?"

"He'll be here on Saturday, to start round two, the same as the rest of us." She then asked if they had more questions. They took turns answering for each other until the conversation turned to *what they were going to do with their week off* and that kind of thing.

One by one they said goodbye and trailed out of the lodge. Ash was the last, seeming to wait for a moment alone. "Is hiring him really the right decision?"

She didn't have to ask who he meant. "What do you have

against Devin?" she asked, realizing it sounded almost rhetorical, but she meant it sincerely.

If Ash raised a real objection, she could undo the hiring. But after a moment of contemplation, Ash admitted, "I guess nothing."

Then he added, "I'll see you in a week." And he left.

Roz could only wonder what might happen in that week, and how he might process the information, and what he might do with his new knowledge that Devin would be here and that Brandy was staying.

CHAPTER SIXTY-NINE

Ash hated this. And he hated that he hated it.

It was stupid. He was afraid that Brandy would fall madly in love with Devin. Afraid of small blonde and redheaded babies running around the Sanctuary. It was ridiculous to think he would be stuck here all next spring, watching them fall for each other simply because they actually got along in each other's company.

He knew that. The likelihood of it was small. But he couldn't shake the thought.

Ash also had to accept that it meant he was nowhere near his goal of getting over her. He was nowhere near his own peace, which was the whole point of letting go.

He was so tangled up in all of it that he couldn't even see straight. He now desperately considered what might happen if he gave her a second chance, which was just as ridiculous a thought.

Brandy might have wanted one several weeks ago, but did she even want him back now? He didn't know. She might have had enough of him and, if she had, it would be fair.

What if he asked her to come back? To be with him? What if

it worked out? Couldn't people learn and grow? What if he begged her to come back and all he taught her was that he could be stepped on?

If she walked away again, could his heart break any more than it possibly had for the last month? Because right now, if he really admitted it to himself, he was shattered.

He was supposed to be putting himself back together, finding his own life. In a mad twist of fate, for the most part, it was *working*. He finally had a job that he loved. A place he wanted to stay. He even really liked Beck, which was surprising given that he'd been kind of standoffish to the guy at the beginning.

He was impressed to find out how much he admired the other man. Now Roz had begun paying Beck's full salary again and Ash had noticed that the tattoos across his knuckles had begun to fade more.

And Lynzee, whom he'd doubted in the beginning, still looked like a goth teenager, but she worked like a mad horse and she was fantastic with the dogs. In fact, Ash's fear now was that they would lose her because she'd go to school to become a veterinarian herself.

That felt good, too. He wasn't sure he'd inspired anyone before.

He adored Roz and understood what she was doing here. He even liked the mountain and the view.

What if he begged Brandy to take him back and three years from now she left him again? Would that change anything for him? At least he could have a few years with her. He tried to imagine every possible scenario.

He wasn't sure he wanted kids, so he didn't have a ticking clock. Maybe he should throw himself into it and see what they could make of it. It just seemed that no matter what he did, he would always doubt her, at least until . . .

He'd been so tangled in his own thoughts that he hadn't seen her, not until he almost stepped on her. She was sitting on the steps to his cabin. Just the sight of her made his heart break again.

"What are you doing here?" he asked. Which was stupid, because he'd spent the whole walk from the lodge over here thinking about begging her to take him back.

"I'm staying for six more months," she said.

"I heard."

Though his response was rude, she ignored it. "I'm staying because I want to be with you. You can keep telling me no, but I know that what we had was good and I hope that there's a way to find it again."

He opened his mouth to tell her it wasn't possible, that she'd broken it. That broken things couldn't get put back together. *But they could.*

If they were smart, they would repair the cracks with something stronger than what they'd started with. He took a deep breath and asked, "What would that even look like?"

"I don't know." Her replies were honest at least. "These cabins aren't really big enough for two." She smiled and motioned over her shoulder to the adorable little log building that they'd spent plenty of nights stuffed into together. "If you want, we can date, but I'm already in love with you."

She paused for just a moment and seemed to think about something. "Is that what you doubt? Do I need to find a way to prove that I'm in love with you?"

"I don't doubt that," Ash sighed, shoving his hands into his pockets for something to do with them, to keep from reaching for her. He looked at the cold, hard ground near his boots. "I need you to *choose* me. I don't know how that would even work until the opportunity arose. And I don't know when it will again . . . But I do know the last time you had a chance to, you didn't."

She frowned at him as if she needed an explanation.

He tried. "As soon as Theo asked you to go back, you went back to him. You picked Theo."

Now Brandy stood up, her chest puffed out. Whatever he'd said she didn't like it. She was two out of three steps up and towering over him. That shouldn't have been sexy. He was too confused to be turned on and yet, here he was.

"That's not what it was," she told him. "You've got it all wrong."

CHAPTER SEVENTY

Brandy looked down at Ash, trying to hold back her anger. It wouldn't help. She tried to take a deep breath but only managed a shallow one. "When Theo came back, you waved me away. You seemed to give me every signal that *I should go back.*"

"Well, *yes*, if that's what you wanted, you should go, because I can't stop what you want." His hands were out of his pockets, gesturing to his sides.

"I didn't know what I wanted." Brandy flailed for words. "I knew I wanted you. And I knew I wanted to figure out what the hell had gone wrong at my own wedding."

"And you chose Theo!" He practically yelled it.

She wondered if anyone else could hear. Then she decided it didn't matter. The sanctuary was a small place, and they probably already knew everything anyway.

"No!" She yelled back. "I chose my *family*. I chose figuring out the *truth*. I didn't go back to be with Theo."

"It looked like Theo thought it was exactly that!" Ash shot back.

Brandy admitted that much was right. "He did think we were going to fall back into our old routine. But I didn't stay with him, I stayed with my family. And I listened to him explain how it hadn't been his fault." She paused, her lip quivering. "Do you have any idea how bad I felt? Thinking that I had been the one who was wrong! That I had left him at the altar, and he hadn't even cheated on me."

Ash raised his shoulders and his hands, as if to ask *why would I even care?*

But Brandy kept going, maybe out of spite. "I felt bad because I had to tell him that I had fallen in love with someone else. That it wasn't even his fault, but that it was entirely mine. I was the bad person in that scenario."

She watched as Ash visibly stilled. *Good, he needed to hear this and he hadn't been listening.*

"I was trying to figure out how to break it to Theo that I wanted to be with you when I found out that he actually was a lying, cheating piece of shit. I guess I got lucky that I never had to admit that to him." She watched as Ash's eyes changed to a darker shade of blue. "So, yes, I left with Theo. I chose to go back to Los Angeles and to go back to see my family. And I chose to find out what the truth was. But I never chose Theo over you."

She paused and added. "I know there's no way for me to prove any of that. But I wasn't going to choose him. You disappeared and never let me tell you that!"

Ash opened his mouth, but she was wound up and on a tear. Maybe she didn't let him speak because Ash could rip her to shreds with just a word. Perhaps it would be best if somebody heard her so they could come and scrape her off his step when he was done.

"You keep saying you need me to choose you. And you're right." She huffed out, looking down into those dark eyes that she couldn't let pull her under. Not this time. "I'd love to tell you that I knew how I felt the moment we met, and *I didn't*. It wasn't until I was in Los Angeles, and with Theo, that I realized I was never going to go back to him, no matter what. Because what I had found with you was even better than what I had with this man that I thought I was going to marry." She was sniffling in the cold air, the emotion bubbling up like her breath forming in front of her face. Her hands waved back and forth, as if gesturing harder might make her case stick better with this wonderful, brilliant, handsome, stubborn man.

He opened his mouth one more time.

But she was just done with all of it. Now that he was finally standing here, a captive audience, she wasn't going to stop. Brandy just kept talking, everything falling out. "I choose you! And I have been choosing you over and over *and over*. I chose you when I gave my money to the sanctuary—"

He cut her off. "You chose the *sanctuary*."

"I love the sanctuary. Yes. And honestly, in part I did choose the sanctuary. But I had enough cash to go start my life over anywhere I wanted. I put that cash *here*." She pointed at the ground. "Because this is where you are, and because this is where you belong. This is the place where you can finally do the work that you were always meant to do without somebody going bankrupt in the process!"

She threw her hands up in the air. "I want this place to survive. I don't know if I'm going to continue working here after the next round, but *you are!* The sanctuary needs to be here for *you.*"

His eyes widened. Though he didn't budge from where he stood, he looked almost as if she had startled him, as if she could knock him over with a thought.

"I stayed at Thanksgiving," she said. "I stayed for you."

"You didn't want to fight the crowds," he said.

"Was I supposed to announce it at the dinner table? *Hey! I'm still madly in love with Ash even though he hates me? And I'm really hopeful that I can talk him into taking me back!*"

He looked away and took a deep breath.

"Would *you* have said that?" she pressed.

"No, I wouldn't."

"And I stayed for six more months! Even knowing that you hate me."

"I don't hate you."

She didn't stop. "Even knowing that you came over the other night. That we are still amazing together. But you got up and walked away . . . I *stayed*. I signed on for six more months of that because I will keep choosing you."

She was sniffling again. Mad that he didn't believe her. Madder still that he didn't see. She spelled it all out. "You don't have to wait until I'm tested. I have been tested every day and I kept choosing *you*."

He'd turned away from her over and over. When he showed up at her door, angry and furious, she'd made love to him.

Now, he stood frozen.

Brandy began to think that it was all wrong, that she'd stitched herself into six more months with this man who was simply going to build his walls back up higher than before.

She stomped down the steps and past him, back toward her own cabin, trying to think what an angry woman could do on vacation for a week.

He didn't come after her.

CHAPTER SEVENTY-ONE

B randy rummaged through her things, pulling out her suitcase and stuffing clothing into it. She didn't have anything for vacation. She threw in a few pairs of jeans, a couple of long sleeve thermal shirts, and her regular sneakers. She promised herself as part of her vacation, she'd go shopping for other clothes.

She grabbed underwear and heard the penny clank as it rolled around, disturbed from its safe hiding spot. She grabbed it and clutched it tight. If only it could save her from Ash.

She had no idea where she'd end up but figured she would drive farther up into the mountains. Once she got aimed in a general direction, she might look up rental houses, stay somewhere in a small town. Go shopping in a nearby big city.

No one had knocked on her door. Aside from a few notifications from social media, nothing had even pinged on her phone. She shoved it in her back pocket, shrugged into her jacket, and felt the penny pressed into her palm.

She fought back the tears that threatened to come. She'd done everything she could. She told herself she loved working with the dogs, and she would enjoy the next six months in spite of that damned man. Wheeling the suitcase behind her, she threw the door open and only made it two steps.

Ash stood ten feet from her front door, hands in his pockets.

She stared at him for a moment. "How long have you been standing there?"

He shrugged, looking a little chagrined. "Since right after you went inside."

"It's cold." A stupid thing to say. As if he wouldn't notice the weather.

He'd been out here for almost half an hour. She wanted to ask, but she almost couldn't bring herself to do it. "Why are you here?"

He didn't answer. "Are you going somewhere?"

"Yes. I have a week's worth of vacation, right? I'm going to try and find a way to enjoy it."

"Where are you headed?"

"I don't know." She sniffled, she was frustrated, as if he couldn't say anything useful, but he prompted her into explaining her bizarre little plan.

He nodded but didn't say anything else.

"Either get out of my way or tell my why you're blocking it."

His smile was soft and sweet. "Because you're right. I didn't see. Because I choose you, too."

She stopped. She stopped breathing. She stopped thinking. She stopped questioning.

She had been building her own walls simply to survive spending every day with the man that she loved but couldn't have. Now it was almost painful to feel those walls crumble. One swift blow from him and they were gone. Pressure pushed at the backs of her eyes. Tears started to form.

He rushed forward, taking her in his arms. The suitcase, already tilted, clattered to the ground behind her.

"Don't cry," he said, stroking her hair. "Don't cry . . . It'll freeze."

She started laughing, her arms sliding into the open front of his coat, pressing herself as close against him as she could.

"I love you," he whispered. "I've never known anyone like you. And I've never loved anyone like I love you."

"I love you, too, you dumbass." She said.

He held her tight a moment longer before leaning down and pressing a soft kiss against her lips. "Do you by any chance want a boyfriend for that random vacation?"

Joy swelled inside her. "That would be wonderful."

"Can I have a minute to pack?" he asked.

She almost teasingly said *no* but shrugged. "Obviously, I don't have any agenda."

Leaning over, he picked up her fallen suitcase and tucked her hand into his. He felt the warm metal in her palm. "What's this?"

"Escape penny." She told him. At his questioning expression she told him. "My grandmother suffered abuse at my grandfather's hands. He monitored everything. So, one day at the library, she learned about mis-minted pennies. She checked every penny that passed through her hands, until she found a few. She left with three pennies and the shirt on her back. She spent two of them getting away. Then she gave me the third on the morning of my wedding to Theo."

Brandy took a breath. "In case he didn't turn out to be what I thought." *Oh, the irony.* "So, I had something he wouldn't see. Something that could fund an escape if I needed it."

In the cold air, Ash softly pulled her fingers open.

She explained, "It's a 1955 double die cast penny. See how it has an echo?"

He leaned down and looked at it, the cold air framing his warm breath around her hand. Picking it up, Ash kissed her palm, then pressed the penny back into her palm and curled her fingers around it. "She's right. You should always have something of your own."

She'd never once thought about telling Theo how her

grandmother had escaped with three pennies. Ash's reaction told Brandy that she would never need that penny with him.

He took her other hand and led her back to his cabin. He tugged her inside, closing the door behind her and setting the suitcase to one side.

He didn't say anything but pushed her up against the closed door and kissed her with everything he had.

Thank you for reading! I love romances with real love and believable characters, and I hope you found all that in these pages. I want to fall in love right along with the characters, and I do, while I'm writing it.

About Savannah

I started writing when I was eight--I hand wrote an 80-page novella that I believed to be (adult) romantic suspense. I'm proud to say, I've gotten a lot better since then. I've grown up to be a nerd at heart! I love neuroscience and people watching, and if you look, you'll find some of that in each Savannah Kade book. Most days you'll find me in my office, looking out my window at a handful of the neighbor's cows, or watching my dogs or my cat roam the backyard.

Follow me, find me, ask me questions! I would love to hear from you.
www.SavannahKade.com
Savannah@SavannahKade.com

www.ingramcontent.com/pod-product-compliance
Lightning Source LLC
Chambersburg PA
CBHW021443240626
47153CB00001B/272

978195919 1032